Memory and Desire

Memory and Desire

Inga Dean

Viking

VIKING
Viking Penguin Inc., 40 West 23rd Street,
New York, New York 10010, U.S.A.
Penguin Books Ltd, Harmondsworth,
Middlesex, England
Penguin Books Australia Ltd, Ringwood,
Victoria, Australia
Penguin Books Canada Limited, 2801 John Street,
Markham, Ontario, Canada L3R 1B4
Penguin Books (N.Z.) Ltd, 182–190 Wairau Road,
Auckland 10, New Zealand

First published in 1985 by Viking Penguin Inc.
Published simultaneously in Canada

LIBRARY OF CONGRESS CATALOGING IN PUBLICATION DATA
Dean, Inga.
  Memory and desire.
  I. Title.
PS3554.E165I6 1985   813'.54   84-26946
ISBN 0-670-80439-8

Printed in the United States of America
Set in Janson

For Deirdre, Caitlin, and John

Memory and Desire

Chapter One

"You're like a cat," a long-ago man said once. He had struggled to explain, while she sat coolly, catlike, assessing. "Your eyes," he had stammered, "green. . . . "

After that Tia had worn green blouses, green sweaters. She learned to take her cues.

"You are lazy," her grandmother would say, coming upon Tia lying in the porch hammock. "Your cousin is sailing."

Gran did not like Tia's indolence, but it was easy to avoid Gran in the big house by the sea. It was shaped and furnished for secrets.

"You want to reduce everything, strip things away," her husband, Sloan, had said angrily. She had just answered his proud confession of the nobility of his family with a remark about everyone's having climbed out of the same mud. She had meant evolution but there had been malice in her heart, and the ensuing argument had gotten suddenly out of control. Sloan, Tia had known, took so many things seriously. "I meant we all started by crawling out of the sea," she said, conciliatory.

It was hard to trace her deficiencies, catalog her assets, when so many of them were part of family custom.

Victoria Valenkova has fine ability as a student, but she seems unaware of many of the "facts of life," the teacher had written on Tia's sixth-grade report. Tia did not understand about races and religions and had confused the two in class. It offended Mrs. Tufo that Tia did not understand. Was there malice then? No, Tia was sure, malice came later. Mrs. Tufo had suffered her pupil's innocence.

Gran's upbringing was a series of lessons, strictures, sudden tangents. She agreed with little that Tia was taught in school, little that was published in the newspapers, though she insisted that they be read daily, and she reserved judgment on everything.

"How foolish," she would say loftily, always looking far taller than she was, or, "How ordinary." Gran would say, "The other girls are very ordinary," when Tia protested the difference between her life and theirs. "Ordinary," she would repeat, drawing out the syllables in her soft, accented English.

"You seem to have a very high-hat attitude," Sloan said. "From the same slime we might be, but yours is more interesting." He looked pleased at having located and attacked her Achilles' heel.

Gran's voice would echo: They are very ordinary. Tia looked out carefully at the world from around the corner of that word. Sometimes they seemed so splendid or interesting: Sabrina Abbott, who was brought to school every day in a Rolls-Royce and never seemed to have parents; Jenny Green, whose mother was the legendary Laura Landsdale.

"You're not ordinary," said Tia's best friend, Jenny, "you're weird." That was, in their private lexicon, a compliment.

Later it was Sloan, saying, "You're so strong. . . . I love you because you're so strong."

Well, how could he know? A psychoanalyst didn't analyze his own family.

"When I'm not working, I'm pretty insensitive," Sloan always assured their friends. "It's true," he said to Tia, "and if I tell them maybe they'll stop treating me like a priest."

"Hey, Vicki!" Jake Streeter, her editor at *Capital Roundabout*, would yell. She hated to be called Vicki. "We got lots of calls on your Petit Chien review. Maybe you ought to go a little easier."

They had wanted her to be vicious and sensuous when they started the magazine.

"Washington food is the pits, Vicki, so go in there and tell it like it is but make it sexy," Jake had said. The magazine had lost lots of its restaurant advertising.

"What are you doing working on that tacky magazine?" said

Jenny, who was then married to a corporation lawyer and teaching yoga at a settlement house.

"You're a pretty girl, Tia, so why don't you do something about your posture? And your hair? Darling." Aunt Elizavetta smiled in her kindly way when she said that. "It's that you look so . . . bohemian."

"Darling, you're one of a kind and absolutely lovely, but you must learn to smile. Don't look so solemn," said Laura Landsdale, Jenny's legendary mother.

"Tia, your cousin is graduating from medical school," said Gran. "Amazing. She was always such a fat, ordinary child." Gran thought about Robin for a while. "Well, most doctors are ordinary, aren't they?"

"You could be anything you want, for God's sake," said Sloan angrily. "You're a spoiled brat." He would get angry about her indolence too. Later he would say that the one thing he had learned from life, from his practice, was that children need their mother at home in their early years. His mother had worked, hated to cook, dressed badly; she was a Catholic convert who wrote books on Christian morality in a changing world. Tia liked Althea Ensear.

"Sloan can be very manipulative," warned Althea, shortly before the wedding. "Be aware. You often seem out of touch."

Tia was far more aware of the warning than the manipulation.

V. V. Ensear is an ignorant snob, said one of the letters about her Petit Chien column. *What she knows about French food could be written on the head of a pin.*

"Tia, you are my bright little star," said the faraway ghost of her dead father.

"Be careful, watch out," her mother's voice would call out when Tia went down to the sea. "She's far too reckless on that pony," said her mother.

"Nonsense," said Gran.

"Mommy, you are the greatest mother in the whole world!" shouted Daisy one evening while she was having her bath. "I hate you," she said later that evening.

"Tia, that's not a bad painting. You should get back to it more," said Sloan vaguely. "You really are quite good," he said, sounding surprised, "though I don't know too much about art."

"You live such a materialistic life," said Jenny, after she divorced the lawyer and met Wayne. "Remember Gran talking about ordinary?"

"Jesus," said Robin, still exhausted from delivering a breech baby. "Sometimes I wish I could go off to Aruba."

"Aruba!" screamed Jenny, whom Tia saw a lot of that year because of the peace movement. "Typical!"

"Women are always at the mercy of men if they work for them or marry them," said Sabrina, who did neither.

"Lucky for me that Wayne married me for my money so he's totally at my mercy," said Jenny.

Chapter Two

The chocolate mousse is rich and velvety, flecked with flakes of bitter, dark chocolate, Tia wrote. Either *flecked* or *flakes* would have to come out. She was tired of thinking up new ways to describe chocolate mousse. *The mousse was velvety, rich with flakes of dark, bitter chocolate*, she typed.

"Mommy, Peter knocked down all my blocks," said Daisy, standing in the doorway in tears.

"Send him in here," said Tia, fighting for time.

"It's not fair," said Daisy, hands on hips, having become suddenly resolute while Tia typed a sentence about the crème caramel.

"No?"

"Peter is never punished."

Tia walked over and picked Daisy up. Tia could rarely resist Daisy for long. Small and firm, her fair hair in long braids down her back, she always returned hugs so warmly. "Um, you smell good, Daisy."

"I washed with Daddy's new soap." She held her hands in front of Tia's nose.

"You can come with me today and we'll have lunch at the Red Door."

"Oh, can we?" Daisy wriggled down in delight. "Can we go to the China Gardens?" Daisy always bargained, even her surprises.

"Got to be the Red Door. We have to try their new menu. Okay? Five minutes, washed and dried."

Gran always used to say that. Tia had believed it was exactly five minutes and no more and would rush through the long halls of Gran's apartment, drying her hands on her skirt.

"Well, well, and what are you two ladies up to?" Sloan came in the study and gave Daisy a hug. He was returning from the regular Saturday tennis match he had been playing since the first year of their marriage. "Saw Joe Sykes, and he and Liz want us to come for a sail tomorrow. Can Priscilla work?"

It was their usual Saturday morning argument. He and Ned must have lost the game.

"Sloan, it's not fair to ask her."

"I'll ask her, if you don't want to." He looked stubborn, his jaw set. I need to relax, he would say defensively, daring her to say that she did not like to leave the children on Sunday, that she did not like to ask Priscilla to work weekends, that she hated those sails with Joe and Liz and their chilled Chablis. Somehow, in the end, he would always accuse her of being spoiled, of having had sails and Chablis while he was delivering newspapers and washing cars.

He bent over her typewriter. "Velvety mousse again?"

Tia shrugged. "Even my thesaurus has run dry."

"Just this Sunday," he said, tucking her against him and kissing her. "Then, tomorrow night, we'll all go to the China Gardens," he said in a stage whisper, "with Daisy and Peter."

"I really prefer BMWs," Sloan was saying as Joe sailed slowly out of the harbor. "Letting Italians build the Mercedes has wrecked it."

"God, there they go again," muttered Liz, lighting a cigarette and puffing hard on it in the wind. She stretched her long legs, looked at them critically, and reached for her wineglass.

"Chris has bought himself a little Cessna," said Joe.

"Every shrink in D.C. who already has his Mercedes is getting his plane," murmured Liz.

"Is that before or after the house in the country?" asked Tia.

"Definitely after West Virginia, not long after Virginia and maybe Maryland. The Grays just bought a place in Easton. That's not a Cessna but maybe it's—what, on a scale from one to ten—maybe an eight?"

"Then there are the Baldwins," said Tia.

"Oh, inheriting is definitely a ten. Maybe an eleven."

"Or the Littletons?"

"Mmmm, very bad. A minus two. Inheriting a place like that! They didn't have the class to keep it a secret." Liz drank the rest of her wine and poured some more. "Drink up, Tia, Joe has just discovered the most disgusting pâtés. They're worse after an hour on the boat."

"You know, I really like that small Cadillac," said Joe.

"Oh, God, a Cadillac. Now they'll know he's Jewish," said Liz, already slurring her words.

"Poor Liz," said Sloan as they drove home.

Tia's face burned from the sun and wind. "Yes."

"She shouldn't have given up her job."

"Probably not."

"You ought to spend more time with her."

There was no point in spending time with Liz. She was always drunk, and as she got drunker she would mix them all into her bitterness.

"She's like a Cuisinart."

"Mmmm?"

"Another food reference. I've got to get another job."

"Why? It's a great job."

Sloan enjoyed it more than she did. Feeling the depression that usually followed a few hours with the Sykeses settling into her, she decided not to argue. It was like the Saturday morning argument, when their animosity flared and left them both puzzled by the breach.

"Liz seems to hate Joe."

"She hates herself more," said Sloan.

"Yes, she does." It was that bitterness Tia saw often in women, a rancor so fetid that it seemed nourished in a dark and guarded place. "Is it disappointment?"

"Hey, it's Sunday. My day off." Sloan laughed. He seemed to lock away his brain at 5 P.M. Once he had practiced his profession on everyone but now he had settled down, and after office hours he played tennis or squash, tinkered with his shiny little sports car, read the ads for vacation houses, supervised the planning of a dinner party. There always seemed to be someone coming for a drink, dinner, joining them for an evening at the Kennedy Center, a meal at one of Tia's restaurants, or they would be off with a group to a benefit for some slightly liberal cause or Congressman, or to someone else's house for drinks or dinner, or a swim, or tennis, or a sail. Summers at the shore, a few weekends in New York, occasional trips to Europe, a winter week in the Bahamas were to take the edge off their routine.

"You have time to do what you want but you're so damn lazy," said Sloan when she protested. He had latched on to her indolence.

"It's just that what we do together . . . " Her voice trailed off.

"If you'd sharpen up your tennis, you and I could play together," he said. "You've just let it go."

Yes, that and so many other things. To Sloan Ensear, of the noble lineage and unfairly impecunious childhood, Tia was too careless. She casually, he seemed to think, discarded what he had struggled so hard to acquire. Her dower, so promising that glittering day they met, had drifted away.

Chapter Three

It was in June, on a blazingly beautiful day, when Sloan Ensear arrived at Gran's house in Easter Cove in his mother's rusty, rattling Dodge. He was someone's houseguest, delayed along the way by a broken fan belt, arriving smudged and apprehensive, clutching the map and cheerful message that had been left for him on a screen door. He had paused below the long porch, looking up and then back at his note, searching the faces above him. Someone had finally recognized him, told him to go around to the front door, gotten him a drink, introduced him, abandoned him again. Tia had watched the whole entrance while she perched on a corner of the porch rail, trying to keep her back in the sun. It was always painful to watch a stranger arrive, especially a young one, a shy one, and see him struggle in this sea of solidarity. Met with indifference, ranging from friendly to glacial, allowed only to stand on the edge of a group, the newcomer had to take extraordinary measures to be noticed. It was really what everyone wanted, someone new and interesting in Easter Cove, but they were vacationing, after all, suspended on summer time, bound by small roads and the sea, both wary and idle.

Sloan had stood that day, sweat beading on his upper lip, looking out beyond the sloping lawn to the sea. He had tried to bend casually against the porch rail, sipping his drink. When lunch was announced he looked around in a panic, trying to find his weekend host, hurrying after the crowd moving into the dining room.

"Why did you let me founder so?" he asked, years later. It was part of her malice and she had rested easily on it then.

She had exchanged a glance with Robin when they both saw him try to find a place at one of the tables for six in the large, dark dining room. They had giggled.

"My dear boy," Gran had said, noticing his awkwardness, "aren't you Edward Cartwright's college friend?" She put her hand on his arm. "Masha, get this young man a chair. There, put him between the children."

Gran never allowed her malice to make people suffer on the spot, though she used it for her own amusement later.

Sloan had tried to make himself narrow as Robin and Tia moved aside for him. Robin had started talking to him and Tia had pushed the food around her plate and listened.

"I thought you were younger than you were," Sloan said later. "Mummy was very beautiful, but she had her hair in two long braids and she looked rather young for a sophisticated college man. Aunt Robin looked forty, however," he would say, laughing.

Robin, also just seventeen, had more liberties than her cousin and took advantage of them. Short, fair, and rosy, she had a lushness that threatened to ripen too soon. It gave her a rather breathless, vulnerable quality. Aware of her effect on men, she presented herself artfully. Tia had mourned the passage. Close as children, spending their summers together with Gran at Easter Cove, it had suddenly put a distance between them. Of course, it had been Tia, tall and graceful, who had reigned over her fat little cousin until this summer.

That day Tia was grateful to Sloan. He did not go into the trance that affected everyone else after a few minutes' exposure to Robin's voluptuous presence.

"Summerlea?" Sloan asked. He had seen the worn lettering on the gatepost.

"Well . . . " Tia started vaguely, wondering how to answer.

That first day the name had been on the gatepost and on some yellowed sheets of stationery in the drawer of a wicker desk in the library. "Summerlea?" Gran had asked, in her soft, accented voice. "What's that?" "Summerlea," the real estate man had said proudly. "Summerlea?" Gran asked again. Both of them had stood, confused, in the dusty, partially furnished library.

"It's a beautiful name," Sloan had said.

It must have been his first sight of the house on Easter Cove, its massive, brown-shingled back hunched over the sea, that alerted him to the possibility of reclaiming his rightful inheritance. It was always too much with him, this sense of inequity and loss.

"Tia," he had said. "Is that short for something?"

"Victoria," she had answered.

"Ah, Victoria of Summerlea," he had said, smiling.

"Oh, we don't call it that," said Robin disdainfully.

"Where will you be going to college?" he asked.

"Radcliffe, both of us," answered Robin, through a mouthful of lobster salad.

"Well, you must let me show you both around," Sloan had said.

"You at Harvard? Oh, yeah, you're Cartwright's roommate," said Robin, wiping her mouth. She examined the lipstick stain on Gran's white napkin. "Oh, Jesus, Tia, she'll kill me."

Years later, Sloan would suddenly face Tia and demand to know why she had been so unkind to him that day. "You just let me hang there!" he cried. Remembering that day, she could recall the intensity of her discomfort, but not his.

Chapter Four

"I make this special for you, Mrs. Ensear," said Chef José of
Mexican Matador. He put a plate down in front of her and stood
over her. She could feel his belly against her shoulder. "And for
you too, Mr. Ensear." He stood back. "Now I leave you alone,"
he said, leering.

"What does he think we're going to do with it?" said Tia.

Sloan didn't answer. He looked down at his plate sullenly. He
hadn't wanted to come here, but the magazine was rating Mexican restaurants, and it had been a year since she had been to the
Matador. The article was already three days overdue, and Jake
had called to remind her that morning.

"I thought you were supposed to be anonymous. Doesn't
Mary Morton wear a bag over her head?" He looked at her
gloomily. "If they know who you are, well . . . " He shrugged.

"Yes, Mary Morton is incorruptible."

"She's very conscientious," said Sloan righteously. "But then
she works for the *Post*. . . . "

It was Sloan's way of fighting: letting his sentences float to
their own conclusions. He had learned that, he once confessed,
to skirt Althea's rigidly literal sense of fairness.

"Are you still angry about the house?"

"No, Tia, I'm not angry." He poked his enchilada. "I just
don't understand why you want to stay in a house that's too small
for us. In Georgetown you could walk to your office and I could
see my patients in the basement."

"In the basement?"

"You know what I mean. That basement apartment could be fixed up."

"We have a perfectly nice house. You have a wonderful office. I hate to walk."

He wanted that big Victorian house, imposingly turreted, planted solidly between its Georgian neighbors.

"Tia, there's all that furniture from your grandmother's New York apartment in storage. This is the perfect house for it."

That was probably it. Suddenly she had a vision of heavy mahogany tables, covered with silver-framed photographs and little birds. Gran had inherited her mother's collection and greatly enlarged it. Anyone baffled by what to present Gran when they arrived at her house, or on her birthdays or Christmas, came with a little bird. They were everywhere, tiny and large, in china, porcelain, glass, wood, metal. They had spread from New York to Maine, more and more of them.

"Go see it with Gran's furniture in mind," Sloan was saying. He had abandoned his enchilada and was digging canals in his refried beans.

Would it smell of Gran and of their apartment overlooking the river? Gran said she liked to live near water because there was always an avenue of escape. "I remember, you see," she would whisper, stroking the lace at her throat, eyes dreamy. "You don't know . . . but I remember." Gran's perfume was musky and filtered through the smell of beeswax and soap and spring flowers that always struck one first. "Ah," she would sigh, when she had their attention, "one can always escape by water."

"Tia?"

"Yes?"

"The house?"

"I'll take another look."

It was larger and darker than she remembered. Sloan had insisted on bringing Daisy.

"Oh, Mommy, can I have this room?" she cried when she reached the first turret.

Sloan looked smug. "We'll see," he said. "Daisy loves it," he whispered loudly.

Tia walked slowly through the house. It was empty, its walls and floors scarred, testimony to other histories.

"It feels sad," she said.

"That's because it's empty and needs a little work," said Sloan.

Gran's apartment, that vast maze of rooms, must have looked like this when the last of the furniture was gone. Only there the river glittered below, and here a narrow street passed the door.

"It's not enough," said Tia, looking out the window.

"Not enough!" Mrs. Pierce, the real estate woman, was angry. No doubt she'd had enough of them all, especially Daisy, now racing up and down the bare stairs. "It's one of the finest properties in Georgetown."

"That's not what my wife means," said Sloan coldly.

"Well, of course, I didn't mean . . . " Mrs. Pierce struggled. "It's just that I—"

"Thank you," Tia said to Sloan. He took her arm affectionately. "You've been awfully patient with us," said Tia. "We really do appreciate it, Mrs. Pierce. Won't you come out with us and have some lunch?"

"No, maybe another time," said Mrs. Pierce, regaining her poise.

They left her in the kitchen, checking fuses.

"I'm sorry," said Tia. They walked slowly while Daisy ran ahead.

Sloan sighed. "I did like it."

"Yes, it's going to be difficult." It would be best to stay in their own house, but she knew that they were on the verge of a change, that Sloan, now chastened, would regroup and try again. His restlessness would never be assuaged. In Gran's static house, Tia had welcomed that part of him, seen it as vitality. He had, she thought, helped her to escape.

"Why does it have to be a man?" her old friend Jenny had said. "Why can't you just leave? You've got to learn to use other escape routes."

Chapter Five

It had seemed impossible to leave. One had to know Gran to understand, know her toughness and resolution, her labyrinths, her deceptions. Tia could not remember an earlier time, when life had not hardened Gran, when she did not wear long black dresses and cover her fingers with rings. Her apartment was full of dark corners, tables cluttered with her private memorabilia, her own vivid canvases on the walls. What she told Tia, and sometimes Robin, about her life was carefully presented to mystify instead of illuminate. Only old Masha, who had come with Gran from Russia, knew everything, and Masha, as abused as anyone Gran sheltered, would never tell.

"There's probably nothing to tell," Robin would say sometimes, when they tired of the game.

And entirely too much, they both knew. It was frightening, this volcanic center of the old woman, the secrets that obscured it, the mysteries that allowed her to float where they could only trudge. It showed sometimes in the small wiry frame, coiled always, and the deep-set dark eyes that blazed from her pale face. It was also, for Tia, and often for Robin, a fortress. The apartment over the river and the house by the sea were guarded by Gran and made safe.

"My mother knew the location of every spa on the Continent," Gran had remarked with bitterness once. Her mother, Natalia Alexandrovna, was beautiful and, said Gran, not really frail at all, but indulged by her rich parents and then by her husband.

Serge Valenkov, Gran's father, was always proud and grateful for the marriage, which had been opposed by Natalia's family, who, conscious of their own rise in the world, had disdained the decline of the Valenkovs. When Natalia tired of summers in her husband's large, rough, isolated country house, so unlike the elaborate Italianate villa her grandfather had built for his family, she made medicinal pilgrimages to France and Germany. She returned to St. Petersburg before the New Year, in time and refreshed for the round of balls, theater, and dinners that she enjoyed with her renewed health.

There were two older brothers, Constantine in the civil service and Serge in the army, when Gran was born. Gran's surprising arrival in her mother's middle age had been regarded by Natalia Alexandrovna as her liberation from further duty toward her husband. Exhausted and weak from pregnancy and birth, Natalia persuaded her husband to find her an apartment in Paris, where, with a large retinue of Russian servants, she stayed most of the year. There would be several months in St. Petersburg between New Year's and Easter, but Natalia never again went to her husband's big wooden house in Kaluga. Gran, christened Helena, went to Paris the first few years, but her father insisted she spend the summers at Kaluga. Gradually her time in Paris was shortened, first because her mother found it difficult to travel from spa to spa with a lively young daughter, and later because Helena did not want to be separated from her father.

While Natalia hated the house at Kaluga, on the plain between wheatfields and pine forests, Helena loved it. There her father taught her to ride and shoot and gave her all the freedom she needed. With her cousins she would explore the labyrinth of storerooms under the rambling house, follow the two brooks that traversed the property and emptied into a lake deep in the pine-woods, drive with her father into the village and sit in his coach while he made his visits, and play for hours in the tiny log house that her father had built for her in the grove of birches. There were always lots of aunts, uncles, cousins, and friends, filling the house, playing endless games of cards or croquet, laughing and talking all at once. Gran would lie in her bed and hear the hum of voices as she drifted off to sleep.

In St. Petersburg they lived in a more orderly fashion, in a large quiet house on the Neva that Natalia's grandfather had bought at the peak of his prosperity. He had given his grand-daughter and her husband an apartment on the third floor, and young Helena spent hours lying on the window seat in the library, watching the traffic on the river. In the summer, before they left for Kaluga, they often cruised the river in a boat from the yacht club, or sometimes headed out into the wide Gulf of Finland in her father's bigger boat, loaded with several enormous hampers filled with cold meats, cheeses, bread, fruit, wine, and vodka. When it was time to return, Helena would stand on the bow and watch for the huge gold dome of St. Isaac's, glittering in the evening sun. She would hurry to her station before they got to Kronshtadt, to watch for the busy wharves of Chekstooshi, the granite quays, the bridges connecting islands, the long unbroken lines of palaces that ran to the grain wharves on the other side of the Liteynaya bridge.

"The river was so white and clean," Gran would say. The river below her apartment in New York was dark and dirty.

Her father liked to walk, and when he came home from the bank he would take her for a stroll along the Nevsky Prospect, where he would stop and introduce his young daughter a dozen times, standing bareheaded in the early dusk of a frigid afternoon, until his daughter pulled him away. She would often get him to walk down the narrower streets, where she liked to stop in front of shops that advertised their wares on large, bright posters. She would stand and admire the magnificent painted array that had so little to do with the modest wares inside.

"There was my favorite—a jeweler who had pictures of the most magnificent tiara, ropes of rosy pearls, sapphires, rubies, emeralds, rings, bracelets."

Her father, tiring of her solemn admiration, had taken her inside. There had been half-empty shelves, some modest watches and rings, dirty children who peered out from behind back curtains.

Helena Valenkova loved St. Petersburg, with its wide streets, large painted stucco houses, vast squares, water, gardens in the spring, troika races on the winter ice. Later, she claimed, she realized that most of all she loved Kaluga. Or so she said. Tia always felt that at one time Gran had considered it ordinary, had felt the sting of her mother's contempt for it, had longed for her grandparents' Italianate country house with its alleys of hedges and roses and its conservatory full of orange trees.

"Those wooden houses used to burn down all the time, and the thought terrified my mother, who loved all her little treasures so. Nothing could ever last there: books, paintings, furniture. My father's family had so little to hand down," she would say, as if explaining her own ambivalence.

It had all ended so soon. Her father and brothers watched the unrest in St. Petersburg grow. It didn't seem to have anything to do with Kaluga, but in town, even Helena, just fourteen at the start of the Great War, felt the tension, saw riots break out in the street, heard shooting, heard her cousins talk about strikes at the university. Among her brothers, her grandparents, her father, there were loud, angry discussions. After her oldest brother, Constantine, was killed in the last months of the war and the Italianate house was burned, Serge Valenkov decided to try to take his daughter to Paris, where her mother had stayed when the war began.

"We'll be back together soon," said her brother Serge when he kissed her goodbye.

"Come as soon as you can," her father said as he embraced his son.

Helena had stood in the great hall, feeling the dampness of the river through the open door, tracing patterns on the marble floor with her foot, listening to her grandfather's last pleas that they go to his sister's villa on the Caspian Sea instead. But they had left Russia and gone to Paris. It was for Helena a frightening, arduous, spiritless journey.

Natalia Alexandrovna greeted them passionately. That month they all spent together, her eyes seemed perpetually wide with fear. Living in the Paris apartment with its delicate Louis IV furniture, shelves of porcelain and china, ceilings frescoed with cherubs and grape leaves, there seemed nothing left of Russia. The smells, the light, the sounds were all different, subdued, smaller. Natalia spoke French and affected a lisping accent when she spoke Russian.

"Please don't go, Serge, please," Natalia Alexandrovna had begged. Helena had heard them one night when she paused outside her father's room. Helena had thrown open the door and run to her father, who had been standing at the foot of the bed while his wife prostrated herself before him. Throwing her arms around his waist, Helena begged him to take her with him.

He had left them both, early in the morning, so that they found him gone before they could renew their pleas. He had written them precise instructions about their financial arrangements, the name of the man to contact at the Paris bank, the name of his Paris attorneys. For Helena there was a short note, evidently interrupted as it was written, promising to return for her in the spring.

He died that spring, at Kaluga, where he had gone to check on reports that the house had been sacked. He had come, as he always did, by the straight road from the railway station and had seen, in the pale dusk, the silhouette of the house against the last of the season's snow. It was not until he drew near that he smelled the smoke and realized it had been burned. Its walls, still smoking, rose darkly in the night, bright embers glowing, with the muffled explosions of bottles breaking in the heat, acrid smoke rising slowly from the debris. He had returned to the village and spent the night at his friend the doctor's house, stayed up most of the night writing Natalia, Helena, and Serge. In the morning, the doctor found his guest dead. A stroke, the doctor diagnosed, brought on by the strain of events, he wrote to the widow and children.

Serge never came to Paris. Natalia tried to find him, but he had vanished. She was sure that he had died trying to defend his grandfather's house in St. Petersburg, but Helena, remembering his sad eyes and resigned patience, wondered if he had not simply chosen to disappear. She could see him coming down the winding staircase of that house with his small valise and going out into the white winter morning, not turning once to look back but walking softly through the snow, leaving them all behind.

"Perhaps it was just that I wished I could, a million times," she would say.

Left with her ailing mother, an entourage of Russian servants, the last bitter letters from her father, Helena had been forced to take charge. There had been a time, right after the doctor's cable, when she had faltered.

"I was such a sheltered young girl and so terrified," Gran would say.

The spoiled daughter of St. Petersburg lay on her bed in Natalia Alexandrovna's exquisite French apartment and cried. She would not leave her room, ceased her fervent nightly prayers in front of the triptych of the Virgin Mary and infant Jesus that her father had given her when she was confirmed, stopped sketching in the leather-bound books her mother had always sent her from Paris, stopped the piano-playing that had been her first passion. Her mother, not by temperament or inclination able to extend much aid, hired the cook's daughter, Masha, to look into matters. For Masha, only months older than her charge and as baffled and wordless, the job was bewildering. In a small, straight chair by Helena's bed, Masha sat, clasping her wide flat hands, pursing her lips with anxiety.

"She looked so silly, sitting there with her peasant clothes on, in the middle of all that Parisian elegance, not knowing what to do with me," Gran would say later.

Tia could not imaginne Gran staying on her bed too long. Once Natalia Alexandrovna's entreaties to abandon it were exhausted, Helena would have been ready to seize any excuse to rejoin the world. Masha's dolorous presence was enough and Helena arose, weakly at first, but after a few days strong enough to greet the callers that had begun to stream to the apartment. Among them she found a doctor for her mother. After years of vague and imaginative symptoms, Natalia finally had a diagnosable disease. Since it confirmed years of unrecognized suffering, Natalia went triumphantly to bed.

Helena arranged for French lessons every morning. In the afternoon, with Masha at her side, she walked through Paris. In shops, at galleries, in restaurants, she spoke to anyone who would speak to her. Later she would come home and write her exercises over and over in her sketchbooks. Often she had people to tea. More and more old friends and family came to Paris, and young Helena Valenkova began serving early Russian suppers twice a week in her mother's long, mirrored drawing room. Her father's friend, the banker who handled the Valenkov deposits, was Helena's first supporter. He succumbed to the strange charm that would draw people to her, fascinated and wary but soon unable to pull themselves out of her orbit.

"It must be her eyes," Robin would say. Wide-set eyes that darkened with intensity or paled with disdain.

There was no doubt that Natalia Alexandrovna was dying. The once-fair and delicate woman was gray and coarsened by illness. Finally realizing the nature of true illness, terrified by its demands and prognosis, Natalia clung to life. While the banker found more specialists, brought great bouquets of her beloved white lilacs, Natalia begged God in tearful prayers to spare her.

"The terrible smell of that place," Gran would say. Her mother's bedroom smelled of medicine and death and lilacs, and Gran could smell it everywhere. "It stayed in one's nostrils."

"But we were lucky, really," Gran would add. In the rain and cold of that first winter, in the midst of death and grief, Gran knew she was lucky. Surrounded by family treasures, cushioned by her father's financial foresight, in the large apartment, with life forming around her, Helena never doubted her good fortune.

Gregory Valenkov was not so lucky. A distant cousin, he arrived in Paris with his German tutor and a small suitcase. His father had been killed by a stray bullet in a skirmish near the Kremlin. All his life a devoted civil servant, with portraits of the Czar and Czarina in his house, he had heard the gates of the Kremlin were being stormed and had started home to see that his family was safe. After his death, the tutor had begged the family to leave Moscow but only Gregory made the journey with him.

"What could I do?" Gran would say. "He was only twenty-two and prepared for a life as an estate manager. Crops and cows —that was all he knew. What could I do?"

What she could do was marry him, but what she really must have wanted was someone to help her sort out the chaos. He probably tried to help, but Gran had no doubt been too impatient, too strong, too angry, to allow him much latitude.

"Poor man," she always said. Robin called him the P.M. A portrait survived. He had been tall and dark-eyed, with a soft, boneless face. Sometimes Gran said he died of pneumonia in the late twenties, another version of his demise was a riding accident, and once she was heard to say that he had drowned swimming in Normandy. Whatever the event, he was dead before anyone really noticed him. His son and daughter could barely remember him, consigning him to an ancestral limbo where he was perpetually assigned the resigned composure his portrait captured.

"A decent fellow," said Valery, "but hard to know."

Not so Valery. A big, noisy, ugly man with a crop of wild red hair and narrow gray eyes, Valery Malachenko had seen the revolution as an opportunity to free himself forever from the legal career his family had insisted he begin. His sudden appearance in Paris was regarded with surprise and suspicion by the early émigrés. In Russia, trying to escape the family and career he disliked, he had spent more and more of his time with a group of young writers and painters and less and less of his time at the bar or at family gatherings. He had started painting in the large studio he had rented for his new friends, arranged to publish some of their poetry, and put off his marriage to the daughter of a prosperous Moscow businessman.

His artist friends' euphoric faith, their joyful plunge into the new fellowship, had not been contagious. "Don't criticize my cynicism, Tia," he had said once. "It saved me." He had not stayed in Moscow long. His euphoria seemed to arise from his penury. "I came to Paris with nothing," he would bellow, his voice mixing with his laugh. Out of Russia he brought only a small trunk with some clothes, his paints, and one lawbook. He was never sure why he brought the book.

It had not taken him long to hear about Helena Valenkova and her largesse. He arrived for Sunday supper with a folio full of drawings. "I terrified your grandmother." He laughed. "The first and last person to do so." Usually he would add, "Because I was what she wanted to be." He would smile: big, red-faced, dropping tobacco from his pipe, paint under his fingernails, roaring like a lion. She had bought some drawings, engaged him to teach her, helped him find other patrons.

The Gran he described was a beautiful, dutiful, rather sharp-tongued young woman who was still grieving for her father. She had married Gregory Valenkov three months after she met him, was caring for her mother and supporting a large group of relatives and friends. At first it had seemed to her that she was bringing order out of chaos, that she had enough money to support them all in relative comfort, and that it was her job to re-create the lost world.

"But really, I was building a shell. There was no substance. I was too young to know how to use my strength. After a while I noticed they all looked at me, followed me about. Poor Mama. Poor Gregory." She would pause, remembering. "I thought I'd go mad," she would add, delicate hand over her heart.

As children, Robin and Tia grew so used to her dramatics that they paid little attention to them, but later Tia would think about Gran, growing desperate, more and more alone as her strength surfaced.

They heard often about Gran's departure from her mother's apartment one cold morning in February. She had run, tears flowing, cursing fate and her husband, through the streets of the city, until she found herself in Valery's houseboat on the Seine. She found him sketching by a coal fire, drinking tea from a big ceramic pot he kept on the stove. What it was that drove her out that particular morning and whether she had been to Valery's houseboat before were questions no one dared ask. Valery was vague too. Apparently it had something to do with her discovery that Gregory had gambled away a great deal of the money she had centered her security on. There might have been more, because Gran once told Tia that she had thrown a beautiful porcelain vase, one of the few relics from Kaluga, at Gregory because he had done something she felt she could not forgive. As she had picked up the broken pieces, shattered beyond mending, she vowed never to look back again.

Once Valery told Tia that Gran had stayed with him for a week, until Gregory had come to the houseboat and taken her home. Gran just said that after that everything changed. She must have grown fiercer, sinewy, older.

Gran did not like stories of struggle. With an airy wave of her bejeweled hand, she would skip from that February juncture to the studio near the Luxembourg Gardens, where she painted portraits of rich Americans until she decided to move to New York. That encompassed twenty years, during which she gave birth to Peter and Tinka, buried her mother and then her husband, established herself as a fashionable portrait painter, and supported her family and Valery.

They were all familiar with the second juncture. Valery never tired of describing it.

"One day your dear grandmother looked at that bored, rich woman in front of her and said no, that was not what she had

worked for, and she threw her brushes down and out she went."
Valery would roar with laughter. He had told the story so many
times he thought he had been there, could describe the woman's
petulant face and Gran's temper.

Gran would sigh. "You embellish so," she would say irritably.
Later, Tia learned that Gran had watched Valery paint his soft,
delicate watercolors, draw his frail ink flowers year after year in
his cluttered, dank houseboat, and gladly accept her support. He
sold virtually nothing and he never seemed to falter.

"But I was painting portraits to pay his bills." No more, she
decided. Perhaps something else had gone wrong between them.
They never spoke of that time.

She had met someone from New York who urged her to trans-
plant herself again. It was another of those mysterious sponsors
she ascribed no gender or history to, who seemed to have come
and gone without anyone knowing what they were doing there.
War was coming, that seemed clear in 1937, and Gran was curious about America. Since her children were French citizens, she
was afraid Peter would be drafted into the army. In the months
since she had stopped painting portraits, she had sold some of her
small, detailed Russian scenes to a New York gallery.

A "Russian Grandma Moses" she was later called, but they
were far more complex, haunted, hard-edged. There was, on
close examination, a frantic quality to the motion of the people,
the horses drawing carriages, birches bent in summer storms,
snow swirling in the night. She would paint them quickly, lock-
ing herself up with them for ten hours at a time, drained when
she was finished.

In New York she acquired a certain mystique. A Russian princess, they were sure—and Gran did nothing to disabuse them—
whose wit and vitality kept them at bay but fascinated, who lived
with apparent ease in a big apartment on the East River. Perhaps
it was her mysterious patron, or perhaps Gregory had died before he could finish spending her inheritance, or maybe the years
of portrait painting had enriched her. She certainly told no one
how she managed the apartment, the house in Maine, what she
called her "comforts."

One sponsor Tia could remember was Edward Ramburg,
whose family owned a big jewelry store on Fifth Avenue. "That
dear, dear man," Gran would say. Mr. Ramburg persuaded

Gran to design jewelry for his store. He was a tall old man with a slow, tenuous gait and Tia could remember him at Easter Cove, always wearing a three-piece suit and staying in his room until noon. He brought Tia and Robin records and would play them on the big gramophone in the library and stand back, hands dangling at his sides, head tilted back, listening intently. He would turn to them and smile expectantly. "Just tell him you enjoy them too," advised Grayson White, Robin's father. When they did, Mr. Ramburg would murmur, "Yes, yes."

Mr. Ramburg's daughter summered in Camden, and he saw the house in Easter Cove while he was visiting her. "His advice was always reliable," Gran would say.

Still, at first she hesitated. Then, in the spring, upset about Tinka's approaching marriage to Grayson White, she allowed Edward Ramburg to drive her to Easter Cove. The house reminded her of Kaluga, stained dark by the early spring rains, its big rooms shadowy in the afternoon dusk. As Gran walked over the muddy lawn above the sea, she closed her eyes and smelled the salty air and mud of St. Petersburg.

"I'm sure Edward thought it would take the sting out of Tinka's marriage." Gran would laugh. Tinka's news had been greeted with coolness, then tears, later supplications. Gran had disliked Grayson White, but when she finally realized that her daughter's mind would not be changed, she threw herself into preparations.

The house was bought, flowers were planted, rooms painted, paneling oiled, and floors waxed. Gran and Masha spent the summer supervising the work. Boxes that had been in storage since they had been packed in Paris were opened and their treasures distributed in the house. Valery's paintings, and Gran's, lined the walls. Books filled all the high glass-front cases in the library. Chairs were covered in flowered chintzes, rugs covered the floors, vases were filled with roses from the hedges that fronted the house. By August the house was ready for the dreaded wedding.

That year Gran was too busy to notice the shy young woman Peter was bringing home. "I didn't realize it was the same girl," she complained. Anna Westcott was slight and fair, as pink and delicate as a child, with long golden hair that hung straight down her back. Her looks belied her age. At twenty-three she was two years older than Peter and already at work on her master's degree.

"It was quite a test," Anna told Tia once. "Gran talked to everyone a mile a minute. French, Russian, German, and every so often English." Grayson's family had stood awkwardly to one side of the celebration.

Grayson told Tia about that day. "No one but your mother and my family seemed to speak English. My poor mom and dad."

"Such a plain man and so dull," Gran said about Grayson, often. "How could someone as vital and beautiful as Tinka marry someone like Grayson?" Gran would sigh. "And poor little Anna Westcott."

Gran, her malice always in control in public, had greeted Anna as warmly as any other guest, taking little note of Peter's obvious infatuation. Anna, relieved by Gran's welcome and misunderstanding its significance, had shed her timidity. Anna and Peter had been inspired by the beauty of the clear blue day, the gaiety of the guests, the radiance of the bride, the champagne, and Anna's afternoon transformation. They had driven back to New York, spent the night together in Anna's tiny apartment, and then, still exhilarated, driven to Maryland and gotten married.

The ceremony dampened their spirits a little. The judge's pants had been unzipped, his house smelled of stale wine and cigars, and he had stumbled over the vows. Driving home, they were caught in a blinding rainstorm, and as they sat in the car waiting for it to subside, water dripping from a leak over the windshield, they decided they would tell no one. Sobered now that the euphoria of the past forty-eight hours had left them, shaken by the actions they had taken, they nervously made their plans. Anna would finish her thesis and with her master's degree find a job that would support them both. Peter would start law school in the fall. Privately they each felt that they had made an awful mistake and that the year they were putting in suspension would allow them to obviate it. Somehow, the marriage would fade from disuse.

That August evening they parted at Anna's door, each hoping

the other would not enforce the vows they had taken in such a fever. What they soon found surprised them both. The mistake they had made, they decided, was in doubting that they loved each other. It was the discovery that Anna was pregnant that forced them to admit it. Each had been careful of the other, fearing they would destroy what little fabric seemed to hold them together.

In their renewed marital transport, Peter and Anna rushed to share their rapture with Gran. They found her in the studio she rented, not far from her apartment. It was a mistake to interrupt her work. She sat, in her faded blue smock, hair protected by a cotton kerchief, paint on her naked hands, listening to them. Anna remembered later that she had never seen Gran's fingers bare of rings, her wrists without bracelets. She wondered if they had seen Gran as she did not like to be seen.

"Gran is so vain," she would muse to Tia, "and she looked so plain in that studio."

But Tia, knowing Gran better, knew it was not vanity but a sense of drama that she cultivated, and that the plain, stark studio and her smock and kerchief were what she stripped down to when she was not onstage. There her focus was so intense, her work so much from old memories, that she had banished any color, instrument, furnishing that was not essential to her process.

That Anna plainly did not understand must have been another mark against her. Tia had often imagined her mother, sitting with Peter, so hopeful and happy, being slowly annihilated by Gran's distress. Her feet barely touching the floor, her bright hair loose around her shoulders, wearing her best dress and speaking in the soft Virginia drawl of her gentle Blue Ridge home, she had failed to disarm her fierce mother-in-law.

"It only made Daddy and me love each other more," she told Tia. It was just the sort of thing her mother would have wanted to believe.

"Your father was brilliant," Valery had told Tia, "but he was always being crushed by your grandmother's strength. It was hard to escape that comfortable, safe haven she made for them all."

Chapter Six

Tia was in the kitchen testing recipes for her Weekender section supplement.

"Other restaurant critics don't have to do recipes," Tia had said ineffectually.

Jake smiled. "Mary Morton is coming out with a cookbook next month, and she—"

"Yes, I know, and she works for the *Post.*"

"'From Humble to Haut.' Great, huh? Sam will love it," he said, pleased with himself.

Now her kitchen was bubbling with chili and béarnaise and she was creaming butter for the cake.

"This is too spicy if you ask me," said Priscilla, tasting the sauce. "Needs more lemon juice."

"The chili seems too bland, don't you think?"

"Mmmm, it's okay. My other people made better, though."

"Do you know how they made it?"

"Mmmm," murmured Priscilla again, grinding some pepper into the pot. "This is good," she granted, tasting the cake batter. "I better pick up Peter, but you just leave everything. I'll wash up."

"Thanks. I've got to get Mr. Ensear's mother in an hour. I'll put on the timer—can you take out the cake?"

"She staying long?"

"For the weekend."

After Priscilla left, the house was luxuriously empty. Tia

turned off her sauces, put the cake in the oven, and then walked slowly around the house. It was fragrant, rooms bright with the noonday sun, everything waxed and dusted by Priscilla that morning. In a few hours the curtains would be pulled against the dusk, the children's toys would be scattered through the rooms, Priscilla would be arguing with Daisy about finishing her dinner, Sloan would be on the phone, Peter would be refusing his bath.

"You must get tired of eating out," said Althea, toying with her béarnaise.

"We thought you'd like eating at home your first night here," said Sloan testily.

"I love it," said Althea firmly.

"We'll be out for both lunch and dinner tomorrow," said Tia.

"There's no need to apologize," said Sloan. "Tia has been cooking all day for this dinner."

"For goodness' sake, Sloan," said Althea irritably, "I'm enjoying it."

Sloan always resented his mother's lack of nesting instinct. "Not only did we move every two years," he would complain, "but the place was always a disaster area." The first time Tia had seen one of Althea's apartments she had been surprised by the drawn shades and dishevelment. It seemed to reflect a lost, sad part of her that was not otherwise evident.

"I'm buying a house in Columbia County," said Althea, pushing away her plate and lighting a cigarette.

"What?"

"It's a lovely place, Sloan. About two hours north of New York." She inhaled and blew the smoke out sharply. "I can finish the book there."

"Mother, suburban life doesn't ever agree with you. Remember New Canaan?"

"Oh, God, what a horrible place!" exclaimed Althea.

"And Morristown?"

"Yes, ghastly." She paused and inhaled. "But darling, this is real country. I've got several acres and people breeding horses all around me."

"Why there, Mother?"

"It's so lovely. Your father's cousin, Perry Cornwall—you remember him—has been urging me to come up. He and what's-her-name—the wife—found the place, and it seemed like a good idea." She looked doubtful for a moment and then, stubbing out her cigarette with force, said, "It will be wonderful."

"I'll visit you on the way to Easter Cove," said Tia.

"Yes, do that. Maybe I'll drive up with you and pay my respects to your grandmother."

Sloan snarled something under his breath. His other chronic gripe was that his mother never stayed home. Pervading all the complaints was his sense of the grave injustice of Althea's being his mother, an injury further compounded by the early loss of his father, which had deprived him, again thanks to Althea's eccentricities, of a secure place in the Ensear clan. This sense of deprivation was only barely mitigated by Althea's gift of several Ensear ancestral portraits, sea trunks, and silver when he married Tia. "They always gave me false hope," he would say sadly, surveying his booty.

"Gran would love to see you," said Tia politely. It would be a problem, because Gran did not like Althea and failed to understand Tia's attachment to her.

"Oh, it's such a lovely place, Tia," said Althea. "If Columbia County doesn't work out, I think I'll see if I can find a house in Easter Cove."

A weekend with Althea was a long time. Sloan would try to bring a professional detachment to her visits, promising himself aloud that he would not rise to her bait, but Althea was always ready to escalate.

"You escape the brunt of it because she's never sure when she has your attention," he told Tia. Sloan never escaped for long because Althea knew she had his keenest attention.

So she surprised him when she liked the house in Georgetown.

"You do? Tia thinks it's not very distinguished," he said, warily.

"Distinguished?"

"You liked it then?"

"Yes, it's a wonderful house."

"I think so," said Sloan triumphantly. "I can have my office downstairs and write off part of our expenses."

"I don't know about distinguished, Sloan," said Althea thoughtfully, "but it's very like you, the house. Maybe not quite Tia, though."

"Me?"

"Conservative—" she started.

"Okay, Mother, enough," he said, holding up his hand.

Chapter Seven

Peter had not told Gran about the baby on that strained afternoon in her studio. She would misunderstand about the marriage, he had told Anna. Anna, acutely aware of the baby growing inside her, had found it difficult to honor his misgivings. As the weeks went by, with Peter still refusing to tell Gran, Anna had made up her mind to spare him.

"I knew Daddy wanted her to find out but he just hated to tell her anything she didn't know," Anna told Tia.

Tia had often imagined the scene between Anna and Gran. Anna, in a loose cotton dress two sizes too big, to hide her growing stomach, sitting on the edge of one of Gran's deep wing chairs. The room, always so muffled by the velvets and brocades that covered windows and chairs, the layers of Oriental rugs on the floor, the crowded tables, was lit only by a small lamp next to Gran and the long windows framing the gray winter afternoon. Gran had sat quietly, her hands resting on the arms of her chair.

"You have courage," she had said, after a long pause.

Anna had been so scared, she told Tia, that she was afraid she would faint. She had sat so stiffly, trying to breathe, trying to concentrate, that when Gran came over and kissed her cheek she had burst into tears.

Their embrace was one of the few moments of communion they enjoyed, but that day, when they met as strangers and adversaries, it was an almost holy moment which neither of them ever denied.

"She was so tiny," said Gran sadly, many years later. "So frail. It hurt to think of her having a baby and being so alone."

She was alone; even Gran understood that. Peter loved Anna, that no one doubted, but he was not yet more than a lover. He caressed her back at night when she came home to their tiny apartment near Washington Square and made love to her when she was exhausted and frightened and then fell asleep while she wept quietly into her pillow. Those vignettes of her pregnancy were offered to Tia as lessons in not marrying early, in being careful and cautious: all the things Anna Westcott had seemed to be and had not been after all.

Peter had not been able to find a job and Gran offered to resume his allowance if he returned to law school. He must have felt that he had little choice. Anna's job as a secretary in a large accounting firm would be over as soon as her pregnancy showed, and they had not managed to save any money from her small salary. Anna had refused to move into Gran's apartment, though she had readied a suite of rooms for them. Peter, torn and anxious to avoid both women, spent most of his time studying at the library uptown. Gran would arrive at the Washington Square apartment every Saturday morning with baskets of food that her driver carried up five flights of stairs. Gran would sit, recovering from the climb, and tell Anna that she looked sickly.

"Oh, she wept all the time," Gran said once, with disgust, when she thought Tia and Robin were in bed. "Thank God Tia is so like me."

"Helena, you are so hard on fragile people," said Valery.

"Yes," said Gran in a hard voice.

"But she was stronger than we all thought."

"Yes. She was. It wasn't easy for her."

It must have been very difficult. The woman who looked like a little girl, whose widowed father had called her his princess, was round with child. Her father had remarried when Anna was eleven, and Mildred, her young stepmother, had been kind but somewhat indifferent and soon involved with her own babies. When Anna's father died, in her sixteenth year, he had left her a small trust fund to pay for her college education. Hard work, scholarships, and her plaintive charm had allowed her to add two years of graduate school and a trip to Europe with her French professor's family before the money ran out. Mildred Westcott had not approved, resenting Anna's "private wealth," as she called it, and had written her scolding, bitter letters. When Mildred came from Virginia to New York to see the new baby, Anna had sat back against the pillows of her hospital bed, wondering why she once had tried so hard to win that woman's love.

Peter had bought Tia a crib with a pink canopy and several huge stuffed animals from F.A.O. Schwarz. He brought his wife and daughter home with great expectations. But the apartment was small, and Tia's cries were easily heard in the rooms where her father tried to study and sleep. She cried louder when he picked her up, reaching for her mother. Polly, the day maid that Gran had hired to help them, would rock Tia in the rocker that always creaked from the magnitude of her weight, singing a series of half-remembered hymns in her low voice, talking to herself and kissing the top of Tia's dark little head.

"Your mother loved taking care of you," Grayson told Tia often. "When she wasn't pushing you around the square or feeding you or bathing you, she was knitting for you."

Anna used to tell Tia that the best time was right after Tia's bath when she was clean and powdered and would fall asleep while Anna held her.

When Peter came home it was different. Then Anna's stomach would tighten every time Tia cried out. When Polly left, always careful to close the kitchen door softly, Anna would wait nervously, hardly able to concentrate on anything else, for Tia to awaken. When she did, Anna would rush into the nursery. Peter would peek in and say, "You're spoiling her." When Tia was sick, Anna would be raw with anxiety and Peter would explode and leave the house.

In Tia's second year, to supplement their income, Anna typed manuscripts at night. "You were lullabied every night with an old Royal portable," Anna would say. Gran still offered them three rooms in her apartment, but Anna was adamant. Peter started spending more time at Gran's. He found his old room a good, quiet place to study. It was hard to study, Gran told Tia later, with the noise of Anna's typewriter and a young child in the house. Of course, Gran would add, it was all very hard on poor Anna.

It was a relief to both of them when Peter insisted on enlisting the day after Pearl Harbor. He was in his last year at law school, but once he decided to go he could not wait. Gran was furious. She ordered him to the apartment and sat, her small body tense with rage, listening to his explanation.

"You are a ninny, just like your father," she said.

"I'm your son too, Mother," he had answered, kissing her cheek, catching her off guard.

"Yes, my dearest, you are," she had said and got up to embrace him. He was tall like his father and she bent her head against his chest. "My dear Peter."

He knew she would start to weep, so he pushed her away gently and bid her goodbye.

"Women and their tears," Tia's father had often complained.

Valery had come to New York that month, just before Christmas. It was a time neither Gran nor Valery discussed. She must have been glad to see him, with Tinka married, Peter off to war, and perhaps she had sent him the money to come.

"I had to leave Paris." Valery would laugh. "The Germans were even worse than the French."

Gran had found him an apartment and a gallery.

"Your grandmother found half of Europe places to live, jobs, money," Valery would tell Tia and Robin.

During those war years, Gran's apartment was full of friends, relatives, people who had been given her name. Often she found them jobs in the jewelry designing company she had started, with Edward Ramburg's help, or with one of the "dear souls" that she called on when she needed something.

Anna found a job as a secretary at a publishing house soon after Peter enlisted. As the young editors left for war, Anna was swiftly promoted. By the time Peter was shipped out to the Pacific, Anna could ask Gran to discontinue the allowance. Because she was still typing manuscripts at night to pay Polly's salary, Anna's refusal of any financial aid struck Gran as foolish and puzzling. For Anna it was the freest, happiest time of her life. She started having friends from the office, Tinka and Grayson, even Gran, to dinner on the weekends. After Grayson joined the Navy, Anna and Tinka often spent their Sundays together, wheeling their daughters through the city, ending the day at Gran's for an early dinner, their faces flushed from the walk, the babies sleeping soundly in their prams in the kitchen. When the children were older they went to puppet shows and museums, to watch the seals in Central Park, to tea at the Plaza with Gran's cool stare to keep them well behaved. In the summer, Anna and Tia joined Tinka and Robin in Easter Cove for two weeks.

Saturday was Tia's favorite day. She and Anna dressed together, in front of the long looking glass in Anna's pale blue bedroom, picking their dresses carefully, taking pains with their hair and then catching the Fifth Avenue bus uptown to Anna's office. While Anna worked, Tia sat beside her at the desk, boosted by several phone books. She lined up her crayons, pencils, erasers, squared the pad of precious drawing paper. Slowly, carefully, she drew her pictures until it was time to leave. Usually it was a drawing for Daddy with airplanes and palm trees, variations on the photographs he had sent them from New Guinea. Often Anna was so absorbed in her work that Tia was afraid to ask her for the fruit and cookies they always brought for a midmorning repast. Usually, Tia was happy just to sit and draw until Anna looked at her watch and said, "Oh, my, how time has flown today," and looked at Tia and said, "What a good girl you've been!"

In the early afternoon they would walk slowly back to the apartment through streets full of shoppers, looking into store windows, making plans for dinner. Polly was off on weekends, so Anna and Tia would cook their dinner together, take it into the living room, and eat by the window that overlooked the back gardens of the houses on the square.

The Sundays that they didn't join Tinka and Robin they would take a bus up to the Cloisters or the ferry to Staten Island or the subway to the beach. On the way home they would stop at the small, dark restaurant on their corner, where the proprietor always came out to greet them and bring Tia a bag of crisp, sugary cookies to take home.

"When Daddy comes home," Anna would say, prefacing yet another glimpse at their glorious future. When Daddy came home, Anna would stay home all day and greet Tia after school; they would rent a lovely house near Easter Cove in the summer and Robin would come and visit. "We'll have a puppy, and I'm going to lie in the sun all day and get fat and listen to all your wonderful stories, and then when it's time to go back to New York we'll all pile into our great big car and you and Daddy will sing all the way."

Once Tia said, "But I like it now," and Anna looked worried. "When Daddy comes home," she said cheerfully, "it'll be so much more fun."

When the war was over against Japan, she and Anna went out in the street and blew paper horns and sat on someone's stoop and Tia was allowed to have a sip of champagne.

The day Peter was to arrive, Polly baked a ham and Tia and Anna hung red, white, and blue crepe-paper streamers on the front door. Anna put on a new dress but was so nervous that she spilled a whole bottle of cologne on herself and had to change. Tia sat in her room listening to the radio Tinka had given her for her birthday, carefully tracing out a WELCOME HOME sign for her father. She drew red flowers and airplanes between the words.

It was all a great disappointment. She did not like having her father's rough face brush hers at bedtime and would wait hopefully for her mother to come and tuck her in and read her a story. But Anna would come quickly, pull the shades, draw the curtains, give her a kiss, and hurry out again.

"Your father wants to take you out for a special lunch tomorrow," Anna said often those first months.

"But Sunday is our day together," Tia would say.

"Daddy wants to get to know his little girl again," Anna would answer.

But her father did not listen to her the way her mother did. His eyes would wander around the restaurant, and he would smoke cigarette after cigarette and not notice that the smoke was making her sick. He talked too fast and sometimes gave her an impatient tug when she stopped to look in a store window. He said no, a dog was impossible in a small city apartment, and instead bought her lots of presents she didn't want. He didn't understand that she didn't like playing with dolls and he gave her books she already had. She hated sitting at the table with him. It took him so long to finish his meal, and he got mad at her when she wiggled or slumped in her seat. Her mother would turn away when he reprimanded her.

"Don't step on your shoes like that," he'd bark at Tia. "They'll wear out. Do you have any idea how much those damn shoes of yours cost?"

"Peter, don't," Anna would say when he berated Tia, "you're hurting her."

"Not me," Tia had said defiantly one night. Even then she felt tears pressing her lids, a constriction in her throat. Then she stood up and shook her head at him. "I hate you," she said.

"Why—" He started to roar at her and then, suddenly, he stopped. "My God, look at her! She looks like Helena."

Anna had smiled.

"She's Mother in miniature." He laughed, sweeping Tia up in his arms.

She pushed against him, ducking his kisses. For a moment, when she stood in front of him risking everything, she had felt wonderful.

"So you're going to be a crazy little Russian." He had laughed again.

"Let me go!" she had screamed, until finally he put her down, still laughing.

But he never made her cry again. She was torn between pity and anger when she saw her mother's eyes fill with tears. Sometimes she'd rush at him and pound him with her fists but that would always make him laugh. Then he'd pick her up and carry her to her room and dump her on her bed and tell her she was to stay there. "No supper for you, missy," he'd say. Usually he would relent, bringing in a tray and sitting down near her, trying to talk.

"Just like your grandmother. Heartless," he would tease. "Pity your poor old father," he'd say, wheedling a smile from her, making faces, until she'd relent. If she smiled, said she was sorry she had been rude and naughty, he would go. Later Anna would come in and hug her, help her into bed, sit with her for a while. "Try and be sweeter to him," she'd beg. "He's having such a dreadful time."

But inside Tia there was such a hard center that she could feel nothing for him, not even pity.

"You'll get used to him," Robin told her, having to adjust to her father's return too.

But Tia did not get used to Peter that first winter in New York and was glad to go to Easter Cove in June, packing her clothes, toys, and crayons herself. Her mother took her to the station in a cab and chatted about the picnics they would all have when she and Peter came to Maine in August. Tia stared out the window and didn't answer.

"Darling, please, it's difficult for us all at first, but Daddy loves you and the three of us could have such a good time together if you'd give him a chance," said Anna as they were walking through the station.

Tia walked as fast as she could and let her mother hurry after her. Last night Tia had heard Peter yelling and Anna crying.

"Please, darling, try to understand," Anna said and started to explain some more, but Tia saw Robin and ran ahead. Robin's nurse waved at them impatiently.

"Yes, Mrs. Valenkov, I'll see that Victoria writes to you," she had said, pushing the children ahead of her. Anna jogged alongside them, trying to take Tia's hand, went into the compartment with them and made sure Tia had her box of sandwiches and fruit, hugged and kissed her, and then stood outside on the dark and grimy platform and blew kisses at Tia while the train pulled out.

In August, Peter and Anna came up and stayed in the small green gardener's cottage at the end of Gran's driveway. It was dark and damp and Tia's pillows smelled of mold. It was cold and rained most of the month, and she had nightmares almost every night. Once she wet her bed and her father was angry, walking quickly around the room, jerking the sheets off the bed, telling her in an angry voice that she was far too old for such nonsense.

"She's upset, darling, don't be so hard on her," her mother said.

"I know, I know," her father said, pulling her roughly into his lap and rocking her. He held her tight and she pressed her face against his shoulder. Her mother came and kissed the top of Tia's head.

The next day they were all subdued. They took Gran's car

into Camden and went to a movie, and Tia was amazed to see her father laugh until tears rolled down his cheek, trickles that caught the light of the film and fell on his sweater and made spots that were still wet when they drove home. She asked him to put her to bed, looking over his shoulder when he carried her into the bedroom to see if the request had pleased her mother. It had. Anna was beaming.

It was never anything like the dream she and Anna had spun together, but when they went back to New York in the fall, Tia had begun to like her father and discovered ways she could be alone with her mother too. Anna had quit her job, as she promised she would, and Tia would hurry home from school, running the ten blocks faster than the bus could carry her, and dash up the stairs. Sometimes they would take a walk, go window shopping, stop at the bakery for hot chocolate and cake. There was always at least an hour before her father came home.

Still, her mother was moodier now, would not always put her book down when Tia came into the room, and snapped at Polly, whose mouth would tighten angrily.

"She's got too much time on her hands," Polly would mutter. "She ought to have another child."

"We don't need a baby here, Polly," Tia answered.

"No, missy, you sure don't, but it would do everybody a world of good. Another baby in the house is what everybody needs, and none too soon, I'll tell you."

"And what news of Miss Westcott?" Gran asked at tea. Peter took Tia to Gran's for tea on Sunday but Anna had begun to beg off those weekly visits. Tia had heard her parents argue about them.

"Mama, you know Anna has quit her job." It infuriated Gran when Anna used her maiden name at work. "Westcott." She'd sniff. "What is that supposed to mean?"

"Ill-advised move, I must say. I think she might have waited until you were back on your feet."

"We can manage. And there were men coming back to the company, so her job was in question."

"Your sister has managed to stay with the school and it has certainly made it easier for Grayson to get his practice started."

"Mama, it was always understood that Anna's job was temporary. Let's not discuss it in front of the child."

"Dearest boy, if you would let me help you a bit. That dreadful little apartment. Grayson and Tinka are buying a wonderful house. It seems a pity to see Robin have so much more than Tia."

"Not now, Mama, give me time."

Gran would sigh. Tia, watching them both, would nibble her cookie. Peter would light another cigarette and change the subject.

"Well, perhaps you took too much time about it," she heard her mother say one night. "After all, there are so many people coming back now."

"I wanted some time, damn it, after four years. Was that too much to ask? I felt like an intruder coming back here."

"That was your perception, Peter. I tried to make it easy. I quit my job when you asked me, didn't I?"

"It's not you, darling. I'm sorry. It's me."

"It's both of us. I'm sorry. I know it's difficult."

They didn't fight much anymore. She could see her mother felt sorry for her father. It was sad to see him come home and fall into his chair with a sigh. He would sit silently, staring vacantly ahead. He and Anna went out after dinner, and Tia would lean on the window and watch them walk slowly up the street, hand in hand.

"Go to law school and I'll give you a place in my firm," Grayson had said.

"No, I'm not going back." Peter was always sure of Valery's support on that issue.

They spent a lot of time together: Valery not painting and Peter not looking for a job, Gran would complain. It was Valery's contempt for the legal profession that had infected her son. "What a narrow escape I had," Valery would say, leaning back in the comfort of Gran's library, Peter across from him, a willing apostle.

Anna went to work at Grayson's firm as a secretary and for weeks spent her evenings practicing shorthand. Peter would walk her to the subway station in the morning and then walk uptown with Tia to school. Often he was in the apartment when she got home. "Poor man," Polly would mutter. Gran was paying for Tia's school and Polly's salary.

Peter had been home over a year when Valery helped get him a job managing a small bookstore a few blocks from Washington Square. Tia would stop there on her way home from school and sit in a corner looking at books while her father's friends sat around his desk, drinking coffee, smoking, and talking. After Peter closed the store, some of them would walk back to the apartment and stay until Anna's weariness and patience dictated an invitation to dinner.

"They're all writers, Anna, far hungrier than we are," said her father when her mother complained. "We can stretch our meals a bit." Anna did not really seem to mind except to say that they stayed too late and the apartment smelled of stale cigarette smoke in the morning. Polly grumbled about the unexpected guests but she, too, seemed to enjoy them.

Peter had begun to write short stories. One was published in a small magazine, and though *Harper's* turned down others, they once sent an encouraging note. "I thought I'd married a lawyer and we were going to live on Park Avenue." Anna laughed. She was so pleased with her husband's first publication that she had family and friends to the apartment for a surprise party the day the magazine appeared.

That was the night, when a few of the bookstore group remained to finish the wine and Tia was curled up beside her mother, pretending to be asleep so she wouldn't be sent to bed, and the windows were open and the noise from the square drifted in with the summer breeze, when someone suggested a printing press.

"That's it," Peter cried, leaping up. "That's it!"

For weeks Peter went out every day looking for presses, and when one that he could afford was finally located, he sublet the back of a butcher shop for it.

"Are you mad, Peter?" Gran said. "A press? In the back of a butcher shop? With a group of Marxist writers? Do you have any sense of your responsibilities to Tia and Anna? I can't go on paying for things indefinitely, you know."

But Peter was too excited about the press to worry about his mother's irritation. Anna had reservations, Tia could tell, but she shared them with no one. She typed manuscripts, helped carry boxes of paper and press type through the dark, rancid alley to the shop, stayed up late helping Peter set type.

"Anna is the only one I can count on not to get drunk and forget to show up for three days," he said and Anna beamed.

The apartment was full of manuscripts, designs for covers, stacks of printed books, extra cartons of paper. Every Sunday morning there would be a meeting of the members of the Phoenix Press, with loud arguments and occasionally laughter. Anna, chronically exhausted, would come into Tia's room with a lunch tray and then fall asleep on her bed. Tia would sit at her table and look at her mother and watch the blue veins in her temples throbbing under the pale skin.

The printing press became the center of their lives. As soon as Peter closed the store for the day, he and Tia would go to the Press. Anna would come and bring them home for dinner, but Peter would often go back later if he was in the middle of printing a book, or stay up late in the littered living room of the apartment, studying manuscripts, correcting galleys, going over cover designs. Anna would set her typewriter up in a corner and spend her evenings typing manuscripts or copy-editing ones that were due to be published. Tia would stay up as late as possible, trying to be unobtrusive so no one would look at her and say, "What are you doing up?" She loved looking at jacket designs.

Her father gave her a corner at the Press, well stocked with paper and colored pencils and, after her birthday, colored inks and fine pens, and she worked quietly until Anna came at six.

Best of all was Gena Celli, the daughter of Peter's principal partner. A very sophisticated fifteen, Gena allowed nine-year-old Tia to accompany her to the bookstores where books were to be delivered. Often they were not welcomed too warmly and Gena would have to argue with the manager, and sometimes they got thrown out. More often, Gena would put her hand on her hips and start what Peter called, admiringly, her con, and they left with their two sheets of invoice paper and sometimes even a book in the window.

Anna knew nothing about those afternoons and Peter, who did, made sure she remained ignorant.

"Where were you this afternoon, Tia? I called the Press and Daddy said you were helping Mrs. Celli?"

"Yes," said Tia, avoiding her mother's eyes.

"Did you help cut the paper for Daddy's book?"

"Yes," said Tia, glancing at her father. He gave her a wink. "I help lots of times."

"How nice," murmured Anna absently.

The Phoenix Press books were beautiful but their beauty was expensive. Gena told Tia that the Press was losing money but that Peter and Richard Celli were raising enough from benefactors to keep it going. Being with Gena was so wonderful that Tia was able to contain her apprehension when they entered a store, her embarrassment as they approached a new manager, her humiliation when they were thrown out, or her relief when they were given an order. The best times were when they were walking home with an empty satchel and a few extra orders and Gena, relaxed, would tell lurid tales of the rapes, murders, dismemberments that she had witnessed or heard about on good authority.

"And then the subway came and it ran over his legs and chopped them off. . . . "

"No, Gena, really? Not really?"

"The man stuck his head in the polar bear cage—I swear, my uncle saw it—and the bear just chomped the man's whole head off."

"Oh, Gena." Tia would gasp, nauseated, imagining the scene over and over: the headless body, the blood, the pain.

"And that's not the best part," Gena would say, with that intense, tumbling voice. "Wait till you hear this. . . ."

Tia tried to imitate Gena's walk and the way she threw back her head with an insolent flip, the way she crossed her arms and stood on one leg with her hip thrown out. Tia learned how to say "Bug off, buster," when someone bothered her on the street, how to move quickly after dark so no one would try to grab her, how to ignore the legless men who sat on carts and sold pencils, the blind men with tin cups, the drunk men in doorways, how to slip candy bars in her pocket while Gena distracted a clerk. It was intoxicating and perverse. Tia stewed with guilt about it. When Anna, her face gentle and weary, sat on the edge of Tia's bath at night, rubbing soap on her back, and then later came in and helped unplait her long braids and brush her hair a hundred strokes, Tia would be wretched with the weight of her deception.

Once, shyly, she confessed her anguish to her father. They were at the Press and Peter was setting type for a book of his poems. He bent over the lines of type as she spoke.

"Mummy would be really angry if she knew about Gena and me going to stores, Daddy."

"Mmmm."

"She wouldn't like me being out after dark when there're lots of criminals out."

"What?" He turned and looked at her.

"Gena and me sometimes do dangerous things, I think," she said nervously.

"You do, do you?" He laughed. "Just what sort of peril are you in?"

She stood and looked at him.

"Go on, sugar pie," he said. "Let Daddy get this straight and then we'll go off to dinner at Monte's." He bent back over his box of type.

That night, when Anna was brushing Tia's long hair, Tia gathered her courage one more time.

"Mummy, do you like Gena?"

"Oh, yes, Gena seems like a lovely girl."

"I play with her sometimes."

"Do you?" Tia could see Anna's face in the mirror. "Isn't that nice. Isn't it fun when an older girl plays with you? She must think you're very grown up."

"She tells me a lot of stories."

"Stay still, Ti-Ti," said Anna, concentrating on a braid.

"We go to the candy store on Tenth Street."

"My, what fun. Remind me to give you fifty cents tonight so you can treat Gena to a soda."

"Mummy, is lying and stealing a sin?"

"Who told you that it was a sin?"

"Masha."

"Well, it is a sin to her. It's wrong to be dishonest or hurt other people on purpose."

"Do you burn in hell?"

"You mustn't let Masha tell you all sorts of scary stories. Little girls are too good and innocent to sin and burn in hell. God loves children, and He blesses them so they can be happy."

"But what about me?" Tia turned her face to her mother.

"Oh, Ti, your braid. Here, turn around. Oh, sweet angel, of course you're the very best girl in the whole wide world." She gave Tia a hug with one hand and held the partially plaited braid with the other.

That spring, Tia begged her parents not to send her to Easter Cove in August.

"No, pie, you're not going in August," her father said, "you're going in June." Peter and Anna had not admired the changes in her and were anxious to see her off. Tia cried, sulked, whined, and pleaded, but even Anna would not weaken. She took Tia to Gran's apartment the night before they were to go.

"My dear, I'm so glad you've turned to me," said Gran, kissing Anna delicately on the cheek. "And you, my little one, come here to me. Peter is mad. You must get away too, Anna. Tinka and Robin will be there all summer." Gran's voice flowed smoothly. "I'll send you tickets next week and you can come up with Tinka."

"You were really weird that summer," Robin used to tell Tia years later. Tia could not remember much except that she felt uncomfortable all the time, odd and restless. Everything she loved so much in Maine—the rocky beach, the pinewoods, the cold wind from the sea, the long porch on Gran's house, the sails on the morning tide, the rainy days in the attic, sitting in the kitchen with Masha eating honey cakes warm from the oven— had lost their appeal. Everything was boring. Tia would move from one activity to the next, start a book, put it down and then start another and not be able to finish that.

"Bored!" Gran roared. "Nine years old and you tell me you are bored?" She put Tia to work in the kitchen and cleaning the house. "Don't let her be idle for an instant," she told Masha.

"Just tell her you aren't bored anymore," Robin said.

"No!"

Anna put off her trip, writing Tia that the Press was very busy and that Peter's new book of poetry had been delayed. Finally Tinka was dispatched to New York to investigate. She reported that Anna looked thin and haggard and that Peter had lost his job at the bookstore. Tia and Robin hid under the hall table and listened to Gran on the telephone.

"I don't care, Tinka. I want you to bring her up here immediately."

Gran called Anna. "I want you to come up with Tinka next
Friday."

Tinka came back the following week without Grayson, Peter,
or Anna.

"They're impossible," Gran said angrily, while Tia and Robin
listened on the stairs. They could see the fire reflected in the wall
of windows overlooking the sea. It was raining hard, beating on
the old shingles, blowing in the open windows.

"Mama, they love what they're doing. And the books are good
and getting better. Did you see all the reviews they've been
getting?"

"Nonsense, child, in absurd Marxist rags that nobody pays
any attention to. Look at Anna: she's aged ten years running
about for those creatures Peter admires so. And Tia! An urchin."

"They've promised to come up. Mama, they're completely
broke. Grayson is going to offer them five thousand dollars free
and clear and then he thinks we should all back off."

"Oh, Tinka, Peter will go through your five thousand dollars
in no time. He consumes money. All with the best intentions.
He left Anna penniless during the war and he's never succeeded
in anything. So like his father. As much as I disliked Anna, poor
little sparrow, she does stand by him, and when he was away she
wouldn't take a penny from me. Without her he would sink."

Tia turned around and went quickly back up the stairs.

The next day Tinka kissed them all goodbye. She was going to
drive to New York and bring Anna and Peter back with her. The
car, a shiny black Buick, had been a present from Grayson and
she adored it. It was one of the first new postwar cars and Valery
said Grayson had had to wait two years to get it. She had driven
the children everywhere they wanted to go that summer. Once
they had gone to Boston for a weekend in it, but usually they
drove up the hill to see the harbor and sunset, down to Camden
for dinner, to the Seafarer in Easter Cove, or up the winding,
narrow coast road to other fishing towns along the rocky land
edge.

Chapter Eight

If that's supposed to look like an appetizing dish, then I'm an eggplant's uncle, the letter started. Jake thought it was funny and wanted to publish it.

Jake had been at Tia's house for dinner one night and had seen the vegetables, fruits, and flowers she had painted on her kitchen cabinets. The project, started on a gray day shortly before Peter was born, had taken weeks, with lots of turpentine and rubbing out and repainting. Peter's birth had interrupted, so that for a long time there was a huge half-painted eggplant, leaning against a finished onion, reminding her of the day she started having labor pains, timed and painted, until she left for the hospital. Sloan did not like the paintings. He thought that kitchen cabinets ought not to be embellished.

"Function gets obscured," he'd complain. "Cabinets should be cabinets and paintings should be paintings."

Jake, however, did like them and commissioned some for Tia's articles. The first set was quite conventional and unremarkable: a collection of artichokes, cucumbers, and tomatoes to illustrate an article on summer soups. Then Jake decided they should "jump a little," when he contracted for another set. She took the term under consideration.

She was uneasy about mixing her painting with her food articles. When her first article appeared in *Capital Roundabout* she read the italics at the bottom of her page with surprise. *Restaurant critic V. V. Ensear has written about food for* Maine Monthly *and co-*

authored Russian Cookery *with painter Valery Malachenko (Washington Roundabout Press, $8.95).* Then there were newspaper ads for restaurants heralding her as "restaurant critic Victoria V. Ensear."

It had all started so casually. Not part of any dreams or ambitions. She had been sitting, heavily pregnant with Daisy, on the lawn at Easter Cove, with Gran and Masha, when the editor of *Maine Monthly* dropped in for tea. An old friend of Gran's, he had asked her for Russian recipes for his Christmas issue. Gran had turned to Masha and Tia ended up spending a week translating, explaining, and, finally, helping Masha cook and serve the dishes for the photographer. It was Gran's idea that Tia should get partial credit and after that *Maine Monthly* called her several times a year to gather ethnic specialties for the magazine. In italics, at the bottom of her column, it said, *Frequent contributor Victoria Ensear has lived all over the world with her grandmother, noted Russian artist and jewelry designer Helena Valenkova. Growing up with the vibrant Madame Valenkova, who is well known in New York and Maine for her teas, picnics and dinners, Mrs. Ensear became well versed in exotic cookery. She tries out her dishes on her husband, Washington psychiatrist Sloan Turner Ensear, and her children, Margaretha and Peter.*

In the small gallery that had shown Tia's works, the photocopied statement tacked to the wall near her canvases read simply, *Tia Valenkova grew up in New York City, studied with Paul Kirburg at his Pine Island School, with Valery Malachenko, and at the Corcoran. She has exhibited at the Unicorn II in Easter Cove, Maine.*

Sloan had bought one of the paintings and given it to Althea for Christmas. Tia had been grateful though embarrassed. "You know, dear," Althea had said, examining the painting, "if you painted those really sweet little watercolors, like the ones you make for the children, you could sell them to a greeting-card company."

There were many suggestions from people trying to help. Now there were angry letters about her paintings in *Capital Roundabout. Do you call that a vegetable? It ruined my appetite. Cancel my subscription.*

"Come on, Vicki baby, people cancel subscriptions over anything. Oh, this is good. Listen to this: 'That Mrs. Ensear ought to get her husband to treat her and help her stop abusing vegetables.'" Jake laughed so hard he started to cough, deep in his chest.

"You wanted them to jump. That's what vegetables look like when their editor wants them to jump," said Tia, trying to cover her hurt feelings.

"Sure, sure. I guess from now on we stick to the usual kind. But I kind of liked these." Jake bent over her drawings, tapping his cigarette against the edge of her desk. "I need a box with Bob's piece on the administration's dining habits—about three or four inches with names, addresses, hours. Maybe something on the likelihood of getting a table if you're Joe Blow."

"Mommy, you're late," Daisy called out indignantly when Tia churned up the school driveway. Daisy was standing alone with her teacher.

"I'm terribly sorry, Mrs. Potter. Something came up—an emergency came up—at the magazine."

"That's all right, Mrs. Ensear. Daisy and I had time for a wonderful chat." Mrs. Potter's face was malice bracketed by sweetness. Gran could not have done it better.

"Oh, how nice. Thank you," Tia babbled. "Come on, Daisy."

There were days when Tia felt overwhelmed by the army of disapprovers. Even Althea had suggested Tia make lists. Lists, said Althea, will help you be more efficient. But Tia already made lists and had decided not to say anything more on the subject. Oh, Tia's hopeless, Sloan would say. Woolgathering, her teachers had complained.

"Mommy, you were really late."

"I know, angel, I'm sorry."

"That's okay," said Daisy after a pause. "I told Mrs. Potter about how sometimes Peter and me go up and listen to Daddy's patients."

"Oh, Daisy."

"Only sometimes. Only we did it once."

"Really?"

"No, we never did it. But sometimes I think about it."

"Never, Daisy. That's private. Okay?"

"I know." She giggled. "Mrs. Potter was so surprised. Her mouth opened, like this. Look, Mommy, like this."

Chapter Nine

It had been a beautiful day in Easter Cove: blue cloudless sky and a light breeze from the ocean. The sun had felt so dry and hot after the weeks of cold and rain that Tia spent the day lying on the rocks, dipping her feet in the water, reading, watching sailboats. She heard Masha call but knew they would make her come out of the sun, and she felt too good, too like a cat stretched across the warm stones. She hid in the pines when Masha came down to the shore to find her, and then scampered along the rocks around the point. She spent the afternoon walking up through the hills and back down to town.

In town she wandered around the harbor, watching boats come in and out, noting how many more there were this year. She went up to the Seafarer and looked in the bowed front window at the row of tables stretching out to the plate-glass back, set with white cloths and thick amber glasses. Then, as the afternoon grew cooler, she started back up the hill to Gran's.

She always felt later that she had known immediately. There were so many cars in the drive and no party had been planned. No sound of voices or laughter, no one out on the grass playing croquet. She stood in the front hall and felt the dampness all around her, hearing only the tick of a clock and soft voices. Gran came out and stood for a moment, looking at her.

Tia made her last bargain. Please, let Gran be mad at me and I will never wander off again. But Gran stood in the hall with her old face collapsed in grief and said nothing. Someone had come up behind her and whispered something, and she did not turn but said, "No, I will."

"No, don't tell me. I don't want you to tell me," Tia had screamed, as loudly, as powerfully, as she could. "No, no, no."

She ran backward, slipping, tripping, scrambling. Someone had caught up with her, carried her back to the house.

The prized car, carrying Peter and Anna and Tinka, had been hit by a truck that lost control on a curve, ten miles south of Easter Cove. Grayson had stayed in the city, though for a few hours everyone thought he had been in the car too.

They didn't know what hit them, they didn't suffer, the police told them. The phrases kept running through Tia's mind for years. She thought about those last moments over and over, sure of the horrible anguish that just that second had allowed her mother to suffer. There must have been an instant, some immeasurably short piece of time, before impact, before death, when Anna had known.

Gran, Robin, and Tia existed together for two months. Gran had bent and contracted. She never went to her studio or gardened, but would hobble across the lawn with her two spaniels behind her and sit on the bench under the pines, looking out at the sea. Robin spent all her time on her pony, or Tia's, grooming them, feeding them apples. Tia walked. Never again the route that she had taken the day of the accident, but as far as the rocks. She would look at them stretching down to the sea and think, The last time I was on those rocks my parents were alive.

Gran's friends came. Tia could see that they were shaken by Gran's sudden enfeeblement, that they felt sorry for Gran and her two little granddaughters. Tia found it a balm to be able to act the role with them. Always a favorite, she became a pet. There were lots of people who wanted to take her home in the fall.

Grayson White arrived in September. Robin had told Tia that his hair had turned white from grief. He had also gotten quite fat. He wanted to take both girls home with him.

"You will never take Tia!" cried Gran.

"Madam, you are too old to bring up a child. Tia and Robin are like sisters. They have each other. You'll have them here all summer."

"Never!"

Gran was transformed. Lawyers flew up from New York. Tia was spirited off to stay with old friends who had a cottage nearby and was not allowed out of the house. Gran called her every night to tell her all would be well, that they would not be torn apart, that Tia would not have to live with the dreadful Grayson. Gran's voice was strong and sure. Gone was the cracked, soft voice of grief.

Tia was moved twice, crouching on the car floor, covered with a blanket. She spent a week in Connecticut with Gran's dearest friend, Elizavetta MacLeod. Elizavetta's son, Ivan, was there too. He let Tia drive into town every day with him to buy the newspaper and read to her every night. Tia would lie in the narrow bed under the eaves, afraid that the glorious Ivan would tire of her, and try to stay wide awake while he read. He had startling blue eyes and thick gold hair and a deep voice. He let her come fishing with him, found her a pole, put a worm on the hook, and laughed happily when she caught a fish. At the end of the week he packed for college and he let Tia sit on the edge of his bed and make a list of the clothes he had stacked on the floor. She went to the station with him in Elizavetta's old Studebaker, and after he kissed his mother, he bent down and picked Tia up and twirled her around. Long after the train had disappeared around the bend, she could feel the imprint of his arms around her waist.

Elizavetta drove Tia to another house, nearby, where she shared a room with a six-year-old girl who kept staring at her. Everyone seemed to avoid her. When she came into a room, everyone was suddenly cheerful. No one asked her any questions. They would say "You had a good sleep last night" or "You like chocolate cake." She wanted to play on the swings with the little girl but everyone expected her to be quiet and sad, so she stayed inside and stared out the window at the six-year-old flying through the air. When Gran called, Tia wanted to ask her what was happening but she did not dare. Her hosts sat nearby, forever sympathetic and tense.

It was a relief when Elizavetta came back to get her. Tia ran across the front garden and flung herself into Elizavetta's arms. They drove through Connecticut in the Studebaker with its stale-smelling gray plush seats, the brass key ring tinkling against

the ignition, and the leaves starting to turn yellow and red. Elizavetta told Tia that she was a very lucky little girl because her
Uncle Grayson wanted her to live with him, her grandmother
Helena wanted her, her step-grandmother Westcott had offered
her a home, her half-uncle Buddy Westcott in Morristown, New
Jersey, said he would take her. Tia sat gripping the seat, tracing
the corded edge with her fingers.

"I don't remember Uncle Buddy," she said finally.

"Oh, darling, I don't think your mother ever saw him. But
isn't it sweet of him?"

Tia remembered the picture of step-grandmother Westcott in a
black dress and a black hat that looked like a bird was sitting on
it. Her mouth turned down at the corners and her eyes were
close together.

"Where does step-grandmother Westcott live?"

"In Ohio or Tennessee or one of those places."

Anna had told Tia that Step-grandmother Westcott loved to
clean all day and say that you could eat pudding off her floor.

Tia stayed with Elizavetta MacLeod until all the leaves had fallen
from the trees and snow had started to fall in swirling flurries,
covering the ground and then blowing away again. It seemed like
a year. Professor MacLeod came up from their New York apartment every Friday afternoon on the train and left Sunday afternoon. He wore a tweed jacket that smelled faintly of sweat and
tobacco smoke. Elizavetta talked a great deal, and he murmured
responses occasionally from the depth of his armchair.

"And you, young lady," he would always say. "Learned anything this week?"

Gran called almost every evening but sometimes she just
talked to Elizavetta. Tia would listen intently to Elizavetta's part
of the conversation. It was the only way she learned anything
about what was going on.

"Oh, Helena, you must not let him take you to court.

"But Helena, she shouldn't be missing so much school.

"Helena, I think she's lonely and confused.

"Helena, what can I tell her?"

One morning Tia woke up and Ivan was standing in the doorway calling her.

"Hi, there, Princess Victoria," he said. "Time to get dressed. You're going home today."

She dressed and packed and hurried downstairs. Ivan was eating breakfast in the kitchen, his hair falling over one eye as he bent over his cereal. Elizavetta threw her arms around Tia.

"I'm going to miss you so, my dearest little baby," she said, tears flowing.

Tia stood stiffly, her face smothered in the folds of Elizavetta's dressing gown.

"Okay," said Ivan. He stood up, kissed his mother's cheek and reached for Tia's hand. "Ready?"

Tia nodded. She followed him out to the car.

"I'll drive back with Father on Christmas Eve," Ivan called to his mother.

They drove down a narrow road in the shadow of a high, bare, stony ridge. Ivan lit a cigarette. He inhaled deeply and blew the smoke out slowly like her father had.

"Did they tell you you are going to live with Gran?"

"No."

"Are you disappointed?"

"No." She felt nothing.

"It'll be interesting, Tia," he said, looking over at her. "Just keep reminding yourself, 'At least I'm not bored.'" He laughed and patted her hand. "Don't worry, Princess Victoria, you're going to survive them all."

Tia never saw the Washington Square apartment again. When she arrived at Gran's, her books and toys were already in her new room. At first she was not sure, finding them only after a tour of the new shelves and cabinets that had been built along one wall. Against another wall was a large four-poster bed with a white eyelet canopy. A chintz-covered love seat and low table were in front of the fireplace, and a towering painted armoire rose between two narrow windows. The rug was thick and pale and when she moved across it her feet sank into the pile. Heavy cream-silk curtains were drawn against the dusk.

"Pretty nifty," said Ivan, dropping her bag and looking around.

Gran stood in the doorway, watching Tia. She walked slowly

around the room. In a corner near the bed was the only piece from her Washington Square room, a small rocker that her father had given her soon after he came home from the war. It had been an early peace offering. It looked shabby and the paint had worn off the arms.

Tia saw her reflection in the mirror. She looked like the little hazelnut doll Valery had made her: pinched, stiff, with large, dark eyes that stared out of immobile flesh. She was wearing a plaid coat with velvet collar that Anna had bought her almost a year ago, and her bony wrists extended from its fraying cuffs, her dress trailed below its hem.

They had a quiet Christmas Eve.

"We are still in mourning," Gran said.

Valery came and brought a bottle of champagne, which they had in the long, dark salon before dinner. Tia sat on a large, slippery chair across from Gran, in a velvet dress and patent leather shoes, counting the scallops in the fire screen. Valery and Gran talked, sipped champagne, and glanced at Tia from time to time. When Masha announced dinner, the four of them sat down together and Valery told stories about people Gran and Masha knew. They laughed, lapsed into Russian sometimes, told Tia to be sure to save room for dessert. Tia tried to eat but she could barely manage to swallow.

After dinner, Valery came to her chair and pulled it back and bent over to kiss her head.

"Come and see what I have for you," he said.

She followed him solemnly to the other room. Masha stood in the doorway and grinned and Gran sat by the fire, smoking a cigarette in a long holder.

"We'll have to see how it works out," said Gran.

"Let her see it first," said Valery.

They had no tree that year, and the presents had been stacked on a low table in front of the fire while they were eating dinner. Valery bent over the table and pulled up the largest box.

"Open it carefully," he said.

Tia kneeled in front of the box and slowly undid the ribbon.

"Oh, not that slowly," said Valery, stooping to help her.

He pulled up the lid. Tia peered into the box and saw something move. She jumped back.

"Don't be frightened," said Gran.

A small black-and-white puppy stood up, blinked, and looked over the edge of the box.

"Oh, Valery!" cried Tia, gathering up the dog.

"That's the first time I've seen you smile all day," said Valery.

"Is it mine?"

"Of course," said Valery.

"We'll have to see how it gets along here and if it doesn't fight with Willy," said Gran, referring to her ancient spaniel, which slept with a snuffling snore by her feet.

"Ivan and I picked him up this afternoon," said Valery. "Ivan said he had big, dark eyes just like Tia."

"Valery, really," said Gran.

Apparently they had been unable to resist the puppy, of uncertain breed, in the pet-store window. It had taken much negotiation with Gran to allow the dog, with its potential size and temperament so unpredictable, into the lineup of Christmas presents.

"What'll I name him?" said Tia, letting the puppy chew on her fingers.

"Ivan kept calling him Charlie," said Valery.

"Oh, Tia can think of something prettier," said Gran.

"No. I like that: Charlie."

Gran was not pleased with Charlie—his name or his spots on the rug or his increasing size—but she tolerated him because Tia's attachment to the dog was immediate and getting rid of him would have been, in view of everything, impossible.

The Phoenix Press remained the only link with Tia's past. Gran had not been able to close it. It had meant so much to her son, she told her wary advisers. Tia, listening to the discussion, understood that Peter Valenkov had left so little that Gran could not obliterate the one part of his vision that was still tangible. So the machines and materials were moved out of the butcher shop to a building farther uptown, where they shared facilities with another small publisher. Gran hired a friend who had published a newspaper in Germany before the war and lately had been night manager of a launderette.

Without Peter and Anna and the apartment on Washington Square, and with the humorless new editor and the new offices and Gran's bookkeeper, few of the old group stayed on. The Cellis sold their shares to Gran. Gena and Tia were no longer allowed to deliver books. Tia, Gran would insist, must accompany her to the offices on her monthly visit.

"It meant so much to your father and to Anna," Gran would say.

Tia tried every deceit in her repertoire to escape these excursions. Still, sometimes she ran out of sore throats, nausea, and too much homework and had to go. Standing by Gran's chair, she would look out into the back room with the big, black presses and the men setting type and remember her father. The smells, the noise, the stacks of paper and type were so evocative that her heart would start to beat fast, her head would spin, and she would hold on hard to Gran's chair until they left.

It had been strained the first months: Tia wandering around the apartment like a stranger, racing back to her room when she heard voices in the library, sitting in her rocker and rocking for hours, holding Charlie, staring sightlessly at the windows. Masha came in at dusk to draw the curtains and be sure the lamps were on. Tia liked the rustle of Masha's skirts as she bustled about the room and the smell of sugar and vanilla on her hands. After dinner, Masha drew a bath while Tia sprawled on the rug with Charlie, finishing her homework. She would look up and see Masha's shadow on the wall as she moved around the bathroom, listen to the sound of water rushing from the taps into the big porcelain tub, smell the bath salts and lavender soap.

"Come on, come on," Masha would call, always impatient.

After her bath Masha wrapped her in a big, rough, white towel and fiercely rubbed her entire body. "Circulation, circulation," she'd explain when Tia cried out. When Tia was burnished and her skin red, Masha held the towel to ward off any curious eyes that might have threatened their privacy while Tia slipped into her pajamas.

When the lights were out, Masha sat on the edge of the bed and told Tia stories about her childhood. They were about pigs and cows that foretold earthquakes, women who saw the future in flames, men who could read minds. Masha's world was as haunted and supernatural as Tia's.

Tia tried every night to remember her mother's face but it had begun to blur. Sometimes her father's face came to her more clearly. Often she would get up and go and sit in front of their pictures and try to memorize them again, but that made it harder and she began to see them as photographs, frozen on a summer day in Easter Cove with unfamiliar smiles. Gradually it became easier not to remember them at all. When Elizavetta or Gran would talk about them, Tia refused to listen. She put away the photographs and the toys that she had had in Washington Square, moved the rocker to the back of her closet, left the room when anyone played the Chopin or Bach pieces that Anna used to play. When Masha braided her hair every morning and evening, Tia welcomed the harsh strokes and tight plaits because her mother's hands had been so gentle.

By late spring, when the air was warm again, when she could open her window and breathe in the river smells, watch the trees far below begin to bud, Tia felt some of her tension recede. Perhaps it was being able to play with Robin again. Some sort of truce had been reached with Grayson, and Robin came over Saturday afternoons and sometimes spent the night in the big four-poster with Tia. Gran went off to Paris in May. Valery came and had dinner almost every night. He brought flowers for Masha and a bottle of wine and sometimes asked other friends, and they sat in the long tiled kitchen and ate and drank.

"Don't tell Madame," warned Masha. "She'll be very angry."

But Masha seemed happier serving soup and bread in the kitchen and talking Russian so fast that Tia could not understand a single word. Valery would bring Tia books that her father had printed and try to show her why they were so beautiful. Tia would always jump up and throw her arms around his neck and giggle, and he would forget about the book and tell her stories about Russia and Paris and escaping from the Germans and being smuggled in the trunk of someone's car to Lisbon. His friends would laugh at him, add their own stories, sometimes fall silent when their humor failed them.

Just before Gran returned from Paris, Tia and Charlie went to spend the weekend with the MacLeods. It was fair and warm, trees blurry with pale new leaves, the grass a deep dark green. Ivan was home with a tall, pretty girl with long red hair. Tia climbed up beside him, eyeing the red-haired girl over his shoulder, while Professor MacLeod bent over the outdoor grill, searing hamburgers.

"Will you read to me later, Ivan?" said Tia.

"Sure," said Ivan. The red-haired girl smiled.

"Darling, you've burned the meat," exclaimed Elizavetta.

"It's just a bit charred," said Professor MacLeod, his face bright red as he turned back from the grill.

"You should have let Ivan do it," said Elizavetta crossly.

"I believe in charring too, Mother," said Ivan, laughing.

"How do you like living with your grandmother?" said Ivan as he put a wedge of blackened meat in a bun for her.

"Oh, it's such a beautiful apartment," said the red-haired girl. "Ivan took me to meet Mrs. Valenkova at Christmastime," she explained.

She and Elizavetta discussed the beauty of the apartment. Ivan put his arm around Tia's shoulder.

"Eat up, skinny," he said. "When I come up I want to see you beating Robin at tennis. Okay?"

She nodded. "Okay."

"When I come up I'll take you on."

"I'd love to see your home in Maine," said the red-haired girl, bending around Ivan. "I'll bet it's really wonderful." She put her hand on Ivan's arm. "Will you take me up there?" she said archly.

"Gran doesn't have guests in the summer," said Tia crossly.

"Tia," warned Elizavetta. "I'm sure Helena would love to see you again, Peggy."

Ivan forgot to read Tia a story that night. He went to town with Peggy to see a movie.

Chapter Ten

"Why don't we look at the house before you go." Sloan looked across the steaming bowls of chowder.

"I thought someone bought it."

"It fell through."

"This chowder is awfully tasteless, isn't it?" said Tia.

All the reviews in the September issue would be negative and Jake would be upset.

"What about the house, Tia?"

"Mrs. Pierce called me about one on P Street."

"Really? Where? Why didn't you tell me."

"Near Liz and Joe."

"Great," he said happily. He looked pleased. If the chowder hadn't been so terrible she probably would not have mentioned it.

"We can see it at six."

"Great, pick me up at quarter of." He reached over and took her hand. "This could be a new beginning for us," he said.

"We haven't even seen it," she said quickly, wondering why he had said that about a new beginning. "We can have an early dinner at the new place on Wisconsin Avenue."

"Can't," he said, abruptly. "Told Klein I'd come to his narcissism seminar tonight. God, that man is so controlling. Today he—" He shrugged. "Oh, well."

The elderly Klein, Sloan's former mentor, had been the focus of much of his frustration this year. Once he started, Sloan's resentment boiled to a rage.

"I guess you're not interested," said Sloan.

"Of course I am," she protested automatically.

"You're saved by the bell," said Sloan, looking at his watch. "Maybe I'll call Joe and see what he knows about the house."

The house was dark and narrow with a small, barren back garden.

"Of course the Morrisons were quite elderly and they did let it go a bit," said Mrs. Pierce. "But you could do marvelous things with it."

Tia could tell Sloan was disappointed. He walked into the dining room and ran his hand along the edge of the mantel. Paint was curling off and he flicked chips with his thumb.

"Those are Delft tiles, Dr. Ensear," said Mrs. Pierce.

"My wife needs a good kitchen."

"Oh, yes, but you have the space here and it might be better— since you use the kitchen in a professional sense—to do it yourself." She smiled at Tia.

Tia, only half listening as she walked along the dusty hall, was caught by surprise. She turned to share her discomfort with Sloan but he was telling Mrs. Pierce that Tia would need a large gas range which would not fit into the small space.

"Oh, but it has such a lovely view of the house across the street," said Mrs. Pierce gaily. "You know that's the best row of Federal houses in Georgetown. Wouldn't that be an inspiration, Mrs. Ensear?"

"My husband had hoped to have an office in the house."

"Well, that's what made me think of you," said Mrs. Pierce.

There were three tiny, windowless rooms in the basement. Two metal beds and a bureau had been left in one, an old couch in another.

"You could make a private entrance where the coal chute was," said Mrs. Pierce.

"I think, Mrs. Pierce," said Sloan in his professional voice, "that this isn't really what we're looking for."

"It is a nice house," assured Tia.

"Yes, it is. But not right for us."

"Well, of course then," said Mrs. Pierce coldly. "The price, I thought, might suit you better."

Sloan flushed. "Price, he said, "is not a major consideration." He stood very straight and walked out of the house.

"Why did I let that get to me?" Sloan moaned as they walked back to the car.

"She meant it to," said Tia. "I think she's getting impatient."

"Her job is to show houses. Considering the commission she'll make when she sells one of those overpriced piles . . . " He glowered.

"I know, I know. She guessed your vulnerable spot."

It was probably the same spot in almost all her clients. It irritated Tia to have been caught in that flock. Coupled with the remark about the professional kitchen, it depressed her.

He turned to her as they were getting into the car and leaned across the seat. "You okay?"

"Yes, fine."

Chapter Eleven

Tia sat silently on the window seat in the library at Easter Cove, hoping not to be noticed. She knew that if she was quiet Gran would not send her to bed, would only be vaguely aware of her presence. Sitting on the floor by the fire, leaning against Gran's chair, Tia wished Robin were still downstairs, but Robin usually giggled or interrupted and was dismissed early. Tonight Ivan's fiancée, Kathryn, was visiting and Tia and Robin had spent most of the day spying on the engaged couple. Since Kathryn paid little attention to either cousin, following her around all day was the only way they could avenge themselves.

Gran's summer visitors were always family and friends. Elizavetta, Valery, Laura Landsdale, Russian cousins, Paris friends, friends of Valery's from Berlin, young painters Gran had met in New York during the winter. In New York she invited her patrons—women who wore her jewelry to balls and openings; people who owned galleries, bought her paintings—rarely mixing them with her own friends. There Tia would sneak down the hall and watch the beautifully dressed women and men as they sipped their drinks, lit their cigarettes, laughed, flitted lightly from subject to subject.

"Go back to bed," Gran would say if she caught Tia. Gran would be tense and irritable.

In Easter Cove, Gran was relaxed and happier, though often her guests were neither. It was Gran, with her large airy house by the sea, her aura of confidence and expectation, and Valery, with his roaring laugh and bear hugs, who tipped the balance. Women and men who had lost everything would come to the small Maine town with battered suitcases and disappear into the brown house on the top of Easter Hill. They sat on the lawn on sunny days, on the white Adirondack chairs that faced the sea, and some walked along the piny paths in the hills or stayed in their rooms. Some dove into the icy Atlantic and swam out into the gray sea with strong, steady strokes.

If Tia was quiet at night, after dinner, sometimes they would talk about life Before. Valery told Tia and Robin little, would caution them not to ask questions. Gran planned the days carefully so that all her visitors were exposed to as much fresh air, exercise, fresh fruit and vegetables as possible. Many balked, and while Gran spent the morning in her studio, they would sit and read or join Masha in the kitchen and drink coffee or walk to town and buy cinnamon rolls and jelly doughnuts at the Sweete Shoppe in Easter Cove. Sworn to secrecy, Robin and Tia were often drafted for those expeditions, trading their proficiency in English and Maine inflection for a brownie or tart.

"Oh, it's so depressing," Kathryn whispered to Ivan. "These people are so depressing," Tia had heard her say that morning.

"Not Valery and Helena," Ivan had said.

Tonight, her head on Ivan's shoulder, Kathryn sighed. Lise Thulin was talking about the big house she had grown up in in Lübeck. "It was right out of *Buddenbrooks*," she said, "and so was my poor father."

"Ah, then that explains your colors," said Gran. Lise was one of her protégés.

"Yes, a variety of grays." Lise laughed.

Everyone laughed except Kathryn, whose mouth turned down at the corners. She pushed a lock of silky hair behind her ear, ran her finger back and forth along the small gold earring and then stood up.

"This has been a wonderful evening, Mrs. Valenkova," she said, "but I'm just dead."

"What a pity. The sea air, it must be," said Gran sweetly.

"And all that delicious food," said Kathryn. "I'll say good night."

"I'll see you upstairs," said Ivan, leaping to his feet.

After they left the room there was a long silence.

"Oh, dear," murmured Elizavetta. Professor MacLeod cleared his throat.

"Well, I'm dead too," said Tia, imitating Kathryn's drawl. Valery burst into laughter.

"Tia!" Gran rose from her seat.

"I'm sorry, Gran," said Tia quickly.

"Go to your room at once."

Humiliated, she hurried up the stairs, but when she got to the landing she heard the room burst into laughter.

"She sounded just like her," said Elizavetta.

Ivan and Kathryn were married in New York at St. Bartholomew's in December. Gran bought Tia a new black velvet dress with white collar and cuffs for the occasion. It was, thought Tia, disappointingly childish for someone twelve years old, when Robin was wearing red taffeta and stockings.

"Oh, how unspeakably vulgar," said Gran.

Ivan stood at the altar with his hair cut very short, his face rigid, watching Kathryn walk in stately fashion down the long aisle after a team of pink velvet bridesmaids. Her stepfather, small and ancient, seemed to be leaning on her arm.

"She is very beautiful," said Gran to Elizavetta, who was weeping.

Very beautiful, thought Tia, feeling overwhelmed. She would never be as old, as poised, as lovely.

"But heartless," wept Elizavetta.

"She wouldn't like anyone marrying her darling," muttered Valery crossly to Tia.

They went to Kathryn's mother's large Park Avenue apartment for a reception.

"Hey, skinny," called Ivan when he saw Tia. He swept her up and gave her a crushing hug. His face was flushed and there was sweat beading on his upper lip. "You are going to be a beauty," he said. "Give Kathryn a kiss."

Kathryn smiled down at Tia and gave her a flower from her bouquet. "You'll have to come and visit us, Tia," she said, brushing cool lips against Tia's cheek.

Tia rode up Fifth Avenue on the soft, plush seat of the limousine Gran had bought that year, and sold the next, covered in a gray rug, while the wind blew the falling snow against the windows. Valery had put his arm around her, Gran smelled wonderful, the car was warm, the streets were full of Christmas shoppers, and they were on their way to tea at the Plaza.

Chapter Twelve

"Don't be too Radcliffe tonight," said Sloan as they drove down the hill toward the Potomac.

"What?"

"George and Mary are . . . " He paused and glanced over at her.

"Stupid?"

"There you go again, goddamn it."

"Watch it."

He swerved around a parked car and accelerated through a yellow light.

"Mary went to junior college."

"So?"

"So don't try to talk to her about Proust."

"Would you care to suggest a topic?"

"Don't get angry," he said, roaring across the Key Bridge and sweeping across two lanes of traffic. "Mary's a Hipwell."

Tia's education had failed her on the sort of name recognition that Sloan expected of her. It infuriated him when she didn't understand about Hipwells and Ensears.

Despite the Hipwell connection, George and Mary lived in a development of freshly built frame houses, set on a treeless ridge. The house was sparsely furnished. Everything looked new.

"Hey, look who's here." Liz and Joe rose to greet them, Liz with her obligatory wet cheek kiss.

Another couple stood awkwardly aside. Introductions were

made. Tia never listened to names being announced. "God, this is going to be a Klein evening," Liz whispered.

"Oh, no," said Tia.

Liz raised her eyebrows. "Can you believe this house?"

"No kidding!" Joe exclaimed across the room. The men stood in a tight knot.

"I'm going to show them the wine cellar," called George, starting out of the room, the men following him in single file.

"Do you share this passion for wine?" asked Mary.

"No," said Tia.

"I poured Gallo's finest into a bottle of Joe's Lafite-Rothschild the other night and he never noticed," said Liz.

"Did you?" Mary smiled, her face stiff, obviously somewhat taken aback.

The four women sat uncomfortably together until George led their husbands back from the cellar. The men boomed into the room, laughing.

"Why is it that men always seem to have such a good time together?" said Liz sourly.

Tia glanced at her watch and found that only fifteen minutes had elapsed since their arrival.

"They try harder," said Mary. "They're content with show rather than substance."

"Are you girls generalizing about men again?" said George, jovial.

"We were just saying what fun you guys seem to have together," said Mary, with a lush laugh and tilted head.

"Not fair," said Liz, whose speech was already blurring.

"Oh, you gals, you spend plenty of time cackling together," said Joe.

Sloan glanced over at Tia, who remained silent but avoided his eyes.

The doorbell tinkled again. It was Klaus and Annie Klein. Even Liz snapped to attention. Sloan and Joe stood side by side, rubbing their hands, smiling, looking like Siamese twins.

"Sorry we're late," said Klein in the soft, lisping German accent that his protégés often affected. "Last-minute phone call." He smiled. Actually he beamed.

Annie, her stiff blond hair streaked and curled for eternity, beamed too. His former student and second wife, Annie was, at least in public, his most ardent supporter. "Tell them, Klaus," she said. She brushed some lint off her sleeve and looked at him expectantly. "Go on, darling," she said—somewhat impatiently, thought Tia.

"It can wait," said Klein, smiling benignly.

"Please," said Sloan. "We'd love to know."

"Yes, Klaus, do tell us," said Liz. She was the only one in the protégés' circle who called Klein by his first name, but since her father had endowed the Klaus Klein chair at Maryland College she felt it was her privilege.

"The President called. Quite amazing, those White House operators."

Yes, so they say, Tia thought.

"No!"

"The President?"

"Tell us, Dr. Klein."

"Tell them where they got hold of you, dear," said Annie.

Klein chuckled. He glanced at his audience.

"Where?" said Sloan.

"At the dentist's."

"At the dentist's!"

"No!"

"The President!"

"While you were sitting in the chair," Tia put in, because Sloan was glancing over at her ominously.

"Well, no, actually, I was in the waiting room," said Klein.

"The White House calling you at your dentist's!" Joe clapped his hands in delight.

"What did the President call about, sir?"

"Ah," said Klein, rubbing his hands together. "George, what about a whiskey for me?"

"Oh, yes, Dr. Klein. I was just so excited. . . . " He stumbled backward toward the bar.

"The President wants me to organize a mental health month," said Klein. He bent over the tray of canapés on the table in front of him. "Mmm, doesn't this look good," he said, picking up a large shrimp.

"A mental health month?"

"Yes . . . mmmm . . . that's right. Sounds like window dressing, I said to the President." He paused. "He assured me that he is very concerned about the issue and that this is the way to get some organizational work started. He thought we could get some distinguished people to serve on the committee."

"That's fantastic!"

"Congratulations!"

"Oh, Klaus, how exciting."

"I'll have to get your input on the matter," he said. Sloan, George, and Joe nodded and smiled.

"Isn't this fun," said Annie Klein, bending over the tray of canapés as her husband moved over to huddle with his protégés.

"Where did you get that marvelous dress, Annie?" said Liz.

It always amazed Tia that Liz could change gears with such ease.

"Klein is awfully excited about the Presidential thing," said Sloan as they were driving home.

"Yes," said Tia.

"You and Mary got into a long conversation."

"She wants to go back to school."

"Good for her. Did you talk to Annie?"

"Not much."

"I wish you'd get to know her."

"Yeah."

"Come on. It isn't too much to ask," said Sloan.

Yes, it is, thought Tia. There was no point in saying anything that would start the usual post-party argument. These evenings filled Sloan with rage and Tia with despair.

Chapter Thirteen

It had started with Valery's suggestion at Christmas dinner. Startled, Gran had agreed. Tia and Robin would accompany her to Paris that spring. Grayson had balked at first. He did not want Robin to leave school early, and Gran had always left after Tia's birthday in May. They had all sat around the table in Gran's dining room overlooking the East River, arguing, while the Christmas goose cooled. The truce with Grayson was so tenuous, had taken so long to achieve, the family had finally reassembled, and as half-uncle Buddy Westcott, invited up from New Jersey on impulse and not expected to accept, tried to arbitrate, Tia burst into tears.

"Tia," said Gran, surprised. "What is it?"

"Poor child," said Valery. "She is upset by the fighting, Helena. On Christmas Day."

"Why don't the girls join you over there after school closes?" said Buddy. "I'll get them to the airport." He smiled at Tia. "Your mom used to cry whenever Richie and I fought."

Tia hastily wiped her tears away and sat up straight.

"Valery, please, do carve," commanded Gran. "Yes, Mr. Westcott, your suggestion is most thoughtful but I only stay in Paris until mid-June."

"Please, Daddy, please," begged Robin, leaping from her chair and rushing around to her father. "I'll finish my assignments early."

"The children are both good students, Grayson," said Gran.

"Why not let them take off a few weeks? We can always have a tutor in Easter Cove this summer to catch them up. Sit down, Robin."

"Please, Daddy, please."

"Well," said Grayson, "I suppose that might satisfy the school."

"Good," said Gran. She looked across the dining room and smiled.

Candles flickered in reflection on the bank of windows. Lights were going on across the river; the tumbling, gray sky was darkening.

While Gran's previous trips seemed to require nothing more than Masha packing a trunk and a solemn farewell dinner where instructions, suggestions, and commands for the coming month were issued, the one that was planned at Christmas dinner took on a pageantry of its own. Tia was taken to Lord and Taylor, Saks, Bendel's, Best and Company, and some of Gran's favorite smaller stores on Madison Avenue. Gran's friend Madame Dreyfus came three times a week to improve Tia's French. Grayson had insisted that Robin would rest on her school proficiency. Presents were bought for Gran's French cousins and friends. Every weekend Tia would journey out to the MacLeods' so that Elizavetta could drive her to her riding lessons.

"Your cousins like to ride, and you'll look foolish if you ride like a little Indian," announced Gran when Tia protested. Actually, Tia enjoyed having two days in the MacLeods' Connecticut cottage. She even enjoyed Professor MacLeod, who made sarcastic remarks about the preparations. Ivan and Kathryn promised to visit, but they decided to stay in Cambridge because their baby was, as Kathryn said, a lousy traveler.

"I can't imagine Ivan with a baby," said Tia.

"Neither can I," said Professor MacLeod.

Grayson impeded Gran's plans for Robin. He refused to let Gran keep her for a month so she could oversee the reducing diet she had prescribed and that was plainly not being followed. Alone in their Brooklyn Heights house, furnished so long ago by Tinka, they defied Gran with breads and puddings and cakes prepared by the Polish housekeeper.

"Polish food." Gran snorted.

But Grayson did allow Gran to add to Robin's wardrobe.

"Gran, these are far too young for me," cried Robin, seeing the plain cotton dresses laid out on the bed for her to try on.

"You'll thank me," said Gran imperiously.

"But my black dresses make me look thin," protested Robin.

"Like a Polish grandmother," said Gran.

"Ohhhhh," wailed Robin.

In traveling suits, carrying new leather handbags with lots of compartments, Tia and Robin followed Gran to Paris. They arrived very early in the morning at Orly, to be greeted by a large group of people all shouting and kissing each other, and took the long drive into Paris, staring out the window and waiting for the city to start looking like it should.

Gran preferred to stay in a hotel in Paris. It was small, on a narrow winding Left Bank street. The rooms had frescoed ceilings and overlooked a courtyard filled with red begonias. The relatives and friends, always in such large and noisy groups that Robin and Tia found it hard to sort them out, swooped in and out of the tiny lobby, their cars blocking the street outside, Gran protesting she was too exhausted for another lunch or visit or drive, and Robin and Tia trying to answer the questions that flew at them. After a few days, Gran allowed Tia and Robin to walk alone around the city while she rested in the afternoon. Tia usually let Robin, with her ungrammatical, badly accented, fluent French, do most of the talking.

"You talk this time," Robin would say. "Your French is so good, Ti."

"I can't, Robin. I get so intimidated."

Before dinner, Tia and Robin would join Gran in her room and tell her what they had done that afternoon. She made suggestions for the following day and always added, "Aren't you glad you worked so hard with Madame Dreyfus, Tia?" with a significant look at Robin.

"Yes, Gran," Tia would answer, and Robin never gave her away.

Then they would be off to someone's apartment for dinner, or to a restaurant for a meal that would last until midnight. "Don't speak English to Tia," Gran would say, always keeping a sharp eye for such infractions. "I want her to improve her French."

Toward the end of the month they drove to Brittany to spend a week with the MacLeods. Professor MacLeod, to celebrate the birth of his grandson, had rented a small house on the Atlantic coast for the summer. It was whitewashed, tile-floored, simply furnished, with a wild garden, on a high dune overlooking the sea. There was a way through the brambles to a precipitous path that led to a small crescent of sandy beach below. Renting it, inviting Ivan and Kathryn and the baby, was an uncharacteristically expansive and optimistic gesture for Professor Mac-Leod. Inviting Gran and her granddaughters capped off the gesture.

The three tiny upstairs bedrooms had narrow beds and thin walls. Robin and Tia shared the largest with Gran. Next door they could hear Ivan and Kathryn and Alexey.

"It's only for two weeks. It means so much to Father," said Ivan, often.

Kathryn's voice was less distinct. "Godawful . . . those brats . . . so wild here . . . Can't we leave early to visit Mummy in Menton? . . . I've had it. . . . Take this damn baby. . . . "

Tia sat on the stairs and listened to the MacLeods and Gran talk.

"She's so terribly wrong for him," said Elizavetta, in tears again.

"She can help him a great deal, Elizavetta," said Gran. "Ivan has always been very pragmatic."

"Of course," said Professor MacLeod. "And she's a beauty."

"Oh, what does that matter?" snapped Elizavetta.

"To a man, my dear."

"Oh," wailed Elizavetta. "Oh, if only Tia were older. They would have been perfect."

"Elizavetta!" chorused Gran and Professor MacLeod.

Tia blushed in the darkness of her hiding place and jumped up and ran back to her bed.

The baby cried early in the morning. Ivan took him downstairs and put him in his carriage and walked up the dirt road that led to the main road to the village. Sometimes Tia got up and dressed quietly and hurriedly and joined him. In the clear blue mornings of that week, they would walk between fields full of wild flowers, Alexey cooing as the carriage bumped along, Ivan bending over and kissing the top of the baby's bald little head.

"Kathryn doesn't like it here, does she?" They had reached the village and were peering into the still-shuttered shops.

"Well, she's used to more amenities. Brittany isn't the Riviera, is it?"

"No, of course not," said Tia smoothly.

"But I love it here."

"I do too."

"Well, skinny, we always like the same things," he said.

"Right," said Tia.

Ivan put his arm around her and gave her a squeeze.

"You're getting tall," he said, surprised, looking down at her. He stopped for a moment. "Are you—what?—fourteen?"

"Fifteen."

"And has it been interesting, after all? With Gran?"

"Yes."

He reached down and stroked her hair. "I'm going to miss my little girl."

Kathryn, Ivan, and Alexey left after a week. They took the train to Paris the day before Gran, Tia, and Robin left. Elizavetta was tearful, Professor MacLeod grim, Ivan conciliatory, Kathryn gay. On the station platform, waiting for the train to come, Gran bought everyone an ice cream. The gesture was so unusual that Tia watched the departure scene with renewed interest.

All the way home Elizavetta wept, speaking in sobbing Russian to Gran, who held her in her arms.

"Lots of drama, right?" said Professor MacLeod to Tia and Robin.

"I think Kathryn will be much happier on the Riviera," said Tia grandly.

"Oh, what do you know?" said Robin. "You don't know anything about the Riviera."

"There are more amenities there," said Tia.

Chapter Fourteen

"Mommy," said Daisy, "you didn't listen to me."

"Daisy, don't be rude," said Tia. She was trying to pack for Easter Cove. Priscilla was ironing Daisy's dresses, and Peter was slowly and deliberately piling up the toys he wanted to take.

"I said," said Daisy, undaunted, "that Peter is taking too much. He thinks he can take all that."

Peter grinned. His pile was growing.

"He just wants to take his favorite things," said Tia irritably.

"He sure has lots of toys," said Priscilla. "He just has too many things."

"Gran and Mrs. Ensear send him so much," said Tia defensively.

"And you."

"Yes!" exclaimed Daisy.

"And to you too, missy," said Priscilla.

Daisy and Priscilla started arguing.

"Don't be rude to Priscilla," said Tia automatically, counting out a pile of underwear. It was hot and humid. She felt sticky. Priscilla hated air conditioning, so they usually didn't turn it on until she had left for the day.

"Dr. Snear said he'd pick you up at six sharp," said Priscilla. "He said you should go out and buy yourself a nice new dress." Priscilla looked over at Tia. "Why don't you?"

Tia shrugged. It was too hot.

"If it was me, I'd buy the dress," said Priscilla.

The party was crowded when they got there. Tia could tell that Sloan was nervous; he kept looking over at her.

"I'm sorry, I didn't have time to shop."

"You look fine," he said tonelessly.

"I'll get some new things when I get back."

"It's just that the Brownlaws are so formal," he said.

Tia looked around the packed garden. Gathered listlessly around the bar, the well-dressed group was wilting in the heat.

"There's Jeanne Jessup. Why don't you talk to her?"

Jeanne Jessup, wife of Jared Jessup, who had just published a book on childhood schizophrenia, was standing at the edge of a group around her husband. Her family's meat-packing fortune had given her a certain autonomy.

"I'm flying now. Bought a Navaho. You've got to come up with me some time, Tia. You'd love it."

"Did you hear," said Annie Klein, "that Bob and Ellie bought the Lees' house on Dumbarton?"

"Well, Bob made partner at Covington," said Jeanne. "It's not a bad house."

"Not a bad house at all," said Annie, raising her eyebrows and giving Tia a significant look. "Tia, I'm sorry you'll miss our picnic. Sloan tells me you're going to Maine."

"Yes, I'm so sorry," said Tia.

Annie Klein regarded her gravely. "Tia, dear, you ought to get more involved in things."

"We love your restaurant reviews," said Jeanne.

"We all have busy lives, dear," said Annie Klein. "But even in our profession"—she smiled, making light of putting herself in tandem with her renowned husband—"we have to politick. After all, this is Washington," she finished brightly.

"I saw you talking to Annie Klein," said Sloan as they left the party.

"I apologized about missing the party."

"You're really going ahead, then," said Sloan.

He was angry. His head would tilt at those moments, just like Daisy's.

"I'm sorry, Sloan." She had been wondering the last few days why she was so anxious to go to Easter Cove when waiting a few days would make life with Sloan so much easier. She had usually given in before.

"You always do exactly what you want to do!" he shouted at her. "You back yourself into a corner, just like Daisy, and dig in."

Perhaps she had, she thought. Still, the thought of the picnic was unbearable: sitting on the Kleins' terrace in the enervating Eastern Shore summer heat, trying to keep track of Peter, drinking and eating and talking too much; driving back in the holiday traffic, feeling irritated and empty, listening to Sloan's jealousy of his colleagues mix with his rage at being a lesser Ensear. A day in the sun with too much time and alcohol would fuel the old sense of inequity.

"Come with me to Easter Cove instead," Tia said suddenly.

Sloan was caught off guard by the suggestion. "You really want me to?"

"Of course."

He smiled. "Well, let me think about it."

She took his arm. "We'll leave the children with Masha for a day and sail out to Pine Island."

"Sounds nice," he said, putting his arm around her as they walked down the hill to their car. "I thought you were so hellbent on going because you wanted to get away from me."

Tia thought that maybe he was right. "Don't be silly," she said.

Chapter Fifteen

Ivan came to dinner on Tia's seventeenth birthday with a sketch of her room in Easter Cove, made from a photograph he had taken the summer before.

"My goodness," he said, when she came into the room that night. "How children grow up."

Seated next to Tia most of the evening, he wove his usual spell. This time, Gran saw, Ivan was less an observer of his effect than a participant. Kathryn, Gran established, was in Barbados with her sister, recovering from a miscarriage. Actually, Kathryn rarely came to Gran's. When she did she said little, looked bored, glanced at her watch frequently, and insisted on leaving early. For the last couple of summers she had insisted Ivan leave her with Alexey in Manchester by the Sea with her mother and stepfather when he drove his parents to Easter Cove.

Mummy counts on this summer visit, and though I'd love to be with you in Maine, I cannot disappoint her, she had written Gran in a thick, round hand on stiff, monogrammed notepaper the first time. The next summer she called and last summer there had been no explanation. Ivan seemed happy to linger at Easter Cove an extra day or so, before returning to Boston, and insisted on coming at the end of two weeks to retrieve his parents.

"Tia and Robin are growing up," said Elizavetta sentimentally, tears glistening.

"Lovely girls, lovely girls," murmured Professor MacLeod, who had been drinking quite a bit since his retirement.

"A toast then, to Tia, on her seventeenth birthday and to Helena for having helped make her such a lovely young lady," said Grayson.

Gran, surprised and moved, reached over and clasped Grayson's hand.

"And to Robin, whose seventeenth birthday I will miss," said Gran, whose annual trip to Paris always coincided with it, "and to Grayson, who has been such a fine father."

Almost everyone was in tears. After so many years it was jarring to be so aware of the absence of Peter, Anna, and Tinka. They drank their toasts in sudden, profound sadness.

Finally Ivan spoke. "Then we must drink to Tinka and to Peter and Anna."

"Yes," shouted Valery, "that's right!"

They all turned to look at Gran. Tears ran down her cheeks. Tia jumped up and went to her.

"It's all right, dear," she said, patting Tia's hands. She raised her glass, nodded at Ivan, and drank.

Tia took her seat, near tears too. The ancient grief, long forgotten, rose again. Fighting its anguish she felt faint, her heart beating too fast. She tried to breathe slowly, staring out the window at the river, counting the lights on the Queensboro Bridge.

"It's okay," whispered Ivan, bending close to her. His arm rested lightly on her back. "We Russians are emotional people," he said, smiling, repeating the phrase Valery frequently employed after one of his outbursts.

Tia started laughing. Robin, who'd overheard the remark, joined her. Ivan threw back his head and roared.

That evening Tia plummeted into love. By the time coffee was served and the presents were opened, it was a matter of embarrassment to everyone that Ivan's sketch was of Tia's bedroom.

"Oh, how nice, Ivan," said Gran firmly. "Kathryn told me you were doing it and I thought Tia would be delighted."

"Oh, darling, how wonderful," said Elizavetta. "Look, he's gotten all those stuffed animals she keeps on her bed."

There was an awkward silence.

"Thank you, Ivan," said Tia, flushed. "It's beautiful."

Ivan looked at her gravely. His eyes were blue and deep-set.

The lamp in back of him gilded his pale hair. Those were the sorts of things that Tia noticed about him that evening.

There was a book, sent the next day. It was Ivan's book about his dig on Crete, with an inscription: *To the beautiful Victoria Valenkova, my little Tia, from her ancient but dazzled friend, Ivan.* For weeks she would feel a breath-catching thrill when she read those words. What a beautiful hand he had, so small and sensitive.

Whether Gran had seen the book or Tia gave signs of bewitchment, Gran started mentioning Kathryn.

"I thought you said she was a silly snob," said Robin.

"Robin, your mouth is full."

"Oh, no, Robin, your grandmother reveres Kathryn," said Valery.

"Please," said Gran warningly. She sighed. "She's lovely— such a sweet little mother." Gran could never resist malice when the subjects of discussion were absent.

There was a terrible time when Ivan came to tea with Elizavetta, and Tia had come running into the room with braids flying, sweaty and flushed, to announce her lacrosse team's victory that afternoon on the fields of Central Park. She came to a stop in front of Gran and then suddenly saw Ivan, sprawled on a pillow in front of the fire, smiling up at her.

"That's wonderful news," said Gran sweetly, smiling broadly. "Isn't Tia to be congratulated?"

"To Tia Victorious," said Ivan, in a wonderful, deep voice, raising his teacup.

"Tia, darling, you're so tall," said Elizavetta.

Tia stood, bristling with consciousness of her damp, red face, navy pleated gym suit, and big feet in bright white sneakers.

"Go shower, darling, and then join us," said Gran kindly.

Chapter Sixteen

"Come on out to Langdon Hall for the day," said Sabrina Abbott. "My ex-stepfather lets me keep my horses there."

Sabrina's mother had bolted again. "She stayed five years this time; she's getting better," said Sabrina as they drove across Chain Bridge to Virginia.

"Where did she go?" asked Tia. Sabrina's mother had always fascinated the girls at Colt School. With her raven hair, pale fur coats, layered makeup, musky perfume, and raspy voice, she swooped into Sabrina's life, fluttered around as nervously as a bird, despite her pungency, and then, as suddenly, took off again.

"She's found some sort of cowboy," said Sabrina, who appeared to accept her mother's mobility as part of her own very private status quo. Living what Gran would call a "very ordinary life" with her stockbroker father in a modern Park Avenue apartment, Sabrina would get a call from her mother and be off to a castle in Ireland, a cottage in Normandy, a Greek island, a coffee plantation in Kenya. There were two years when her mother was a countess, a year as a princess, and for Sabrina never a year without a stepfather, stepbrothers and stepsisters, and, occasionally, a new half brother or sister. Sabrina's room was lined with photographs taken in front of large houses, on sunny beaches, on horses, by swimming pools, on skis, with a changing cast of family smiling around her. Yet Tia knew only the sober, efficient Sabrina who solemnly put her hair up in pincurls every night, turned her homework in on time, always volunteered to head the spring dance cleanup committee, was student body treasurer, and insisted on being home for dinner with her father every evening. "He's lonely," she would say, shrugging. Robin, who also lived with her father, seemed to understand. Tia, who found Paul Abbott very dull, did not.

At Colt, they had all vowed not to marry. Jenny and Tia were the first to break those vows, long forgotten, and all the others followed, except Sabrina. She lived with five dogs in a small house on Capitol Hill and worked for Save a Pet, which she had founded with a stepsister.

"Perry, you look wonderful," said Sabrina in her flat, cheerful voice, lightly embracing her stepfather. "You remember Tia Ensear?"

"Of course," said the master of Langdon Hall. "Your husband is a surgeon."

"Psychiatrist," said Tia.

"Yes, of course. Same thing, eh?" Perry Dunning laughed.

"Almost," said Tia.

Perry insisted they join him for lunch on a wide veranda overlooking breeding barns and pastures. As they ate, Perry sipped his Bloody Mary and discussed his three new foals, the one that was born dead, the three mares still due.

"And by the way, Brina, I've got Ellie Babcock interested in Save a Pet. She suggested opening a shelter in Middleburg."

"Great. I'll call her tonight."

Finally there was a long pause. Perry looked uncomfortable, poked his salad absently. "Brina, what do you hear from your mother?" He flushed.

"She's in Montana."

"Married?"

"I don't think this one will get to that."

"Really?" He looked pleased.

"Lucy and Tommy flew out yesterday to go fishing with her."

"Lucy and Tommy?"

No one found it easy to keep track.

"Von Eignor."

"Ah, yes. Of course." He turned and smiled at Tia. "Number three, I believe."

"Number two," said Sabrina. "Abbott, Von Eignor."

"Seymour, de Revellier, Dunning," said Perry. "I used to be up on that."

"And Dunning was the best," said Sabrina cheerfully.

After their ride, Tia and Sabrina sat on a hay bale in the stable courtyard, warmed by the sun.

"Poor Perry," said Sabrina. "He always asks me to come out and bring a friend and then he sits there talking about horses and Mummy."

"Is he still in love with her?"

"Tia, you're so romantic." Sabrina laughed. "I'm sure Perry would like to see Ma drawn and quartered, but she does always leave something behind."

"Your father used to be the same way."

"Yes, they must hate her and yet they never lose interest."

When Tia got home she had a call from Perry.

"Tia, I found a scarf here I thought might be yours," he said.

"No, I didn't have one."

"Why don't you come out Wednesday. I have a new little mare I'd love you to try."

"I'd love to, but I have to work Wednesday."

"What about Thursday?"

"I have to work all week, Perry."

"Oh."

"Can we do it another time? Perhaps Sabrina can drive me out next week."

"I'd like to see Langdon Hall," said Sloan.

"I don't think Perry is too interested in you," said Tia.

"What?" Sloan looked hurt.

"He likes ladies," said Tia quickly.

"You?" He looked surprised.

"Not just me. He's lonely."

"I don't want you going out there."

"Don't worry. I'm not about to fall into Perry's arms."

"I mean it," he said, his voice hard.

"Oh, come on," said Tia.

"Damn it," said Sloan and threw his glass in the sink, where it splintered against the enamel edge.

"Sloan, what is it?"

"Do you have to argue with me about everything? I'm sick of it." He slammed out of the kitchen. Moments later she heard his study door bang shut. She stood where he had left her, staring down at the shards of glass.

Chapter Seventeen

Ivan drove his parents up for their July visit. Tia sat nervously on the porch most of the afternoon, waiting and reading.

"Tia, my darling little angel," Elizavetta exclaimed, grasping Tia around the waist with her tiny hands. "What a beauty you are turning into!"

"She looks like an Indian to me," said Gran. "She insists on lying in the sun all day."

Ivan stood behind the women and looked out at the sea. He had on a worn blue Shetland sweater over his shirt. It was the color of his eyes. He seemed subdued and thinner.

He was polite but remote as they sat out on the porch having drinks. Tia found him staring at her, but with a cool, angry expression that chilled her. Before dinner, Gran and Elizavetta took a walk around the garden and bent their heads together and whispered. Professor MacLeod dozed over his newspaper. Tia tried to talk to Ivan but he hardly answered her, so she sat silently until dinner was announced.

"What's the matter with Ivan, Aunt Elizavetta?"

The women exchanged glances. "He's having some problems with Kathryn," said Elizavetta, putting her arm around Tia's waist. "But these things happen and we're all sure they'll be fine."

After a strained dinner Tia excused herself and went to her room. She fell asleep reading. When she woke, sometime around midnight, Ivan was sitting on her bed.

"What are you doing here?" she asked.

He said nothing but stroked her hand.

"Ivan?"

"Hush," he whispered. He smoothed the hair back from her forehead. He ran his hand along her cheek. "Don't look so frightened," he said, smiling. He bent down and kissed her gently on the lips. Then, suddenly, he pulled her up toward him in a rough embrace.

"Please, Ivan, don't," she said, smothered against his shoulders.

"My kitten, I'm sorry." He laid her back gently. She had smelled the whiskey on his breath.

Ivan knelt by her bed. He pressed her hands to his cheeks. Then he stood up, bent over and pulled her quilt over her, and left the room.

Tia lay without moving, listening to the sea washing against the rocks. Then she heard the piano in the music room. She jumped up and went out on her balcony and saw Ivan, cast in amber light, playing, bent over the instrument, his hair shining gold. She stood in the damp, sea air, watching him, hardly listening to the harsh sounds he was making, until Masha found her there and scolded her and sent her back to bed like a child.

Ivan left that night. In the morning there was a note of apology to Gran and, later that day, a small box from a Camden jewelry store came for Tia. In it was a small jade heart on a gold chain and a note that said only *From Ivan to Tia*. A week later he was back. His face was brown from the sun and the lines around his eyes seemed deepened. Elizavetta had rushed to greet him and he had returned her embrace. Tia stood in the doorway, watching them, and Ivan had looked up over his mother's head and smiled at her. From the drama of their embrace, his smile seemed so sunny and unexpected.

"That Kathryn!" Elizavetta cried out, still buried in her son's arms.

"No, no, Mother," said Ivan soothingly.

"And poor little Alex," Elizavetta whimpered.

Ivan patted his mother and turned her slowly toward the house. He smiled up at Tia again. "Tia, we are all so Russian."

He seemed buoyed, merry. The melancholy, brooding, intoxicated presence of a week ago had been replaced by laughter, teasing, warmth. "It will all work out," Ivan said softly to his mother. She stopped crying and at dinner that night seemed as buoyant as her son. Even Professor MacLeod seemed to emerge from his whiskey haze and resumed his teasing. There were some of Gran's friends from New York and a special dinner and a festive air. Ivan had brought champagne, and he walked over to Tia and filled her glass until Gran laughingly warned him to stop.

Tia had sat on the edge of the evening, wary, watching. When Ivan spoke to her or smiled, she would feel the warmth and merriment of the occasion, and then he would turn to someone else and she would slip away again. She questioned her pleasure in his appearance, but the lock of hair over his forehead when he laughed, his gesture of pushing it back, the thick, faded sweater, the blue eyes, the long legs, his deep laugh, mesmerized her.

After dinner, Ivan, almost boisterous by now, led a party across the lawn in the moonlight. Tia, tagging along, watched him take the hand of one of the guests and lead her along the path through the pines.

"Wait, everyone," he called. "Tia has to lead us. She knows this path like the back of her hand. Tia!"

"Here she is," someone said and hands pushed her forward. Ivan's hand had been large and cool and he took hers easily and laughed.

"Down to the sea in ships," he called. Then he pulled her close. "Am I forgiven?" he whispered.

"Yes," she said, afraid they were being overheard and observed.

"Hurray," he said, laughing again. "Tia forgives me."

Everyone laughed and plowed along the narrow, piny path to the sea.

He had not come to her room that night as she had expected. Confused, she had gone out to her balcony and looked down at the music room. He was sitting on the piano bench, sipping a glass of wine. She had put on her robe and gone down the stairs and out on the lawn, across to the music room wing. She had stood in front of the French doors and he had looked up.

"Tia?" He seemed surprised. "Can't sleep?"

"Will you play?"

"It'll wake everyone up. I'm not quite drunk enough tonight." He came outside and stood beside her on the dewy grass. "You'll catch cold." He put his arm around her and walked her back across the lawn.

They had walked silently up to her room, both of them careful to be quiet, pausing once when someone behind a closed bedroom door coughed. Then he had taken off her robe and kissed her gently on the lips and tucked her into her bed. He had stretched out beside her, resting on one elbow and looking down at her, stroking her hair. She had fallen asleep and when she woke, an hour or so later, he was asleep beside her. She bent over and kissed him, and he had opened his eyes and looked up at her. For a moment he looked bewildered, and then he put his arms around her and returned her embrace. He made love to her slowly, gently, acknowledging her innocence with his tenderness.

Afterward he held her close and talked to her. He told her that his marriage had long been troubled, and now Kathryn had taken their child and gone to stay with her father in California. He missed Alexey terribly.

"And you. I fell in love with you the day you came running in with your braids flying, in that silly gym suit." He laughed.

"That day? I looked so horrible," Tia protested.

"Or before that. Or tonight when you came out wearing that jade heart. Or maybe last week when I tried to rape you and you looked so frightened or maybe tonight when you took my hand in the woods or just now when I made love to you." He rolled the words out rhythmically, as if he were speaking to himself.

"Do you really love me, Ivan?"

"Let me count the ways," he said, laughing and reaching for her.

Gran had understood from the very beginning and watched the affair with silent distress, but she had stopped making pointed remarks about Kathryn and little Alexey and did not ban Ivan from the house. Tia was keenly aware of the warnings that were never spoken: the sudden excising of Kathryn from Gran's conversation, the sad eyes that met Tia after Ivan's phone calls, the sudden strains and silences.

"I think you miss Robin," said Gran one afternoon. It was as close as she came to trying to explain the turn of events. Robin had gone to Europe with Grayson for the summer. It was the first summer they had not spent together. "I talked to Laura Landsdale this morning. Her play is closing next week, so I suggested that she come with Jenny for a week or so."

"That would be nice. I do miss Robin," said Tia thoughtfully. "And you must miss Valery," she said suddenly.

Gran looked up quickly, her dark eyes wide with surprise.

"I do," said Tia quickly, ashamed.

Valery had married the year before. Claudia, the bride, was thirty years younger. He had brought her to Christmas dinner in New York and had seemed so quiet and subdued.

Gran regained her composure. "Yes, Tia, I do," she said sadly.

"I'm sorry, Gran," said Tia, rushing over to Gran and hugging her.

Gran sighed. "My poor child," she said wearily.

The pain of love was intense. It dug into her, keen as a blade, blunt as a fist, twisting and tearing. There was so much that had never been said, that was not clear. Suspended, she'd wait for him to come to Easter Cove for a day or two, days without context for him, taken from a life he belonged to, a life she tormented herself with, was ignorant of. Waiting, she remained alien to her own life. Then he was there and she would swing from transports of joy to pained anticipation of his departure.

His moods sometimes frightened her. They ranged as wide as hers but they were his own, not dependent on hers. Sometimes he would stand looking out at the sea, the creases around his eyes deepened by his squint, looking like a tired, pale Viking. In other moments he would bound with boyish energy, laughing, telling stories, suddenly reaching over and hugging Tia, arriving with baskets of presents for her and a big armful of flowers for Gran.

She treasured everything he gave her. The last visit of the summer he brought her a ring, inscribed with both their initials. It was a gold band with fluted edges, small rubies and seed pearls set in its center.

"It was my grandmother's," he said. "A Russian ring for us two little Russians."

When he teased like that she was never sure. Sometimes he saw her confusion and softened; at other times he ignored it.

This time he took her roughly in his arms and kissed the top of her head.

"Gran has made me promise I won't see you again until I have divorced Kathryn," he said.

"No!" cried Tia.

He hugged her. "It's a promise I won't keep, little kitten."

Gran put off her trip to Rome that fall.

"I want to finish some work before I go," she said. She was wearing a wide silver choker, studded with large, roughly cut amethysts. She fingered them as she talked. Tia wondered if they would become smooth from the touch of her fingers.

"I'm going to see Ivan tomorrow."

"Tia!" Gran stood up.

"I won't stop seeing him, Gran."

"You must, child." Her voice was soft and she sat down heavily. She sighed. "At first I thought it would be a passing fancy for you. A first affair. An attractive, experienced man. I thought you'd wake up some morning and see him too clearly. I thought you were like me."

"Was it that way for you?"

"I have always seen too clearly," she said harshly.

"What's so terrible about Ivan?"

"You are going to be absurd and blind like your poor little mother. . . . " Gran got up and walked over to the windows. She put her hands on the sill and looked down at the river. "I brought you up to be better than that." She turned back and looked at Tia. "Better than the mistress of an ambitious, unstable man."

Tia stood in the middle of the room. "What about . . . ?" She started angrily and then let the sentence die. The impulse to knife the old woman with her past faded.

"Yes, Tia, but you really know very little," said Gran quietly.

She was right. Tia knew very little about Gran; all her secrets were guarded. For a moment, watching Gran walk slowly into the dining room, Tia wondered again. Then she turned and ran to her room because she could feel her bitterness swelling again.

Tia did see Ivan again and Gran must have known it. They seemed to enter an unspoken agreement not to mention it. In the disjointed life she led that year, Tia had spent the week going to school in her navy blue uniform, playing hockey, singing in the chorus, going out for a soda with Jenny and Sabrina. Then, on weekends, she was with Ivan. On Saturday afternoon he would stride into the reading room of the Society Library. She would wait, as the hour of his arrival approached, so that she could see him as he came through the wide pillared hall. Sometimes he was late, and her body tightened with fear and she would think about his death on the highway or on the street below. Ambulance sirens rang through the afternoon dusk, and she would stiffen as they came closer. Then he would be there, laughing as they hurried down the steps to the street, hugging her, his words half lost to her.

When the MacLeods were in the country, Ivan took Tia to their apartment and made love. They would get up at midnight, dazed by the intensity of the hours they had spent together, and walk to Gran's. In the morning she met him again, hurrying from the obligatory Sunday breakfast with Gran, hoping to find him still asleep. She would slip into bed with him and he would turn to her, his face blurred with sleep, and hold her close. Though they planned to go to the theater, out to dinner, to museums and movies, they rarely did.

"We'll get over this phase eventually," Ivan said once, when they had planned to go to a party at Robin's house.

In February a snowstorm forced the MacLeods to spend the weekend in the city. Ivan said they would "go cold turkey." He reserved theater seats and, when he picked up Tia at the library Saturday afternoon, announced they would have a walk in Central Park and then dinner in the Village.

"I can't stand this," he said as they walked around the frozen boat basin. He pulled her close and kissed her. "I'll give Mother and Father the theater tickets."

The MacLeods, like Gran, had said nothing. Elizavetta, Tia sensed, was pleased, and Professor MacLeod insisted on treating Tia as a little girl that his son continued to treat to occasional outings. When they met, Elizavetta would clasp Tia close to her, stroke her hair, murmur some endearment. "Have they taught you anything in school?" Professor MacLeod would still ask.

"Wouldn't that be too much to ask?" said Tia.

"Oh, Mother will understand but Father will take another drink and tell you not to study too hard," said Ivan. His voice was cold. He turned to her and smiled and his face softened. "It's worth a try."

"No, no, Ivan," Tia could hear Professor MacLeod say. He had not greeted their offer as casually as Ivan had predicted. Elizavetta had seemed nonplused too.

"Come on, Father," said Ivan. His father had called him into the study for a talk.

"The child has to be protected!" shouted Professor MacLeod.

"Oh, dear," murmured Elizavetta, who had brought some sherry out for Tia.

"For Christ's sake, you old hypocrite!" Ivan shouted back.

Elizavetta jumped up and took Tia's hand. "Let's wait in the kitchen," she said.

"What are you doing to that child?" Professor MacLeod was screaming, as they let the swinging door close behind them.

"I'm sorry, Aunt Elizavetta," said Tia.

"Don't look so miserable, little one," said Elizavetta, putting her arms around Tia. "Ivan loves you so," she mumbled into Tia's neck.

"Well, for Christ's sake, you're a goddam married man!" they heard Professor MacLeod shout.

"There's no love in that marriage," said Elizavetta, pulling slowly away. "I know how strong it is between you and Ivan. I've seen it for years, even when you were little. I thought then, if only Ivan could have waited. Not married. And then little Alexey." She sighed. "Of course no one could see it then. But Tia, don't give up. Don't marry someone you don't love as much as you love Ivan. As much as Ivan loves you. Don't!"

Ivan came into the kitchen. His face was flushed and his eyes glittered.

"I'm sorry, Mother," he said, breathless. "Come on, Tia."

"Ivan," said Elizavetta, tugging at his sleeve.

He pulled his arm away. Then he paused and looked back at her. "Poor Mother. Poor Tia. Ivan the terrible," he said, giving her a quick hug. "Come on," he said and took Tia's hand and pulled her out of the apartment.

They went to a bar and Ivan drank one whiskey after another. He bent over the table, his head down, focusing on the drinks.

"Ivan," said Tia timidly.

He looked up at her, his face creased, sour. "I'm sorry," he said.

She sat, prisoner of his misery, for an hour. Finally she got up and went to the bathroom. She looked at her face in the streaked glass and hated what she saw. Her eyes looked like black raisins in her white pudding face. Her hair hung limp and straggled over the collar of her jacket. Her wrists were veined and bony, her clothes hung on her as if she wasn't in them.

She turned away from her reflection and combed her hair, buttoned her jacket, and walked back to the bar.

"I called my old roommate, Jack Keller. He's going off to a party in five minutes. We can go there."

"No, Ivan. Not tonight."

He looked up at her, surprised. "Why not? Oh, come on, Tia. I want to talk to you. But not here." His voice was thick from whiskey.

"I want to go home."

"Please, Tia. I feel rotten. I've made a mess of things. I don't want to be alone now."

"Okay." She took his hand and they walked slowly, not speaking, through the cold night to Jack Keller's apartment.

When they got there Ivan poured himself another drink and sat down. The room was sparsely furnished. In the other room, through the open door, Tia could see an unmade bed.

"Sit down, you've hovering," Ivan said, irritably. It was the way he talked to Alexey.

"Ivan, this evening is going to get worse. Let me take a cab home. Why don't you sleep here and then go back and talk to your father in the morning?"

"Don't leave me," he said, imploring.

"Just for tonight."

"If you leave me now, you won't come back," he said, pronouncing his words carefully. "Why should you?" He put his head in his hands. "My God, what a mess I've made of everything."

Tia went over and knelt by his chair. She stroked his back.

"You're such an angel," he murmured.

She was frightened, in over her head. She wanted to run out the door. The man sitting on the chair terrified her. He looked up. His eyes were bloodshot. "It would be easier for you if you were thirty. You wouldn't look so frightened."

"I'm fine, Ivan. You'll be fine."

"Yes." He sighed. "I will."

She wanted to flee. Her hand, stroking his back, felt numb.

"I do love you, kitten," he said, kissing her cheek. He reached for her and pulled her toward him. They held each other awkwardly, his knees in the way, the chair tipping.

Ivan rose and pulled Tia up, stumbling a bit as he did, catching himself by balancing against her. His arms were tight around her, pressing her close. His mouth was on hers, moist and heavy. For the first time his body against hers did not arouse her. He moved toward the bedroom, his arms still tight around her.

"No, Ivan," she said, as he pulled her along.

He pushed her on the bed and rolled down beside her, pinning her. She tried to twist away, moving her face away as he kissed her. He pulled at her blouse and she pushed his hand away.

"No, no," she kept saying, evading his lips.

He was pulling her skirt up, and his hand was rough on her skin.

"Come on, Ti," he whispered.

"No!" she shouted. "Get away."

He stopped suddenly and sat up. "I know." He pulled her skirt down and looked down at her. "I thought I could make it all better."

"Not this way," she said, edging off the bed, buttoning her blouse.

He walked with her down the narrow staircase to the street, hailed a cab, helped her in, and gave the driver her address. He stood on the curb while she folded herself into the far corner. As the cab pulled away he turned back into the dark entry.

"Tia, what is the matter?" Gran stood in the doorway of Tia's bedroom.

"Nothing," sobbed Tia. She had cried almost constantly during the night and most of the day.

"Of course it's Ivan," said Gran.

"Yes."

"It was impossible. You're free again. Learn to enjoy that freedom."

Tia nodded and sniffled. "Yes."

"Now, take a bath and get dressed. I want you in the library in half an hour."

"I can't, Gran," said Tia, tears flowing again.

"You certainly can. It's Masha's birthday."

"Oh, God."

"Masha is coming back early because she thinks I've got people coming in for dinner."

Masha, of course, was never fooled. Gran would never forget her birthday or have guests in on Sunday. Every year Gran would prepare a high tea, seal off the library all day, gather presents, and Masha would come in, dressed in her best embroidered blouse, and feign astonishment.

"Gran," started Tia.

"Don't whine, child. Masha's very hurt that you've been so indifferent to her lately. If you miss her birthday . . . "

Tia nodded and got up, shuffling slowly toward the bathroom.

Monday morning a basket of white freesias was delivered with a note that said *I love you with all my heart and soul* and was signed *Terrible Ivan.* Tia took one flower to school and sniffed it all day.

"God, that's disgusting," said Jenny. "It's all brown and smells like cat's pee."

That night a basket of yellow freesias arrived with a card that said *Please forgive me* and was signed *Ivan the Miserable.*

"Gran, I don't know what to do," said Tia, because she was so desperate for advice.

"Be free."

"Gran."

"I'm afraid at your age one doesn't have the capacity to be free. Hormones." She sighed.

Tia could smell the freesias the moment she came into the apartment. She dialed his apartment in Cambridge once but then hung up the phone before it rang.

On Saturday Gran insisted Tia come to an art gallery where Valery, at last, was showing some paintings. They lunched afterward with Claudia and Valery at the Plaza. Tia, restless, kept looking at her watch.

"Isn't it just so exciting, Mrs. Valenkova?" said Claudia, wiggling like a child in her oversized chair.

"Yes, Claudia, it certainly is," said Gran pleasantly.

"I'm sure he'll sell them all," said Claudia cheerfully.

Valery, always intensely uncomfortable when he was with Claudia in Gran's presence, smiled and nodded.

"I'm going to the library," said Tia suddenly.

Gran looked up and opened her mouth to speak.

"No, Gran," said Tia. She bent over and kissed her grandmother's cheek. "I'm so happy for you, Valery," she said, bending and kissing the top of his head. "It's wonderful," she said to Claudia, pecking at her cheek.

Ivan was standing in front of the library doors. It was cold and the wind blew down from the park. His coat collar was turned up. He put his hands in his pocket and started toward Madison Avenue, trudging heavily.

"Ivan," called Tia, from across the street.

He didn't hear her, muffled from the wind. She called again and watched as he walked up from the avenue, his pace increasing. His pale hair was visible above the turned-up collar. When he turned, his face was sad and his eyes seemed shadowed.

"Tia," he said, as she ran up beside him. He smiled and waited a moment, looking wary.

She threw her arms around him and stood with him, jostled by the Saturday afternoon shoppers and strollers who eddied around them.

They went to the MacLeod apartment, and their lovemaking was so urgent, so full of desperation, that when it was over they both were in tears. It felt like grief.

Chapter Eighteen

"I like Sunday." Daisy sighed, rolling herself into her parents' goosedown quilt.

"You like this?" Tia looked over the top of the Sunday *Times Magazine*. Peter was playing with his trucks on the floor, and Daisy had brought all her crayons and a big pad and set herself up at the foot of the bed.

"Mmm," said Daisy.

"Come for a cuddle," said Tia, putting down the magazine. Daisy leaped for her. Peter looked up. "You too, Peter." He clambered on the bed.

Sloan had left early for a squash game, and Tia had brought the paper and breakfast upstairs. "Don't let the children eat in the bedroom," Sloan would say, if she started upstairs before he left. Tia tried to confine them to the card table she'd set up by the window, but they usually climbed into bed with sticky fingers.

"Oh, look at Peter," said Daisy. "He's gotten jam on the pillow."

"Daisy did," said Peter, examining his sister's face. "Look."

"I did not!"

"Never mind. Come on. Let's get a clean pillowcase and then everyone get dressed and we'll walk down to the zoo."

There were whoops of delight and the children raced out of the room. It would take some time and coaxing to get them washed and dressed. By that time Sloan would be home.

"The zoo? Okay." He shrugged. "I want to go over to the institute this afternoon for a couple of hours."

Tia started to protest but Sloan left the room quickly. Actually it would be easier with Sloan gone. Everyone always relaxed. "Slobs," Sloan would say when he got home and found the children's crayons and toys scattered around Tia's desk. She knew it reminded him of Althea's house.

Tia was taking a bath when the doorbell rang. Sloan was still at the institute and the children were asleep. She waited for a moment but the bell sounded again. She reached for Sloan's robe, thinking how cross he'd be when he realized she had used it.

"Victoria!"

Tia peered into the darkness. It was Perry Dunning, holding a bottle of champagne.

"I've come from a wonderful party, and I thought you and your husband would like to share my champagne," he said. "Oh, dear, I've gotten you out of bed."

"No, come in."

He walked in carefully, holding up the bottle.

"Is your husband asleep? It's early," said Perry. He walked into the living room, staggering a little.

"Perry, what is this?"

"Why, lovely lady, I—" He looked at her. "You were in your bath."

"Why didn't you call?"

"Was nearby and have this champagne."

"Do you want some coffee?"

"'Do you want some coffee?' Coffee?" He wagged his finger at her. "Coffee?"

Tia watched him stumble against the table, right himself, straighten his back.

"Would you like something to eat?"

He sat down, almost missing the chair. "You look lovely." He sighed. "I'm awfully drunk."

"Are you driving?"

"Drunk and driving."

"You can spend the night here."

"No, no, too much bother." He got up and took two steps and fell down.

"Perry, come upstairs and sleep it off."

"My cousin got married," he said, struggling to get up.

"Here, give me your hands." Tia arched her back against his weight. "Come on, Perry."

"Maybe I better," he said, on his feet. His words tumbled around his tongue. "You want me to stay, don't you?" He stumbled after her. "Where's Slater?"

"Sloan? He'll be back in a few minutes."

"That's too bad," he said, his voice suddenly shrill with laughter.

She led Perry upstairs, gave him a pair of Sloan's pajamas, avoided his embraces, and got him to take his shoes off and sit on the edge of the guest-room bed with the pajamas on his lap.

"I think I'm going to be humiliated in the morning," he called after her. She heard him laugh as she closed the door.

"Did you use my robe?" said Sloan. He had come home after Tia had gone to sleep. Now, standing on a circle of milky morning light, he held the robe aloft.

"For God's sake, Sloan," she said.

"I don't mind. I just don't want the children playing with it."

Tia got dressed and got the children up. She poured their juice and cooked their cereal. Daisy came down, crying that she couldn't find her shoes.

"Peter hid them," she said, wiping the tears from her eyes.

"Come on, Daisy," said Sloan impatiently, coming down behind her.

Peter stormed downstairs with his pajama top on, trying to reach Daisy with his fists.

"I'm getting out of here," said Sloan. He poured himself a cup of coffee. "Have fun."

It took a while to restore order, find Daisy's shoes, get Peter dressed, both fed. They missed their carpools and Tia drove them. "I'll be late, all because of him," Daisy kept saying.

Driving home, she thought of her tasks for the day. There was a review to finish and take down to the office before noon, a sketch and recipe she'd promised *Maine Monthly*, shopping for tomorrow's dinner for a new colleague of Sloan's. She should leave the car at the garage for servicing, but she had to take the children to the dentist after school and buy Peter some underwear and stop at the cleaner's to pick up Sloan's suits.

As she let herself back into the house, she remembered Perry Dunning. She raced upstairs and knocked on his door.

He was sitting on the edge of his bed, rubbing his face.

"Oh, Tia," he said, "how can I ever apologize?"

"Are you okay?"

He moaned and got up. "Are these your husband's pajamas?"

"Yes. I'll get you some coffee."

He came into the kitchen, slicked down from his shower. He drank his coffee, nibbled on a piece of toast.

"You're very good, Tia," he said. "Very sweet."

She smiled. It was almost ten and she had two hours of work to do on her article. She wanted him to go but he looked so pathetic, sitting at her kitchen table, that she could not ask him to hurry.

"Will you come out to lunch with me tomorrow? See my new mare? Take a ride? I feel so terribly foolish. . . . " He came over and took her hands. "Please. You can bring your children. Will you?"

"Of course."

"Wonderful." He put his arm around her shoulder and walked to the front door. "Don't tell Sabrina, will you?"

Perry was plainly disappointed to see Peter. Tia was able to keep him on her lap some of the time, but after lunch she let the house-keeper take him off while she joined Perry for a tour of his barns.

In a darkened corner of the barn he pulled her toward him and kissed her hard on the lips. She had been expecting it and tried to pull away, but he held her tight. It had been so many years since she had been assaulted like that. The years of fending off un-welcome advances had seemed long past.

"Perry, come on," she said, when she freed herself.

"You feel it too, Tia, don't deny it," he said, breathless, his hands caressing her back.

She wanted to laugh, but her sense that the moment had not passed safely forced her to smile instead.

"I'm married, Perry."

He kissed her again, pulling her down on some hay bales. His hands were under her blouse, his body over hers.

"Mr. Dunning," a voice called from the other end of the barn.

"Jesus," said Perry. "What is it?"

"Long-distance call."

"I'll be there in a moment." He got up and pulled Tia up. He kissed her cheek and brushed the hay off her blouse.

"I know you like to be a good girl, Tia, but you wanted that too," said Perry.

"That's what they all say," she said, brushing off her skirt.

Perry wheeled around. "What?" he said sternly.

Tia smiled and shrugged.

"Oh, yes," said Perry, laughing, "very good."

She did not answer the phone when she was alone, spent her days at the office. When Priscilla said, "That Mr. Dunning called again," she would try to look puzzled. He wrote her a letter, carefully phrased, asking her to come out and look at the new mare, sending his regards to her family.

"I'm letting this get to me," Tia said to Robin, who was down for a medical conference.

"Problems with Sloan?"

"Nothing new. Maybe I'm just having a seven-year itch."

Robin looked surprised. "Maybe you should have an affair. Maybe it's just what you need."

"But Perry Dunning? I must be desperate."

"Are you?"

"Come on," said Tia.

Perry Dunning turned up at the office.

"I've come to take you out for that lunch I promised you," he said loudly, so that Jake looked up from his galleys.

"Is Sabrina coming too?"

"This is take-an-old-man-to-lunch week," he said.

He took her arm and guided her out of the building. She waited for him to tell her what she had imagined him saying all week: You are running away from your feelings, you really want me, you are a passionate woman, your husband doesn't understand you. I adore you. I want you.

"Do you like fish?"

"Fish?"

"I thought I'd take you to a seafood place. You never seem to write about seafood restaurants."

They walked down Connecticut Avenue, in the midday

crowds. Perry was tall and he kept his arm firmly through hers. He stopped her at the window of a jewelry store.

"Isn't that a lovely necklace," he said. "Would you like it?"

"No, I would not." Tia laughed.

"You can't be bought, eh?" He laughed too and steered her down the avenue.

They talked about horses, restaurants, the Bahamas, tennis rackets, Sabrina. Perry had an endless, effortless font of conversation. Finally, when the restaurant had almost emptied, he bent toward her.

"Tia, come up to the country with me this afternoon."

"I can't."

"But you'd like to." He stroked her hand.

They walked back to her office. He had switched easily into another conversation about horses.

He looked confident. Sloan would have liked to look that way in a pin-striped suit.

Chapter Nineteen

For weeks after their night at the MacLeods' there was an awkwardness between Tia and Ivan that could not be erased in the ways they had always eased their tensions before.

"We need some time together—without you having to rush home at midnight like a schoolgirl." After he said that he looked stricken. It was part of the tension, obviously.

"Yes," said Tia quickly, though she wondered how she would escape Gran. Tia felt she had stretched her limits to see Ivan and this further incursion would upset the delicate truce. "Though I don't know how I'll manage it." They were walking to Gran's apartment through the rain.

"You can find a way," he said, not turning to look at her. His jaw was set, his head down.

Tia slipped her hand under his arm. For a few moments he seemed oblivious of her presence, certainly unaware of her hand at his elbow.

"Ivan?"

He turned his head and looked at her. "Sorry, kitten," he said. He put his arm tight around her shoulder. "Have Robin give you an alibi. She won't mind."

They had set off in his little car, rattling northward in the spring dusk. The air had been warm and humid, rich with the smell of damp earth and honeysuckle. Ivan had reached for her hand every few minutes. He looked as excited and tense as she felt.

The inn had been on the crest of a hill, overlooking apple orchards and hayfields and the Berkshire hills to the north. They had driven slowly up the narrow drive, the car by this time overheating and backfiring.

"What an entrance." Ivan laughed. It had alerted the couple who ran the inn. They came out to the front entrance and watched as Ivan pulled into the parking area.

Suddenly terribly self-conscious, aware that her blouse and skirt made her look even younger than she was, sure that they knew Ivan was not her husband, Tia stood by him while he took the bags out of the car.

"Okay, Mrs. MacLeod," he whispered. "Hello," he called to the innkeepers, still watching. "Little car trouble."

"There's a Mobil station in town," said the woman, glancing at Tia.

"Ivan MacLeod," said Ivan, extending his hand. "My wife, Victoria."

"Peter Bemis and my wife, Betty," said the innkeeper. "We'll get someone to bring the bags in."

After the car, and perhaps Tia's obvious youth, the Bemises seemed uneasy. They watched Ivan sign the register and exchanged glances several times.

"How will you be paying?"

"By credit card," said Ivan. "You don't want me to settle now?" He looked at them with cold, blue eyes.

"Oh, no, no," they chorused.

They trudged up to a big corner bedroom, with Mr. Bemis leading the way.

"Very nice," said Ivan, still cool.

"We serve dinner at seven."

"Fine."

"They know, don't they," said Tia, after Mr. Bemis left.

"Who cares?" said Ivan, striding across the room to her. "Who cares?" he repeated, putting his arms around her.

They were late for dinner. Ivan, buoyant again, drank a great deal. His laughter and voice grew loud and the other diners in the quiet little dining room kept looking at him. The food was not very good. The Bemises hovered. But the bedroom was beautiful and they retired there early.

In the morning Mr. Bemis came over to their table.

"We've made a terrible mistake, Mr. MacLeod. Your room was booked months ago for Saturday and Sunday nights. We could let you have another room, if you'd care to stay."

"What sort of room?"

"I'm afraid it's rather small and you'd share a bath."

Tia looked down at her plate. There was a long silence.

"Very well," said Ivan finally. "Just prepare our bill."

The morning had been gray and damp and the rain started as they packed the car. As they waited in the gas station for the car to be fixed, Ivan tried to laugh about the Bemises but Tia felt sick.

"Don't look so sad, kitten, we'll find another place," he said, as they drove away.

But she didn't want to find another place. It was as if she'd woken from her trance, into a nightmare world of realities she had long denied. Kathryn, Alexey, her youth, the MacLeods, all intruded. "It's all wrong," she said. Chaotic and unmanageable and painful, she meant.

"God, you're so damn bourgeois. You're just like Kathryn." His voice was twisted with rage. He was driving too fast. Tia had looked over at him and his face had been hard. His glance had met hers and Tia had seen anger that bewildered her.

"Don't start weeping," he snarled.

They drove to Robin's house in silence. He double-parked, jumped out and opened the trunk, handed her her bag, got back in the car, and drove away. She stood on the curb, watching him. At the end of the block he looked back and she thought he was going to come back, but when the light changed, he screeched through the intersection.

She had waited for him that weekend at Robin's. Years later she still felt the humiliation of waiting by the phone for two days. Mercifully, Robin had said little. Back at Gran's there was also a sort of solicitous silence. Tia wondered what they knew and did not have the courage to ask, but as they remained noble and tender toward her, she realized that what she had thought was a nervous quarrel with Ivan was really a far graver rupture. Years later those last two months of school were lost. The graduation photographs, with Tia in a white dress, her long hair restrained by tortoiseshell combs, offered her only the dimmest memory. She had apparently not lost her ability to smile and laugh, as the photographs testified, which seemed surprising. Still, Robin told Tia that she had seemed like a different person, even seemed to look different. The photographs were unlike others. Perhaps it was because they were black-and-white and somewhat grainy, but she looked angular and her eyes were wide and vague.

She did remember that all summer she wrestled with the coming college term. She and Robin were to go to Radcliffe. Ivan had been so pleased.

"Harvard's so big—we'll never run into him," argued Robin. "Don't let that jerk stop you."

There had been a trip to England with Robin and Gran, to a large Georgian house in Wiltshire that belonged to some cousins. It had been an unusually hot, dry summer, and the grass on the downs had turned yellow.

Chapter Twenty

"Vickie," boomed Jake, "this stuff is okay, but we need more copy." He threw some pages on her desk. "Sam liked the chatty aspect. He says more of the same, please."

"I have some new recipes I could stick in under the 'haut' section," Tia said.

"Chatty, kid," said Jake.

"If he wants all this other stuff, then let him raise my salary," said Tia irritably. "I know he paid Ralph a thousand for that little puff piece last month."

"Ralph Percival is a *Times* man," said Jake. He blew some smoke in her face. "Cheer up, Vick, your husband is supporting you in style. Why don't you get on with that cookbook? That might make Sam sit up and take notice."

Sam and Jake wanted her to do the Capital Roundabout Cookbook. "Food for Power" was the title they had come up with after a drunken lunch. "Isn't that great? 'Food for Power,'" they kept saying, leaning over her desk and exhaling martinis.

"Yeah," Tia said. It meant hours on the phone getting Congressional offices to issue her bland little casserole recipes, months of cooking them up, months of eating them. "I always used to put a couple of anchovies in my tuna casserole, but now they're too expensive," said one Congressional wife. "Honey," said another, "my husband always says pie recipes are the safest." Pies and tuna casseroles all fall.

They had one more appointment with Mrs. Pierce before Tia was to leave for Easter Cove. Sloan was seeing a new patient, so she went alone.

"Doesn't sound too promising," he had said, when he saw the address. It was not in a part of the District Sloan had marked on the map he had given the real estate office.

"But it's quite charming," Mrs. Pierce had said over the phone. "I think you'd like it, Mrs. Ensear."

It was on a small side street near the Maryland line. A tall lilac hedge hid its facade from the street. Mock Tudor and colonial houses lined the street, rising from neat lawns.

There was a narrow path through the lilacs, into a small, shady garden filled with day lilies. A pale, rosy stucco, the house rose between stands of plum and dogwood, and at the sill of each tall casement window were boxes of white petunias. Tia stood looking at the house.

"The owners are European," said Mrs. Pierce. "It's a big lot."

Past a small, dark entry there was a large, light room with French doors overlooking the long back garden. Books lined wall-to-ceiling shelves and were piled along side chairs and tables. An obvious attempt had been made to tidy up; the stacks had been squared neatly.

"You must see the kitchen, Mrs. Ensear," said Mrs. Pierce, leading Tia by the arm. "The tiles are lovely, I think," she said when she saw Tia examine the blue and yellow tiles that lined the kitchen counters. "The owners spent time in Mexico."

Windows were open to the front garden. A sweet breeze blew in over the petunias.

"There are four bedrooms upstairs. Two overlook the back garden and two are smaller and face the front," said Mrs. Pierce as they went upstairs.

Tia leaned out and looked at the back garden. Roses tumbled over the high brick wall.

"And Mr. Berger built his wife a little study that I thought would suit Dr. Ensear," said Mrs. Pierce, nudging Tia away from the window.

The study was empty. After the books and papers and paintings that filled the rest of the house, it was surprising. Tall windows opened into the garden, and there was a small fireplace with a coat of arms imprinted on its curved front.

"Mrs. Berger died last year," said Mrs. Pierce with a sweep of her arm at the empty room. "You could clear away a few trees there and put in a side door."

Tia leaned against the windows and looked out at the roses.

"It's lovely, Mrs. Pierce," said Tia.

"I knew you'd like it." Mrs. Pierce smiled broadly.

They stood at the window. They both knew this was not what Sloan had in mind.

"Yes, of course I'll look," said Sloan that evening. His tone was reproachful. He had met her enthusiasm with a stony face. "It just doesn't sound big enough. And it's out of the way."

"You can get out to Rock Creek Parkway in two minutes, Sloan."

"I said I'd look."

The more she said, the less he would like it.

In bed that night Sloan put his arm around her shoulders. It had been so long since they had made love that the gesture was no longer familiar. As his hand stroked her back, she felt leaden with guilt. It had always been that way with Sloan, as if she was not really supposed to be there with him.

Chapter Twenty-one

The first day of college a huge bouquet of red roses arrived, without a card. Every other day another dozen arrived. The bleak, dark room with its blond, built-in bureaus and precarious double-decker beds was filled with flowers. Tia's roommate started to sneeze, and after a week they had to move the garden to the first-floor reception rooms.

It must be Ivan, Tia thought. She called the florist, but he would not reveal the sender. Robin and Jenny, who lived in other dormitories, came to see the tributes and agreed it must be Ivan.

She tried to remain calm. Time had erased much of the pain. In her crowded dorm, in classes, at meals, in the library, she was surrounded by new friends. Jenny and Robin came over often. Young men took her to dinner in Boston. Best of all, she thought, after years of being a conscientious but bored student, she was fascinated by her classes. The atmosphere seemed charged. When she wasn't studying, she was talking about studies. For the first time in her life, her room was no longer her refuge. So when she saw Ivan one morning, crossing the Yard ahead of her, his head bent in conversation with a student, it hurt far less than she anticipated. She had watched him disappear through the tall, iron gates to Harvard Square and waited for the familiar ache. Nursing its inception, she started the litany of anguish: the last angry words, the car screeching across the intersection, the waiting by the telephone, the tearing memory of his arms around her, his rumpled look in the morning, his boisterous laugh, the way he strode into the library reading room to claim her. But only the ghosts of pain and anger moved inside her.

Still, she feared the roses were pulling her back. Perhaps it was the waiting.

"It's like blackmail. Like being a puppet jerked around. He's got some sort of control over the situation and he won't allow me to do anything about it," complained Tia.

"Call the florist. Tell him you aren't accepting any more flowers."

"Oh," said Tia.

She did. A day later Sloan called.

"Sloan?" She couldn't remember.

"Sloan Ensear."

"Oh, yes." She still couldn't remember. There was a long pause. "Well, how are you?"

"I'm glad you stopped the flowers."

"The flowers?"

"You didn't know?"

"No."

"Last summer, at your grandmother's, you said your heart could be won with roses."

Really? She didn't remember. "They were beautiful."

"I didn't know how to stop them and reintroduce myself. I thought you'd know it was me. Didn't you?"

It was Robin who had said that about the roses. Maybe Tia had agreed with her because she had run out of conversation. Robin said it often.

"You're very extravagant," she said quickly.

"Yes." He laughed. "The scholarship committee wouldn't approve."

"Oh, dear."

"No, no."

Another pause. "Well, it was awfully nice of you," said Tia.

"I hope they at least won me an evening with you."

"Oh, yes," she said.

"Saturday?"

"Not this week."

"What about Friday after?"

"Fine. That would be fine." She dreaded it already.

Sloan was, as Jenny said, dogged. He called almost every day. He asked her out often and she found it hard to refuse him. He was amusing and flattering. Sometimes another bouquet of flowers would arrive. Their evenings were well organized and, unlike most of the boys she was seeing, he never got drunk. A medical student, he knew what he wanted to do. There was little confusion about him, which was rare in Cambridge. Gradually, as the weeks passed, he was with her more and more. He learned her habits, discovered her haunts. Often annoyed to see him suddenly at her elbow, she was also touched by his persistence. He asked very little in return.

"He's trussing you," warned Robin.

"He's going to smother you," warned Jenny.

That emptiness at her core, that she thought the break with Ivan had left her, was being filled by Sloan.

"Can't you just be on your own?" said Jenny.

On her own? She thought she'd always been on her own. "I'm an orphan," she said suddenly.

"Oh, bullshit," said Jenny.

Occasionally she saw Ivan in town or walking through the Yard. Once she passed him on the wide steps of Widener Library. He had glanced at her but Sloan was with her, his arm possessively around her shoulders, and Tia had looked away. At Christmas she heard that Ivan was taking a term off and going to Crete.

"You know he's back with Kathryn," said Gran. "They're expecting another child."

That opened some of the old wound. Tia wanted to ask more, find out when they had resurrected their marriage, when the baby was expected, would Kathryn be going to Crete.

"Really," she said. She asked no questions.

In the spring Tia drove to Washington to meet Sloan's mother and brother. She had resisted the meeting but Sloan had been, as ever, effectively persistent.

"But they might misunderstand," she had argued.

"I want you to meet them," he had insisted, sidestepping, as he always did, the central issue.

Althea Ensear and Toby lived in a narrow rowhouse near the Capitol. Althea occupied the downstairs, Toby the upstairs, and a small room and bath at the top of the stairs were Sloan's. The kitchen was neutral territory. In the long, dark downstairs living room, Althea had spread her books and papers. On the otherwise bare, white walls there was a rough wooden cross. There were some large oil paintings of Taos stacked in a corner. In the kitchen there was a confusion of crockery, pans, lists, coupons, maps, open shelves of disordered cans and boxes. The small, round table was covered with a worn oilcloth.

"Tia," Althea Ensear had said when they arrived, "I'm so glad Sloan brought you." She cleared papers off a chair. "Sit down. Sloan, get the sherry. Toby's at practice but he'll be here for dinner."

Conversation was awkward at first. Althea examined Tia closely, watching her with narrow, green eyes. Sloan, tense and irritable, drank three glasses of sherry. Tia wished she had not come.

Toby bounded into the house with a fragrant box.

"Hi," he said. "I got pizza, Ma."

"Pizza!" exclaimed Sloan. "Mother!"

Toby was as round and gregarious as his mother and brother were lean and guarded. He served up the dinner, poured beer, kept the conversation going. Sloan, as the evening progressed, became quieter.

"Let's take a walk," he said suddenly, rising and cutting Toby's sentence in half.

He took Tia's hand and rushed from the house.

"I keep thinking she'll get better," he said. "Damn that woman." He walked down the dark streets. Tia followed him, hurrying to keep pace.

Goddamn, she said to herself. She wanted to be a stranger to private parts of his life. Three more days. She wondered if she could have Robin call her and say she was needed at home.

"You've been wonderful, Tia," said Sloan, stopping suddenly and putting his arms around her. "This must be difficult for you. I'm sorry."

There appeared to be tears in his eyes.

"Don't be silly," she said, patting his arm.

She stayed the three days. Sloan was grateful. He had given her his room at the top of the stairs and only tried to come up once. After Ivan, her born-again virginity was hard to maintain as the pure, white flame that Sloan had chosen to honor. It was not the corporeal temptation he offered, because in healing the wound that Ivan had left, she had shut off much of that part of her, but when Sloan clasped his head and murmured lust-choked apologies, she hated herself. Still, that feeling passed too and it was easier than coming up against his persistence.

Gran was not really pleased about Sloan either. Once she said he was "callow." Valery teased Tia about Sloan's rather humorless description of his future plans. "He keeps telling us about himself," said Valery, "as if he wants us to know he is worthy of you. Doesn't he understand any of us?" That no one in that house on Easter Cove was interested in earnest, impecunious medical students, he meant.

They ganged up on him when he came: Gran with her icy politeness, Valery with his teasing, Robin with her indifference, Masha with her suspicious, inarticulate protectiveness. Tia felt sorry for him, sitting with those conspirators, surely unable to understand their malice.

"They didn't think I was good enough for you," he said later. He still did not understand. Now, he thought, he was good enough because he had a successful practice and he could buy houses and cars and trips.

"I'm disappointed," was all Gran said when, at the end of her sophomore year, Tia said she would marry Sloan. But Gran did not try to dissuade Tia and went ahead and announced the engagement in the *Times*.

"You're just running scared," said Robin, often. "You're such a baby that you won't take any chances."

Tia found it easy. She and Sloan studied together almost every evening. On weekends they went into Boston for dinner and a movie or to the theater or symphony. When boys called, Tia could say she was engaged. When people asked her what she was going to do after graduation, she could say she would have to see where Sloan took his internship. When Sloan could get rid of his roommates, they went to his room and made love for an hour or two. Tia finally had to pretend to be deflowered again.

When conversation failed, they could always plan the future. They could talk about trips they would take, the house they would buy with an office for Sloan and a studio for Tia, children, cities they wanted to live in, how they would keep their marriage happy and solid. It was intensely comfortable. They rarely fought. Tia's grades improved and Sloan was at the top of his class. He phoned her every morning to wake her up, and on the days he worked at the lab and couldn't see her, he'd call again in the evening.

Sloan liked Gran's houses and when she understood that she accepted the engagement. The first summer Sloan found a job at a camp near Easter Cove and Tia would drive over to fetch him on his day off. They would spend the day walking, swimming, talking. It was a relief to Tia that they could not make love under Gran's roof, though that was Tia's rule and she was its enforcer. The second summer, the summer of their engagement, Tia found a job in Boston to be near Sloan, who was planning to work for one of his professors. Then one of the rich Ensears offered Sloan a job on his boat, and even Tia agreed it would have been foolish to turn it down. She went to Woods Hole with him and had lunch with the cousins and then drove back to Boston alone in the little Volkswagen they had bought together.

Tia had rented an apartment in Cambridge with Jenny and Robin. It was on a back street across from a playground, in an area far removed from the university. Every morning the three would set off together. They would walk through the early-morning streets with their brown paper bags and part in the middle of the Yard. Robin went off to her science class, Jenny to her drama classes with Madame Plevisky, Tia to the subway to Boston, where she sold underwear at Bonwit Teller's.

Every evening Tia would retrace her steps alone, passing through the Yard with summer strangers occupying familiar buildings, dust and paper blowing across the browning grass. Exhausted, she would finally reach the house and find Robin and Jenny deep in study. Robin took a corner of the living room and installed herself amid books and papers, and Jenny used one of the two tiny upstairs bedrooms, where she tried to muffle the sounds of her performance with a blanket tacked over the plywood door. They took turns cooking terrible meals that improved only slightly during the summer. After dinner, one of Robin's admirers would pick her up and they would go and study at the air-conditioned Lamont Library, and Jenny would sweep out with one of her swains. Turning on the fan, soaking her feet, Tia would stay home and read or write letters to Sloan.

Sloan sent postcards from his ports of call, crammed with descriptions of the towns they were visiting and the conditions at sea. Gran called several times a week.

"Oh, darling, why don't you leave that job and come up to Easter Cove and paint?" she said.

"I wish I could," Tia would whimper.

"Of course you can. That absurd job," Gran would say soothingly.

But the next day a letter from Sloan would arrive, extolling her virtues. "I think of you toiling away at Bonwit's," he wrote, "and me here acting like a servant and all our wages mounting up. . . . Maybe we'll be able to marry while we are still in school. . . . I figure that if every summer we earn an average of . . . " The card was from Monaco.

"For God's sake, Tia, you are such a bore," said Jenny. "I can't believe you!" Her voice, thanks to Madame Plevisky, had deepened. Jenny moaned and panted several times a day to lower it.

"You're such a zombie. Come on," said Robin.

"You're selling underwear at Bonwit Teller's," said Valery in horror. "Why?"

"Come up to Easter Cove," said Gran.

"You should be painting, not selling that stuff," said Valery.

"No, I can't," said Tia firmly.

Finally she went up for a weekend. She felt pale and thin and stupid and sat on a rock in the sun all day.

"Tia," said Gran that evening. "I know this relationship you have with Sloan," she said, picking her words carefully, "is because of what happened with Ivan."

Tia started to protest and then shrugged. Her face burned and she was exhausted. "You can't marry someone like Ivan," she said.

"Are Sloan and Ivan the only two men in the world, Tia?"

"Please, Gran."

"Tia, there was a great deal of pressure on Ivan to stop seeing you." She reached for Tia's hand. "He did love you. In his fashion."

"What do you mean?"

"His wife wanted him back. There was Alexey. Kathryn was able to help Ivan with his work. It's expensive to be an archaeologist."

"You mean . . . ?"

"You were so young. And Ivan was so smitten he didn't think it out very well."

"Did you speak to him?"

"Tia," she started. She touched the choker at her throat.

"What?"

"On that weekend—" She hesitated a moment. "I called Robin, and the maid told me you were not expected." She sighed. "I called Elizavetta. We realized there was nothing we could do. Of course I think Elizavetta was always caught up in the whole thing. So she begged me to do nothing. But I remembered Ivan met you at the library. I waited downstairs for him. We had a talk. He really wouldn't listen to me, but I did manage to tell him he must desist. My God, you were a child." Gran looked away. "The next day he called and said he had brought you back to Robin's."

"And?"

"That he had hurt you badly but that he didn't know what else to do. Oh, he blamed it all on me, of course. He said, 'I'm sick of all of you.' Elizavetta said a month or so later Kathryn had him back. You know, Tia, even people like Ivan usually take the easiest path."

It was very hot in August. The house baked them. Tia decided to go to the library with Robin one evening because she couldn't stand lying on the nubbly couch, the fan riffling the pages of her book. She found a stall, got a stack of art books, and settled down.

"Thank God for air-conditioned libraries," whispered someone. It was one of the hazards of university life: always seeming to be available for engagement.

"Mmmm," she mumbled.

"Hello, kitten."

She looked down. Ivan was kneeling beside her. "Oh," she gasped.

"You look beautiful."

"I'm engaged," she said, before she could think.

"It's worse for me, I'm married."

She looked away. She did not dare look at him too long.

"Look at me," he said.

"Shhh," someone nearby hissed.

"Come on." He stood.

She followed him outside. He took her arm and steered her across the Yard. They stopped in the shadow of a building. He put his arms around her and held her tight.

"How I've missed you," he said.

"I can't go through this again," she said, trying to back away. "I can't."

"But what can we do?" he said. He said something else too, but she didn't hear the words because she was fighting so hard with herself.

"Oh, God, get him out of your system," said Robin.

"You're bound to this time," said Jenny.

"Go off with him for a month," said Robin.

"That'll cure you. I got over Cooley that way," said Jenny.

"Piss or get off the pot," said Robin.

"He's beautiful." Jenny sighed. "And so sort of . . . European."

"And such a bastard," said Robin. "Make him give a bit too, Tia. See if he'll go away with you."

"We can go tomorrow, today. A colleague has offered me his house."

"And your—"

"Kathryn?"

"Yes."

"Our second try was a farce. She's in California with her father. We'll work something out." He kissed Tia's hand. "Let's never get married or buy a house or have babies. I want you to wear your hair long and paint and I'll finish my book and we'll travel."

"Let's not make plans," she said quickly. There was still Sloan to consider, toiling away in the Mediterranean.

"You'll come on my digs. I'm going to be working with Wilson. We're getting ready for next summer. If I ever finish this damn book."

"Gran told me that Kathryn was pregnant again."

"Oh?" He looked down at her coldly. That glacial stare, face hard and nasty, was frightening. It had been so long, and then months with Sloan where she was never careful, that she had forgotten it.

"Yes," she said, standing her ground.

"Ah, that little deception." He reached over for his cigarettes. He pulled one out of the crumpled pack, straightened it, smoothed it, and lit it. "She came over to my apartment one night, begging me to come back. Rather unusual for Kathryn, as you can imagine. She said she was having terrible trouble with Alexey. Nightmares. He was crying for me. I don't know. I'd been seeing him almost every day. Things didn't seem that bad. But you and I—" He shrugged and inhaled, tapping his cigarette on the edge of his ashtray. "Well, I didn't really give much of a damn and I certainly did care for Alexey. So I ended up going back. Then after two months—God, we did nothing but snipe at each other—I told her it was insane. She announced she was pregnant. 'Do you want me to get an abortion?' she asked. In that cold way. Christ! I couldn't even stand to look at her anymore. So of course I said no, I did not want her to get an abortion. And we went on with the damn thing. Of course, she had some reason for not being pregnant in the end. A spontaneous abortion in the john at the tennis club. I don't know."

"Ivan, I had to ask you."

"Yes." He sat, staring out the window.

"I'm sorry."

"You? Never!" He got up and put his arms around her. "Don't worry. Next summer you'll be sitting in the sun, painting in the most beautiful country in the world. My princess has been rescued from the tower." He laughed, hugging her.

Tia quit her job the next morning.

"What? No notice? You just walking out?" her supervisor screamed. "You'll get no recommendation from us."

Tia rushed home from work, hurrying upstairs to throw her clothes into a bag, pull some books off her desk, write a note to Robin. Jenny was mooing in her room.

"I'm going to Vermont with Ivan, Jenny," Tia called through the padded door. "I'll leave the number on the hall table."

"Christ, are you?" Jenny opened the door and peered out from around the edge of the blanket.

"Yes. Don't tell me I'm crazy."

"And there's a letter from your intended on the hall table," called Jenny as Tia flew down the stairs.

Tia stood and looked at it, with its blue and red airmail trim, addressed in Sloan's tight hand. "Oh, damn," she muttered.

"Going to read it?"

"Probably an update on his savings account," said Tia.

"There's the old Valenkova talking," said Jenny.

There were some things Tia could do well.

The house was small, white frame, with its prerevolutionary date in numbers above the door. Set on the side of a hill, it overlooked lines of smoky blue mountains over the border in New York. It took almost half an hour to drive the rocky, rutted road from town.

Ivan set himself up in the living room, spreading his cartons of books and papers over a long refectory table. The first day he drove Tia down to Bennington so she could buy painting supplies. She had not painted for two years. Ivan helped set her up in the dining room, which overlooked the orchard.

"I can't believe this," Tia said the first night, as they ate their dinner at the big round table in the kitchen. "A week ago I was fitting ten-year-olds with training bras and wondering why I was so miserable."

He drank his wine and sighed. "It's wonderful." He threw back his head and laughed. "You're wonderful," he roared. He took her hand.

"I don't want to think about what will happen next," said Tia quickly.

"Neither do I," he said quietly.

Once, while they lay in bed on a rainy Saturday morning, he asked her if she would go to London with him in January.

"But what about Harvard?"

"I don't know about Harvard."

"Aren't you going to teach next year?"

"Not if Kathryn can help it."

"What could she do?"

"Oh, kitten, money speaks very loud, and her stepfather has made it difficult for me before."

"I hate to leave school."

"You can go to school anywhere. In London. You can go to the Slade."

She mumbled some response but he wasn't listening. He was lying back, looking far away. "This time, we'll do it all differently, Tia. Neither of us was made for people like Sloan and Kathryn."

"Sloan?"

"All the worker bees." He got up and started pulling on his pants. "I've been such a good little MacLeod, and you've been such a good—what was it—West? Westerly?"

"Westcott."

"And we'd end up dull and fat and belonging to the AAA."

"What?" She laughed.

"And you're far too young for me, they'll all be saying. And he left his wife and son for her. His promising career at Harvard. The house on Brattle Street. Seats at the Symphony. Waltz Evenings." He walked back to the bed and stared down at her. "She left her medical student, her nice rich granny, her brilliant college. But we'll know, won't we, kitten? No one else will understand the secret." He looked down at her, his eyes far away, and then walked into the bathroom.

Tia sat up in bed. "The secret?" She called out her question but the water was running and he didn't hear.

Gran met them at the front door, standing erect in her long black dress. Her lips were clamped firmly together, even when she kissed Tia's cheek.

"Helena, you realize of course that you would have done this too."

"Never."

"Tia is turning out like you after all, Helena."

Dinner was tense. Tia described the house in Vermont. Ivan talked about his work. After the meal Gran excused herself. Ivan went over to the bookshelf and took down a book. Tia watched him. The high-cheekboned face looked fleshy and flushed. He looked over at her.

"What's the matter?"

"Nothing," she said.

Tia, have you run off with a girdle peddler? read Sloan's postcard. *Miss you. Returning Sept. 15. Can you meet my plane? TWA 234, 4 p.m.*

"Romantic," said Ivan.

"I've written him a letter," said Tia. "I'm such a coward."

She had coupled being a coward with being malicious.

"Well, how else are you going to get rid of him?" said Jenny.

"Just make him understand," argued Robin. "You don't have to be such a bitch."

"He's so thick," drawled Jenny.

"He's very much in love with Tia," said Robin righteously.

But it didn't seem much like love. It felt like being chased, cornered, trapped, flogged.

"You don't understand what you're doing," thundered Sloan. He called her at all hours of the day and night. He analyzed her need for Ivan. "He acts out for you, but you don't need that," he would insist. "We're engaged," he said firmly. It had been announced in the *Times*. "We bought the car together."

"I don't know what to do," said Tia, and then wept. Ivan was amused, somewhat irritated, not very interested.

"Oh, he'll get over it," said Ivan. He was talking to Kathryn's lawyer about a divorce. Kathryn was still in California with Alexey. "I'm surprised how much I miss Alexey."

"We're causing havoc everywhere," said Tia.

They were sitting by the fire in the house they had rented for the winter on Cape Cod.

"Yes"—Ivan sighed—"and we probably will continue to do so the rest of our lives."

"I don't see myself as a havoc raiser, normally."

"Ah, but you are. A quiet one." He bent over and kissed her cheek. "I tried the other way but havoc won out."

"Not easily, though?"

"No." He looked sad. "I miss Alexey," he said again. "And being so brutal with Kathryn." He looked down at her. "And you with Sloan. See?"

The cottage on the Cape was small, gray-shingled, on the Wellfleet dunes. They usually left Cambridge after Tia's last class Friday morning and returned Sunday night. They lived together those three days in patterns they had established the summer before in Vermont. Ivan taught her to work, to lose herself for hours in her books, to ignore distractions, hunger, the telephone. His work, her studies, were always the pivot of their time together. They were drawn to the core of the house, to the wide fieldstone fireplace, to the tables and chairs flanking it. Beyond that, they wandered back out into the world, blinking at the light, inhaling the salty dampness, walking through the dune grass and wind-whipped sand. At night, when she cooked dinner while Ivan typed up the pages he had written in longhand, she would look out the kitchen window and watch the faint white outline of surf on the beach.

"Wouldn't it be nice if we could buy this place," mused Tia one morning. The fog was rolling up from the sea and Ivan had lit a fire. He looked up from his work.

"Mmmm," he muttered absently.

Tia sat down close to the fire and opened her chemistry text. Perhaps they would have a child later and Alexey would come down and visit them. She could plant lilies and roses along the fence in front of the house.

"Let's miss classes tomorrow," said Ivan, one cool blue Sunday. "Call in and say you were delayed at home and I'll have Larsen take my class." He rubbed his eyes. They were bloodshot, and the lines around them were white.

"You sick?"

"No. Just need a day off." He got up and stretched. "Want a Bloody Mary?"

"Maybe later."

He went downstairs. Tia could hear the icebox door slam, the sound of ice in a glass. He came back into the bedroom, the glass already almost empty.

"Ah, now I feel human. A bit of hair of the dog." He pulled on his jacket. "Come on. Let's go see if we can find someone to take us somewhere on a boat."

All day, while they walked along the docks in Provincetown, and in the boat Ivan finally found, she felt a growing tension mixed with the old familiar sense of foreboding. Sitting on the deck, huddled in Ivan's rough tweed jacket, she felt the cold seep through her until it seemed to ice her organs. Everything she saw, she tried to frame in still life, so that she could hold on to something she felt was slipping away. What it was that was beginning to elude her, she was not sure.

"This is perfect, isn't it?" Ivan's face was ruddy again. He smiled at her. "Cold, kitten? Want my sweater?" He started to peel off the heavy, white sweater Masha had knit him.

"No, I'm fine." She smiled up at him.

"It's beautiful!" he exclaimed, looking out at the sun-dazzled sea.

Straining to feel the beauty he saw, Tia only felt as if she had retreated behind glass.

"Please, Tia, just see me," begged Sloan.

"I'm going away for the weekend," she said coldly.

"You seem to go away every weekend."

"Yes."

"Then, this morning. Come on, Tia, you owe me that."

Finally she agreed. She met him at the cafeteria across from the Yard. He was sitting at one of the long tables, sipping coffee. Watching him for a moment, before he saw her, she was surprised that he did not look marked with grief. He was reading something and smiling.

"Hi," he said.

"I only have half an hour before my seminar."

"You taking a seminar this term?"

She nodded. He seemed so smooth-faced and narrow-shouldered. She missed Ivan.

"You look drained, Tia," he said, putting his hand on her arm. "You've lost weight." He looked pleased. Maybe he thought she was grieving too.

"You look fine."

"You should have seen me this summer. I got black. Stupid thing to do, of course."

"Yes."

"Of course medical students have all the diseases they're studying." He smiled calmly, but his hands nervously worked his napkin.

Years later Sloan had told her how surprised he was by her appearance that day. She had looked so drawn, so pale and tense. Her eyes had seemed enormous and black. "That's when I knew we'd get together again—that it was just a matter of time."

"Because I looked ill?"

"No, of course not," he had replied impatiently. Then he had gotten angry, reliving that time again. "You're damn lucky I did see it—not everyone would have been so loyal."

That day, with the clattering of dishes and the smell of cooking grease dimming her senses, Tia had not seen what Sloan perceived so confidently. She had fled at the end of thirty minutes, running up the steps of Sever Hall as the ten o'clock bells tolled.

Lying in bed next to Ivan, listening to the surf and to the rain on the roof, Tia tried to relax her body and sleep. Ivan's arm across her back, usually so comforting, felt heavy. She got up and walked quietly downstairs. The wind animated shadows cast by the full moon. She sat at Ivan's desk and pulled his sweater around her shoulders.

"Tia?" Ivan padded down the stairs. "Are you there?"

"Over here."

He walked cautiously over to her, banging into furniture. "Can't sleep?"

"No. I've been so tense lately," she blurted.

Ivan bent over and kissed the top of her head.

"Tia, I've been thinking this past month about getting out of my spring schedule and joining Wilson in London after Christmas. Why don't you come too?"

The invitation sounded so casual. "Can't you wait until June?" She had looked forward to spring here. There were lilacs in the garden and a bank of wild roses.

"No, I really want to get out of Cambridge."

He walked into the kitchen and poured himself a drink. "What do you think of Christmas in London? Gran and Elizavetta could come there."

Gran would never leave New York at Christmas, thought Tia.

"Are you sure you want me to come?" She tried to keep petulance out of her tone, but he heard it and laughed.

"Yes, little kitten, I do," he answered gaily.

"Do you think I could go to school there?" Her voice sounded so childlike.

"Certainly. Or we could find a cottage somewhere and you could paint. Wilson lives somewhere in Kent. I'd only need to get up to London a day or so a week if we lived near him."

He told her about the work he'd need to do and the people he wanted to see. She listened like a child negotiating unfamiliar words and ideas, watching his lips move, fighting hard not to lose the sense of what he was saying. Someone called Carlin lived in Cornwall and would have to be seen. Tia could rent a car and see the country. They could take a lease on a cottage or apartment, so if she didn't like the dig she could come back and study in London.

"That way you won't feel trapped." He smiled. She noticed how large his teeth were. He was pleased that he had been able to think it all out in a way that showed plainly that he took her into consideration. She felt that he had added the last, about the rented sanctuary for her, as the climax.

"Gran won't like it."

"So be it."

"She holds the purse strings."

"Ah," said Ivan. "Mmmm."

His divorce from Kathryn was expensive. She had insisted on half of his university salary and all their bank accounts. Actually, in a burst of last-minute generosity, and allowing that she was a rich woman in her own right, she had let him keep the small trust fund his grandfather had left him. In the eight years Ivan had been married to Kathryn, he had forgotten how controlling money could be. In the last few months he had been constantly surprised by the absence of it. He had been shocked by Kathryn's ferocity in claiming it, fighting angrily for more than he thought she needed. "She never seemed interested in money," he would say, bewildered.

"I'll talk to Valery. Maybe he can talk to Gran," said Tia.

"We'll manage," said Ivan, his cheer restored. He rose and walked over to the window and looked out on the moonlit sea. "Oh, God." He sighed. "I can't wait to get out of here."

Chapter Twenty-two

Feeling reckless, Tia accepted Perry Dunning's invitation for lunch in the country. They sat across from each other, talking again about Perry's favorite topics, while the housekeeper served them and the sun poured in the windows. They sat for a long time, drinking wine and smoking cigarettes, talking. It was effortless. Perry did not seem in a hurry to proceed with his seduction.

After lunch he went upstairs to find her a sweater. The wind had started, and the day had turned cool. He put it over her shoulders, and they walked out to the barn. The horses were already saddled, waiting on cross ties. The mare was darting back and forth, ducking her head as they approached.

"Are you afraid?" Perry stopped her and smiled. "You don't have to ride her."

Tia was afraid but she shrugged. "I'll be fine."

The mare pranced and pulled at the bit as they started. They rode down the rolling meadows. Perry trotted off, his big horse taking long strides on the uneven grass. The mare was hard to hold back, and Tia could feel her body stiffen.

"There's a wonderful place for a gallop down here. Okay?"

Tia nodded, fearful. The mare strained at the bit, pulling away from Tia's hands, racing in back of the gelding, trying to pass him. Tia pulled her toward the bushes, trying to regain control, but the mare fought back. What the hell, thought Tia, seeing the path through the field stretch out evenly. She loosened the reins and let the mare go. They flew past Perry, covering the ground so fast Tia could hardly see where they were going. The air rushed at her, tugging at her jacket, loosening her hair. She bent forward, and the mare moved forward in another burst of speed. The beat of her hooves, the speed, the earth flying past them were so exhilarating that Tia did not want to stop. As they started up a hill she could feel the mare begin to tire and for a moment she urged her on and felt the horse respond, and then she started pulling her back and stopping her.

"My God," said Perry, when he caught up with them. His face was drained. "Are you okay?"

"You didn't tell me she was off the track," said Tia.

He looked at her and smiled. "You did very well."

Surviving the ride made her feel more reckless. In the barn she let Perry take her to his dark little corner and kiss her and pull her down on the hay and unbutton her blouse. Then she pushed him away and he helped her up and brushed the hay off her while she buttoned her clothes up again.

They walked back to the house. Sabrina ran toward them.

"I thought I saw your car, Ti." Sabrina jumped up and kissed Perry's cheek.

"You should have seen your little friend on that mare," said Perry easily. "I was going to beg Tia to stay for dinner, and now that you're here I'm sure she will."

Tia called Sloan. "You and Sabrina playing with horses?" he said, somewhat irritably. "Perry Dunning? Oh. Well, suit your-self. I'll tell Priscilla to feed the kids."

"Tia, I know it's none of my business, but are you and Perry having an affair?" asked Sabrina the next morning.

"No!"

"He's awfully lonely. He'd take it more seriously than you would."

"Sabrina! He pestered me to try that mare. That's all."

"He's had lots of problems, you know, Ti. Mummy really hurt him."

"If you think he misunderstands . . . " Tia fought to maintain her innocence.

"Just be careful. I'd hate to see him fall apart again."

Damn, said Tia to herself. "No easy answers, are there?" Valery used to say at times like this.

Perry, with his easy conversation, his smooth gray hair, his well-tailored suits, should have been able to provide one or two, thought Tia.

Chapter Twenty-three

Ivan had left for England before Christmas. He really started on his journey the day he made the decision to go. The last few weekends in the Cape house seemed hollow. Gran had said she would not countenance Tia's accompanying Ivan to England.

"Absolutely not. Don't even bring the subject up again," she had said.

"You're almost twenty-one. Why are you allowing your grandmother to withhold permission?" said Ivan. At first he was angry, disappointed. Then he moved on and left her alone to sort out her options.

"I can't go, don't you understand?"

"No, darling, I really don't." But now there was an impatience in his tone. Not only at her, for being so recalcitrant, but at her disturbing the smooth progress of his departure. For several weeks they did not mention it. Then, one stormy night in late November, he told her he was leaving in two weeks. "I've made definite arrangements now." He paused. "You know we've got this house until June. Do you want to keep it, or should I see if we can sublet it?"

This house without Ivan? What delicious agony that would be. Standing in this room, on another stormy night, perhaps in January, and seeing his table bare of books, the closet empty of his clothes. Eating alone in front of the fire, playing his records on the gramophone.

"Ah-ha," he said. "So you have all sorts of plans." He had misunderstood the expression on her face.

"No, Ivan, I don't want the house without you," she said quickly.

"I couldn't stand it," he said, coming over and putting his arms around her. "You've got to come to England soon, kitten. Don't let Gran spoil this for us."

That weekend he whistled as he packed his books. He played Stravinsky, cooked up a pot of stew, wrote some letters. Tia studied and, while he cooked, took a long walk. The storm had gone out to sea and left the sky blue and the surf churning. The trellis on the side of the cottage had blown down. The beach was slick with seaweed. She stood on the dunes and looked out at the ocean rolling and thundering below and wondered how she would ever survive without Ivan.

It had all been so ambiguous. He had held her in his arms and wept the night before he left. She had been stiff with fear. They had made love so they would not have to talk. It was only clear that he was going and she was not going with him. He had run up the ramp to the plane and then, as if he had almost forgotten her already, hesitated before he turned back and waved. He probably could not see her standing at the big plate-glass window, and his wave was vague. He had turned back to the plane, exchanged a word with the stewardess at the door, and then bent his head and stepped into the darkness.

She had taken a taxi back to Gran's and chatted with the driver and laughed at his jokes. When he pulled up to her apartment house he had reached back and put his hand up her skirt. Already, she realized, she was defenseless.

"Defenseless? Come on." Jenny laughed. "You?"

Jenny was the great puncturer. There were times when people avoided her. Tia hedged a little. It was just that Ivan had made such a complete world for her. Jenny groaned.

"You have a whim of iron," said Jenny. "I've lived with the best of them," she said, referring to Laura Landsdale, "and I ought to know."

It was difficult to elicit sympathy from Jenny.

"I miss him so much," whimpered Tia fearlessly.

"Look at you—you make it so easy for yourself by never really trying anything."

That was not true, thought Tia, but she didn't want to argue about it. Grief had weakened her ability to joust with Jenny. I do so try, she thought to herself. I've been having an affair with Ivan for years, when other people were still playing at serious love.

"And I don't mean screwing some Byronic lush," Jenny said.

Robin was more even-tempered. "Work on Gran. She'll give in. If she doesn't, then you can just go on without her blessing."

"She's old, Robin. She's given up so much for me."

"Come off it, Tia."

Sloan had not given up. He still called, and sometimes he sent flowers. Then he suddenly increased his assault. Tia assumed Robin, who had always defended him, had urged him on. "She's in a weakened state," Robin probably told him.

One afternoon a messenger arrived, carrying a box which he solemnly insisted on giving Tia himself and standing by while she opened it.

"I have to, I'm bonded," he said.

In a blue velvet box was a ring with a small emerald flanked by two tiny diamonds, set on a narrow band of gold.

"Oh, shit," said Tia, when she examined the ring and saw the *S to T* engraved on the gold.

The messenger looked surprised. "Something wrong?"

"No, no," she said, snapping the box shut. "Can you take it back?"

"No, I don't think so. I don't know." He looked uneasy.

"Please, here. I'm sorry." She fled upstairs.

Ivan's letters were scribbled hastily and hard to decipher. It seemed that he was having some difficulties with Wilson. On Christmas Day he called her and told her he missed her but there were noises of merriment in the background and Gran stood near Tia so the conversation was strained.

"I know you're suffering," said Gran, "but you're strong."

"But why? I could be in London with Ivan if you'd let me."

"Do you really want to go, Tia? Do you want to cut off all your roots—your schooling, your life with me—and take a chance on something you are ill prepared to try?"

Of course she was not sure, and Gran understood that. "Yes," said Tia.

"Come down to New York on your weekends. Get away from Cambridge. I'm opening Easter Cove in April. I'll see that you have a car."

Tia found that she could not stand Gran's voice. She avoided her phone calls, but when the plane tickets arrived, Tia, racked with guilt, embarked. She arrived in New York Friday afternoon, about the time that she used to arrive in Wellfleet with Ivan, and tried to return Masha's embrace with feeling, tried to sit with Gran and not allow the anger that made her almost light-headed spill over. She swallowed it down as it rose in her throat, left the room before it spoke. The long dress, the chokers, the musky perfume, the long, jeweled fingers seemed an absurd pose. Nothing seemed to have substance. Masha was stupid, her movements irritatingly slow and clumsy, the smell of onions and sausage strong on her breath. The rooms that had once appeared thick with mystery and beauty now seemed merely dark and cluttered. Gran, the chief martinet, ruled her empire without a crown. Valery was a silly, posturing man with a boring, giggling wife. The conversations that had once held her in thrall now seemed pretentious and self-serving.

That weekend she retired to her room early, abandoning a party that had obviously been arranged to cheer her, and curled up on the window seat. The cold night air and the oily river smell seeped in from around the edges of the window frames. As she looked down she thought of flinging herself out the window, hurling herself away. The impulse was so strong she got down and went into the bathroom. She stared at her reflection in the mirror. A strange, angry face stared back. It rose on a scrawny neck above an ill-fitting blouse. There were dark blue shadows around the eyes and too much lipstick on lips pressed together like an old woman's.

Still, she came again the next weekend, and the ones after that. It was as if she were testing herself, taking a steel point to her skin and puncturing the surface to see if there was still feeling in her body. Perhaps, she sometimes thought reluctantly, she was waiting for Gran to rescue her, to see that something was wrong and perform a miracle. Gran certainly saw that something was wrong and knew what it was but she said nothing. She allowed Tia to retreat to her bedroom, to sit silent and abstracted at dinner, to refuse to go out. Nothing was said about needing a hair-brush or changing for dinner. Moreover, nothing was said about recovering, growing up, getting on with life.

"Get off it," said Robin, who felt no such constraints. "You're such a pain in the ass."

"I can't seem to pull myself out of it," Tia finally conceded.

"Try a little harder," said Robin.

"Time will help. Be patient," said Jenny to both of them.

In April Gran wrote that she had bought a car for Tia and that Valery and Claudia would drive it up to Cambridge for her.

"Oh, no," said Tia when she read the letter.

"Look at Valery," Ivan would say when he discoursed on the perils of marriage. "He's been hideously transformed."

By the time Valery and Claudia arrived, a week and three hours late, Tia had begun to look forward to their arrival.

Valery was excited about the car. "It's wonderful," he exclaimed. He had never learned to drive, so Claudia had to demonstrate. "See, isn't it handsome?" he said. "Claudia drives so well. We had a marvelous trip." He gazed fondly at his wife. She smiled back at him and touched his hand.

"Valery covets your car," she said. They all stood awkwardly for a moment. Gran had cut off Valery's funds. Claudia's teaching salary was barely enough to maintain them in their tiny apartment. "But what would he do with a car?" she said, laughing. She must have been half his age.

"I'd paint it," he roared. "Paint it!"

"He would, too." Claudia laughed.

"Tia, come on—we'll drive to Easter Cove. Claudia will show you how."

They drove up that night. Valery fell asleep, slumped against the door, and Claudia would look over at him from time to time and smile.

It was the first time Tia had driven to Easter Cove from Cambridge. Gran had always insisted she fly. Neither one of them wanted to discuss their fear of that place on the road where Peter and Anna and Tinka had been killed. It was out there, in the darkness, and Claudia was going to pass it at her cautious speed and they wouldn't know. On that spot where they had all died, some spirit must linger, thought Tia. She pulled her coat on.

"Cold back there? Want me to turn the heat up?" said Claudia.

"No, it's fine," said Tia, looking out into the moonless night.

"I thought you might want to spend the summer on Pine Island," said Gran.

"Why not let her stay in New York and study at the Art Students League?" suggested Laura Landsdale, who was recovering from the failure of her last play.

"Pine Island is a much better place for Tia to study," declared Gran.

"Poscko has a wonderful class. I think I can get her in," said Valery calmly.

"I don't think so," said Gran.

"And you, Tia? What would you like to do?" Valery turned to her.

"Am I going to be consulted?"

"Don't sulk, child," said Gran. "I've already made arrangements for Pine Island. I was going to surprise you. I showed Paul some of your work, and he was impressed."

Paul Kirburg had been one of the ghosts who passed through Easter Cove. A painter, Valery's teacher in Berlin in the twenties, Kirburg had not heeded his pupil's warnings a decade later. Enjoying success as a painter and teacher, he had met a young Austrian pianist. The courtship had been difficult, time and distance interfering with its progress, but finally Paul had convinced Hanna to come to Berlin. By the time Valery had gone to Berlin to persuade them to leave, they had a young daughter and were so transported by their joy that Valery's fears did not move them. Valery could understand, sitting in their comfortable apartment, with Hanna laughing as her tiny daughter banged her fists on the piano keys and benignly paternal Paul relaxed in his armchair, why it was hard for them to believe that their life would not always be charmed. Paul and Hanna said they would come if things got worse.

It was too late then. Paul survived Dachau, but Hanna and Lisl died at Ravensbrück.

Paul wrote Valery from a DP camp in Germany and Valery brought him to New York. Of course it was Gran who made the arrangements. When Valery crossed the Atlantic he had changed his style and lost his former patrons and found, with the exception of Gran, no new ones.

Paul arrived in July and came to Easter Cove. His story had preceded him and was never mentioned after his arrival. It was mostly Russians, Robin would point out, who talked. Paul was one of the quiet ones who sat on lawn chairs, almost always wrapped in a blanket, and looked out to sea. Robin and Tia regarded him apprehensively. The weight of his sorrow was more than they could bear. Would he slowly walk down to the sea and end his suffering? Would he despise them for being alive? Poor little Lisl, they said to each other, how do you think she died?

Slowly Paul awoke. He insisted on helping. Gran gave him the gardener's cottage and he tried to take care of the lawn, but he couldn't keep the lawn mowers running. Gran grew irritable.

"Why doesn't he teach again?" she asked one morning while she watched Paul's struggle with the edger.

"Yes," said Valery thoughtfully.

It took several months to remember Pine Island. Gran had bought the small island off Easter Cove for Valery during the war, but he hated being isolated, found the farmhouse too damp and spartan, and could not understand why brush and trees soon overgrew the meadows. One fall afternoon he had swamped and sunk his launch, swum across the channel to Gran's house, and never returned. Now he thought of it for Paul. Paul went over with a Whaler loaded with lumber and supplies the spring that marked his year at Easter Cove, and by fall he had restored the big barn, made the house habitable, and cleared some of the fields. The following summer he started his school.

He rarely came to Easter Cove anymore. Occasionally Tia and Robin sailed through the channel, along the west side of the island, where they could see Paul's house and studio and the cabins where the students lived. They always thought about Lisl and Hanna.

"I don't want to go to Pine Island, Gran."

"Tia, if you are at all serious about your work, you will go."

"Oh, it sounds heavenly to me," said Claudia, trying to temper the growing tension.

Tia looked at Gran. Words like "heavenly" vexed her sorely.

"Yes, it is, Claudia," said Valery quickly. He looked imploringly at Tia. "Perhaps Helena is right."

"Paul is certainly a great artiste," said Laura Landsdale, pleasantly.

"Oh, what a divine opportunity, Tia," said Claudia, warming.

"It certainly is," said Valery. "Tia?"

"Yes," said Tia, "I think so."

"Well then, Helena, it's all settled," said Laura Landsdale in her deep, authoritative voice.

Valery smiled. Claudia reached over and squeezed his hand. Gran rang the bell for Masha.

"Please see that these vegetables are reheated. They were served ice cold," she said crossly.

Paul Kirburg was no longer the tired, gaunt man who had stared vacantly at the sea. While his body had softened and rounded, his wit had grown sharp. His withering remarks kept his students subdued. They waited, often in vain, for a rare compliment. Mitigating some of the anxiety was his new wife, Myra. Myra, with her tall wide-shouldered frame and booming laugh, swept up the debris every evening with her ample suppers, lavishing hugs and food with blithe good spirits. Even Paul would unbend a little, laugh suddenly when needled fondly by his wife, talk about painters he had known in Europe before the war, talk about Freud, to whom he was distantly related, talk about Myra's enormous Hungarian family in Brooklyn.

"It's true, it's true," Myra would laugh. Once his student, she had abandoned her painting to focus all her attentions on him and the school.

He could be as cruel to her as to the others. She shrugged away his taunts, the irascible jibes at her size, the volume of her voice, at her beloved terrier.

"It's okay," she would say, "he does it when he's hurting." She would sigh. Hanna and Lisl were on bone piles in Germany, and Paul lived on Pine Island in Myra's big embrace. "I've been lucky," she would say softly. The students, chastened by her empathy, would go back to Paul.

"Well now, Miss Valenkova, this is supposed to be a human figure? On these legs he can run and bend and jump?"

"Ah, Mr. Popkin, a back without a spine?"

"What, Miss Banks, is that protruding from the middle of his face?"

"Yes, yes, not bad, but it has no life."

The beds in the bunkhouses were narrow and hard. Each student had a bureau, a chair, and a jelly glass provided by Myra so that they could pick wildflowers.

"He's so mean," said Tia, one evening.

"But he's such a great teacher," said her bunkmate, Polly Banks.

Such a mean teacher, said Tia to herself. "Perhaps," she said to Polly.

"Miss Banks, you are simply banal," Paul barked at Polly the next morning.

Tia hardened herself to his critiques, enjoyed the island, enjoyed Myra. In the afternoon she would start out with her sketchbook and end up sitting in Myra's kitchen, peeling potatoes and cutting apples. Sometimes she would sketch Myra in that steamy summer kitchen, her great back bent over the low cutting table, the wild red hair breaking out of its restraints. Myra would talk about her family, her husband, Pine Island in the winter.

"You'll have to come down to New York and stay with Gran, Myra."

"I'd love that," she'd exclaim, "If I can ever get that melancholy Jew out of this winter wilderness."

"Don't you miss your work?"

"Oh, Tia, darling, of course. But I love what I'm doing now." She waved her hand around the big kitchen.

"No regrets?"

"Paul says I'm so busy eating and talking I have no time for thinking." She laughed.

Ivan and Sloan wrote. Tia always read Ivan's letters first. Both men seemed so remote.

The last day Paul spoke to each student privately. Tia dreaded the moment.

"Miss Valenkova," he said, "Tia." It was the first time in the six weeks of school that he had acknowledged their prior relationship. "Tia, my dear girl," he started; then he sighed. "You are very quick, very facile."

"Facile?"

"In the sense of doing things easily, quickly, but also some-

times not working hard enough, not working until you reach inside yourself. You give me what I ask for and keep the rest to
yourself." He looked at her sympathetically. "You have to be
willing to do much more. You take no risks, Tia." He smiled at
her. "You won't be very good if you keep hiding. It will be like
your work this summer—nice, pretty, but meaningless. You are
leaving the interesting part out."

"Was he rough on you too?" said Myra, standing in the farmhouse doorway as Tia passed.

"I think he said I was shallow," said Tia lightly.

"Russians are never shallow," boomed Myra. "Neither are
Hungarians."

Sloan was waiting for her at the ferry slip.

"Robin told me you were getting back today," he said. Then,
because she did not seem glad to see him, he added, "I'm staying
with Cartwright—you know, my old roommate."

"Sloan, why did you come?"

"You know why." He put her bags into his car and drove her
to Gran's, telling her about his last term, his hopes for a residency in Washington after graduation. Tia tried to move her
thighs so that the seat covers did not stick to her flesh.

"It'll take a few years, but eventually I'll be able to give you as
good a life as you ever had with Gran."

"Why should it take a few years?" she said sourly.

"Oh, internship, residency," he said earnestly.

When she returned to school for her senior year, there were
fewer letters from Ivan. He had not come home in September, as
he had planned, not even to see Alexey. He had been offered a
post at London University which would give him more time for
his book and he had taken it. Tia had been busy with her thesis.
He understood, he said pointedly in one letter, why she should
have less time to write. He hoped she would come to London in
June, after her final exams.

She had a hard time remembering what he looked like. She
missed him almost from habit. One day she drove to the Cape
and walked up the Wellfleet dunes to their house, and some of
the ache revived. She wrote him about the sentimental journey,

as she, feeling unsure, called it. Ivan did not mention it when he wrote her. Her last move for mortification was the day she walked to Kathryn's house on Brattle Street and stood near the gate and watched a small boy playing on the wide front porch. He was small, with long, thin arms and legs, and hair as thick and pale as Ivan's.

"Alex," someone called from inside.

He looked up and listened for a moment. He saw Tia and looked at her with Kathryn's cool, dark eyes.

Chapter Twenty-four

Jenny was getting married again. He was a carpenter with three children. The courtship had started while he built cabinets in Jenny's Virginia farmhouse.

"We're going to raise dogs," she announced.

"Why?" asked Tia.

"It's about all we can do together. Dogs are all we have in common."

"Do you want to raise dogs?"

"Why not?" said Jenny, shrugging.

"She's always trying to provoke her parents," complained Sloan when Tia told him. He was, he had announced, getting very tired of Jenny.

"You liked her when she was married to Bartley and giving dinner parties for her mother," said Tia nastily.

"It beats sitting on the floor fending off cockroaches and talking to people who are so stoned they drift off in the middle of a sentence."

"It's just a phase with her. At least she's not dull."

"On the contrary," said Sloan, "she's very dull."

"Everybody's dull," snapped Tia.

"What's the trouble with you?" asked Sloan.

"Cobblers' children," she muttered.

"What?"

"They go shoeless."

"Yes?"

"A psychiatrist's wife . . . "

"Oh!" He regarded her with his professional gaze for a moment. "You don't need therapy, Tia. You just need to keep busier."

"Busier?" That, she thought, had been the trouble.

"I mean, get some exercise. Start running, play tennis, walk more. It'll make you feel better. And do something about your wardrobe."

"What?"

"It's . . . " He paused. "You could pep it up."

"Pep?" She also had begun to seize on his words like Gran.

"For Christ's sake, Tia, what do you want me to do about it?" he burst out angrily, his face flushing. "Don't you think I have enough stress and strain? Jesus, can't you just pull your load?"

"Apparently not." It was the accusation she feared the most. Gran had pulled a million loads, her father had pulled none, and Anna had died trying.

"I'm sick and tired of your attitude," he continued, warming to his subject. "You don't do a damn thing to help me—you can't even be polite to Annie Klein, and I don't care if she is an idiot (oh, yes, I know what you were going to say)—and I'm struggling in that snake pit and my wife won't even lift a finger to help and yet she expects me to go out and eat dinner at every two-bit diner in this damn town." He had not spent his rage and he glared at her while he cleared his throat. "You treat me like some third-rate medical student instead of someone who's done pretty damn well in his profession. Yes, you do—you made me come crawling to you, beg you to marry me, and I had nothing then but my name." He glanced at her, afraid she might seize on that last phrase.

"That was long ago, Sloan."

"Other people respect me. I'm very good at what I do." He was off on a new tangent now, uncomfortably aware that he was beginning to make a fool of himself.

"What are you saying?"

"I just want you to join me, to stand by me. . . . " He sighed. "It's that you're so damn remote sometimes. I've started to envy

Klein and Sykes—their wives are really out for them. Oh, shit, I
don't know." He walked quickly out of the room and slammed
the door.

"Jenny, why are you getting married again?" said Tia.

"I like being married."

"You're nuts." Tia laughed, trying to lighten the bitterness of
her tone.

"I don't take it as seriously as you do," said Jenny.

They were waiting for the justice of the peace to arrive.
Wayne, the bridegroom, was outside playing ball with his children. Sloan and Robin sat in the shade watching them. Daisy
was standing at the edge of the ball game, her hands behind her
back, twisting her knees together. Peter was playing with his cars
in a small pile of construction sand near the house.

"Doesn't Wayne have any guests?"

"He invited some friends. I think his sister is coming."

Jenny sat at her dressing table, combing her hair. She had her
grandmother's silver brushes. Tia sat on the bed and watched
her. She remembered watching Jenny using those brushes at her
mother's dressing table, in the evening, after Laura had left for
the theater. They would go into her room then and look into her
closets, reverently walking up and down the rows of dresses,
coats, blouses, skirts, gowns, racks of shoes. There was a thick
carpet on the closet floor and bright lights on tracks. Sometimes
they'd sit in a corner, under the blouses, talking until they heard
the housekeeper calling them. Other nights they'd tiptoe into
Laura's bedroom and gaze at the white marble ledge beside the
sink, lined with bottles of perfume and boxes of powder. The
whole bathroom was fragrant with them.

"Jen," called Wayne. "Sissie's here, and she says Buck and
Pete are down at the Exxon. I'll just run down for them."

"Send Sissie on up," called Jenny. "He calls me Jen," she said
to Tia. "I wish he wouldn't."

Sissie came upstairs and sat awkwardly on the window seat.
Jenny put on some mascara and looked at herself critically.

"Sissie, you should have brought your children," said Jenny.

"Well"—she shifted and put her handbag on her knees—
"they'd mess up your house."

Jenny wiped off the mascara. Tia could hear cries from Peter, and she jumped up.

"I've got to see what's bothering Peter," she said, grateful for an excuse to leave the room.

Peter was lying on the ground, kicking his legs and pounding his fists.

"Wayne's boy took his car," said Sloan, who was trying to subdue him.

Wayne's ten-year-old son, Rex, stood defiantly some feet away.

"Give him back that car at once," ordered Tia, marching over to the child.

Rex looked hesitant and surprised. "It's mine."

"It belongs to Peter, and you have no business bullying a little boy around," she said through clenched teeth. She could feel herself running amuck.

Rex handed the truck to her, tears welling in his eyes. He turned and ran into the house.

"Tia!" exclaimed Sloan.

Tia stood with the truck in her hand. Peter had stopped crying and was looking up at her. His face was streaked with dirt.

"The kid is a little shit," said Robin.

"Still, that's no reason—" Sloan stopped.

Rex would not come out of the house for the wedding. During the brief ceremony under the locust tree they could hear things crashing in the house. Wayne looked uneasy. Jenny smiled up at him and winked.

After the ceremony Wayne and Sissie went into the house, and the rest of them stood under the trees and drank warm champagne. Jenny's old nurse had sent a box of cookies.

"I should have made sandwiches," said Jenny, picking through the broken bits of shortbread. "Wonder what happened to Rex."

When Sloan, Tia, Robin, and the children stopped on the way back to Washington for a late lunch, they ate hungrily.

"Poor little Rex." Robin started to laugh. He had come out and pointed an accusing finger at Tia. Everyone had pretended not to notice.

"How could I?" said Tia.

"Being with Jenny always makes you act like a kid," said Sloan. But he smiled. The gin and tonic and good lunch had mellowed him.

"You really scared him, Mommy," said Daisy. Now, joining in the spirit of good fellowship, she was being magnanimous. Earlier she had been humiliated.

They all started to laugh. Peter, curled up against Tia, sleeping soundly, his face flushed and damp, stirred and then pressed closer against her.

Chapter Twenty-five

In the spring, Sloan had finally persuaded Tia to spend a long weekend with him.

"I'll plan it," he said happily when she finally, ungraciously, consented.

Perversely, she was pleased when he told her that they were going to the Cape. She sat in the narrow car seat, her shoulder vibrating against the door, and watched the familiar landmarks. There, by the Duxbury marshes, she had once stopped with Ivan, and they had made love while rain drummed on the roof of the car. Farther along the winding shore road was the restaurant where they always stopped for coffee on the way down and sometimes dinner on the way home. Winding up past Sandwich and Barnstable, she saw their favorite bookstore, an inn they had stayed in once, beaches they had walked along on blowing, winter afternoons.

Sloan did not seem to notice her silence as she inventoried the past, digging at old pain. He had gotten his internship in Washington, he was graduating near the top of his class, his great-uncle Ensear had sent him a large check, his rich Ensear cousins were flunking out of Williams and Wesleyan. Sloan complained cheerfully that Althea was moving again, to Baltimore, to live with her recently widowed Bryn Mawr roommate.

"Of course, she's thinking of moving up to Hanover if things don't work out in Baltimore," he said.

Tia listened sporadically, paying greater attention to passing landmarks.

————

She was relieved that Sloan had chosen an inn in the center of Provincetown. By the time they reached it, she had had sufficient time to regret her misanthropic journey. Her dedicated self-pity had erupted into rancor.

Silently she helped with the bags, stood by while, flushed with embarrassment, he registered them as "Dr. and Mrs. Sloan Ensear," followed him up to their small, musty room at the top of the house. She regarded him sourly as he opened the windows and hung up his jacket.

"Well, not the Ritz exactly but not too bad either," he said awkwardly.

She let him go on feeling awkward and responsible while she sat on the edge of the bed and said nothing.

"What about a walk on the beach?"

She nodded.

"I know this is difficult for you, Tia." He came and sat beside her and put his arms around her. "Darling, I don't want you to go through this. It feels sort of like sneaking around for you, I know." He kissed her hair. "That's why I want to get married as soon as the term is over."

"Please, Sloan."

"We could be married anytime after about the fifth of June." He put his arm around her. "With my uncle's check we can make out—maybe even take a trip up the coast."

It was not Ivan she was leaning against. It was a stranger with strange, clumsy gestures. It was a damp, murky room with rough, stained bedspreads and cobwebs on the ceiling.

"The first year or so will be rough." He tightened his grip on her shoulders. "Do you think your grandmother would help us out the first year?"

She started to cry. Sobs tore through her body, tears flowed, anguish coiled in her chest. She pulled away from Sloan and flung herself on the bed and beat against the pillows with her fists.

"My last tantrum," she used to say later, always discomforted by the memory of it.

"I realized how little I knew you," said Sloan, later. "You'd always been so calm and in control."

He really did not learn much. Perhaps he knew that it had

something to do with Ivan, something to do with finally acknowledging the end of that relationship, and was afraid to discover too much. Sloan rubbed her back and mumbled soothingly. Finally, spent, she turned over and looked at him, sitting there in his worn, tweed jacket, his eyes large with bewilderment. He had meant so well with this trip. It had, no doubt, taken weeks of saving the small allowance Althea sent him to ready himself for it. His face was drawn and weary, his eyes shadowed blue, his shoulders slumped. The exhausted, hard-pressed medical student and the spoiled girl who had ridden next to him for hours, wishing he were someone else.

"Ah, you're smiling," he said, relieved.

"I'm sorry." She took his hand. There she sprawled, her skirt up around her hips, her hair damp with tears, her nose and eyes red and swollen.

"Let's go for that walk now," he said, smiling. Then, when she did not answer immediately, he looked unsure. "Do you want to go back?"

"No, let's walk."

He hugged her. "Great. I'd like to do a little running."

He made it easy. He never asked her why she had cried that afternoon or why, during the rest of the weekend, she would suddenly be overcome by tears. When there were silences, when she seemed to drift away, he would talk about medical school, or Althea and Toby, or his plans for his practice. It was carefully presented. There was nothing for Tia to do but listen and learn.

It was only at night, lying beside him, that it became difficult. His hurried, almost agitated lovemaking seemed impersonal. Trying to lose herself in it, she found her thoughts wandering, her body making appropriate movements but her mind occupied elsewhere. Afterward, while Sloan lay sleeping beside her, she felt empty and drained. The next morning she would wake beside him and feel a grudging tenderness. He woke slowly, like a small child, with his hair over his eyes, blinking at the startling light of the morning. He would climb silently out of bed and go into the bathroom and emerge showered, hair slicked down.

"I had a strange dream last night," said Tia the last morning. Actually she had dreamt it the first night but it had haunted her.

"Oh?" He turned warily toward her.

"Yes, mostly about Gran. I went to Easter Cove and she'd moved. The house was completely different—new and with modern furniture. It wasn't our house at all. No one knew where she'd gone. I kept looking for her. It was awful. Funny, I didn't think about Robin or Masha."

Sloan sat down on the bed and put on his sneakers. "Hmm," he said thoughtfully. "I knew you had a nightmare. You called out a few times."

She did not ask him who she called out for. Last month she had woken up twice screaming for Ivan. Someone would rush into her room and wake her and she would lie in bed for a long time, shaken, exhausted, before she could sleep again.

He reached over and put his arms around her. "Don't worry, Tia. You'll be okay." He stroked her back. "Now, let's get going. I want to rent bikes today and go to the state forest."

A week later Toby Ensear was killed in a car accident. Sloan appeared at Tia's dorm, his face ravaged.

"That idiot kid. He was drunk," he kept saying. "That goddam bitch Althea gave him a car, knowing what a kid he was." He said it again and again.

They sat in the small, dimly lit library in a corner of the old dormitory. Sloan would jump up and pace the room and then return to Tia, going over and over the accident and the events that led up to it.

"I can't face her," he said. "I can't blame her but I do. I know it isn't fair. Why did she give him that car? She barely has money to pay his goddam school bills." He pounded the couch. "He was such a stupid, immature little kid."

Tia held his hand. She could think of nothing to say. She had never seen anger in the face of death before.

She put her arms around him and he leaned on her shoulder. "What a goddam fucking stupid world this is."

"I'll drive you down for the funeral," she said.

"Would you?" he said dully. "Thanks."

Althea had been ready to move, and the rooms were almost empty except for packing boxes, stacked against the walls. She greeted Tia with a handshake and Sloan with a careful embrace.

"Oh, what a sad time for you," said Tia, taking Althea's arm as they walked back into the house.

"Everything is an awful mess," said Althea.

"Is the service tomorrow?" Sloan asked.

"We're having it here," she said wearily.

"Here?" Sloan put his hands on his hips.

"Please, dear, don't fuss."

Tia cooked hamburgers in the kitchen that night while Sloan tried to stack the boxes in the cellar. Althea sat on her bed, phoning people about the service.

"It'll be very simple," she would say. "At the house, at eleven. Sloan and Tia are helping me."

They sat together, eating dinner quietly, in the chaotic kitchen. Tia sat across from some drawings of airplanes that Toby had made. The paper was yellowed and curling and fastened to the wall by pieces of masking tape.

"Why was he driving at that time of night?" Sloan blurted.

"Sloan! Don't!" said Tia.

"Sloan, I don't know," said Althea.

"Couldn't you give him any guidelines? Couldn't you discipline him?" Sloan threw his napkin down on the table and pushed his chair back. "Didn't you think your selfish sort of life would ever catch up to you?"

"Shut up, Sloan," said Tia. "Sit down."

"Thank you, Tia," said Althea coldly. She rose with dignity and walked out of the kitchen. In a moment her bedroom door slammed.

"I'm sorry, Tia. How can you stand me?" Sloan put his head in his hands.

"I understand," said Tia, patting the top of his head. "Let's clean the kitchen up a bit."

He jumped up and threw his arms around her. "What would I do without you? God, I'm so lucky!" He buried his face against her neck and wept.

Her head ached and her chest felt tight.

People started arriving when Althea was still in her bath.

"That's all right, we're early," they said in soft, sympathetic voices, even those arriving late.

Sloan, who had been agitated and restless earlier, became calm and solicitous as the house filled. He moved easily through the small, crowded rooms, introducing Tia, excusing his mother's absence, accepting sympathy.

Then, as the sandwiches dwindled and the wine had warmed, Althea entered the room. She was wearing a long, purple dress that fit too snugly over her bosom. She had swept up her hair in a glittery comb, and her bony arms were covered with round leather African bracelets.

"My God," whispered Sloan, grabbing Tia's hand.

"She looks very stately," said Tia.

"I have to get out of here," he said.

"Not yet," said Tia firmly. To her surprise he nodded, his eyes watering with tears.

"Everyone in this room knew and loved Toby. I would like to read a few poems that Toby loved, and then, if anyone has anything to say, I hope they will say it."

There was a shuffling and moving of chairs, coughing, glances exchanged.

Tia leaned against a bookcase. Sloan stood next to Althea, stiff with embarrassment.

"Oh, how blest are ye whose toils are ended!
Who, through death, have unto God ascended!
Ye have arisen
From the cares which keep us still in prison."

Althea read fluently, her voice steady.

Sloan got up and walked slowly between the sitting guests, to the kitchen. Tia waited a moment and then followed him.

He stood, his hands on the sink, head bent. "All those Ensears love it—good old Althea giving them what they came for. They'll have plenty to talk about over their gin and tonics this summer."

They went out into the garden, walking down the narrow path to the back of the house. The afternoon was bright and clear.

They could hear Althea's voice start again.

"Swifter far than summer's flight,
Swifter far than youth's delight,
Swifter far than happy night,
Art thou come and gone. . . . "

"You're marrying him out of pity," said Robin.

"Are you pregnant?" asked Jenny.

"Oh, for God's sake," said Tia.

Gran was predictably displeased. "Come, Tia, he just wore you down," she said. "You know quite well that you don't love him."

"You still love Ivan, don't you?" said Valery.

"No," she said quickly.

"Don't marry yet," he said.

"Dear child," said Gran, "I've talked to my cousins in Paris. They'd love to have you. You could study painting with Loucette. I know he'd take you."

Tia sailed out to Pine Island to see Myra.

"Tia, it's your life. If you love him, it's worth giving up anything for it," said Myra, kneading bread.

"How do you know if you really, really love someone?"

"Oh, Tia, you'd never have to ask."

Sloan offered Tia more than baking bread on a tiny island, more than anxious students and a suffering husband. He knew so clearly what he wanted. It would make it easier for Tia, always fettered by her doubts and perceptions. There would be freedom in having limits to her possibilities.

"Sometimes I feel so tired," she said.

Myra stopped kneading and looked at her sadly.

Tia wrote Ivan. His answer was gallant. He understood. It had been a long absence and he had been so occupied with his work. The age difference, perhaps, was a problem for someone as young and inexperienced as Tia, he wrote. He scratched out the next sentence. He would always love her, he said, and wished her great happiness.

Reading the letter, going over and over each sentence, she felt sadder.

Chapter Twenty-six

The afternoon rainstorm had left the city wet and warm. Tia watched the black clouds roll back toward the river. Priscilla had taken the children to Georgetown to visit her sister, who worked in a house with an indoor pool. When her employers were away the sister invited her friends to the house and they brought their charges as a buffer against discovery.

Tia stretched out in the porch hammock with a book. She watched the honey bees flying around the lavender hedge below her. Her neighbor sat on his deck, shirtless, sipping a drink, reading the evening paper. Vivaldi thundered from his upstairs window. Daisy's friend Melissa was playing a desultory game of hopscotch on her father's recently laid brick terrace. Sloan had scalped the hedge last fall and it had not grown back as he had said it would when, exhausted, he had laid down the shears. "Must have been a very difficult patient," said Liz, who was drinking on the porch with Tia. So, Melissa and her family, their new brick terrace, their occasional outdoor dinners, their new puppy, and their garbage cans were all part of the Ensear view, which pleased Daisy.

Melissa, apparently bored by the hopscotch, was throwing pebbles against the metal trash bin. Her mother was potting geraniums, unbothered.

Tia wandered back into the house and flicked on the air conditioner. No response. She tried a lamp and it did not light. The storm must have knocked out the power.

"Are your lights out?" called her neighbor from his deck when she returned to the porch.

"Yes."

"I thought we'd forgotten to pay our bill." He laughed. "Again."

"Power must be out," said Tia.

"Who turned out the goddam lights?" shrieked his wife from inside.

"Tia says the power's out," he called.

"Shit!" A moment later a head peered out the window. "Sloan home yet?"

"Not yet."

"Come over and celebrate. We'll send out for dinner."

"I'm getting out the gin," he said.

"I'd love to, but I've got to see another house," said Tia.

"Knock on our door when you get back," he called. "Let's have some bridge."

She opened the car windows and drove up Connecticut Avenue, wondering where she would go. Suddenly she saw the street, turned off Connecticut, and slowly coasted down the hill, looking for the Berger house. It took her a while to find it, tucked away from its manicured neighbors, cool and leafy in the hot afternoon sun. She walked through the hedge and up the path between the day lilies and stood looking at the house.

"Can I help you?"

Tia jumped.

A small, bald man in a rumpled shirt peered out over a box of petunias on the second floor.

"Are you looking for me?"

"I'm so sorry," she apologized, tripping over her words like a drunk. "I came with Mrs. Pierce the other day. I love your house."

He smiled at her. "Did you want to see it again?" he said, after a pause.

"If you don't mind?"

He smiled, nodded, withdrew his head. Tia watched the curtains billow, filling the air and sailing over the petunias and curling against the edge of the casements.

"Come in," said Mr. Berger, at the door. He was a tiny man, as small and round as Priscilla, with a tonsure of curly hair and large, tobacco-stained teeth.

"You must excuse everything," he said. "Mrs. Pierce always warns me—gives me hours—and I've begun to pack up some of my things."

"Can I look at the studio?"

"Do you like it?" His smile had vanished.

"Very much."

"I built it for my wife," he said soberly.

He led her to a small hall off the kitchen and pointed to the door.

"Wander around. I'll be upstairs."

She let herself in. Walking slowly around its perimeters, she planned its shape. She would put her desk by the fireplace, her easel and table near the garden door, perhaps have a skylight cut. She walked out into the garden. Bushes of roses with large, pink blooms grew between narrow, brick paths. Their fragrance had blown into the studio when she had opened the door.

"Please, Sloan, look at it soon."

"I told you I would."

"It has something so . . . it's hard to describe the quality."

"Mmm," said Sloan. "Sounds off the beaten path."

"It's peaceful."

"Sounds too small."

"It has plenty of room."

"What about Gran's furniture?"

"Some things."

"Room for a pool?"

She shrugged.

"I want room for a pool."

She cleared the table. There was no point in trying logic, pointing out that the Georgetown houses they had seen had no room for pools, that Sloan had often said having a pool was dangerous for young children, but she reviewed each point silently. She had made the mistake already of saying too much.

"Tia," said Sloan, coming into the kitchen with the place mats and shaking them over the trash can, "don't get perverse about this."

The day was so hot it was an effort to breathe. Sloan had called at noon to say that the air conditioning had broken down in his office and he had to cancel his afternoon patients. He would see some of them the following day, which would mean delaying their departure for Easter Cove. Tia had a feeling he would nibble away at the time until it was gone.

Tia turned on the air conditioning.

"You know that thing gives me a terrible cold," complained Priscilla, but with little force. Still, she did not want a truce without a treaty. "Don't turn it up too high."

With cool air blowing on her, Tia finished typing her article for Jake. It included rather sober interviews with chefs, waiters, and busboys. Jake had wanted gossip. He would complain that it wasn't "lively" enough, but it would suffice. Jake was working with the First Lady's former hairdresser on an article he knew would be difficult to get by Sam. The more sedate Tia's inches were, the easier it would be for Jake to slip his own article in.

"You know, she's got those marine guards running errands for her. She flies all her pals around on Air Force One. She's been dyeing her hair for years but we might not print that."

"Can you suppress the truth?" said Tia.

"Listen, so it's not the *New York Times*, kiddo," said Jake.

"Why do we work on this rag?" she said, looking over his shoulder at the hairdresser galleys.

"Because we like to eat," said Jake, putting his feet on his desk and lighting a cigarette. "We sell out cheap."

"What did you do before?"

"Freelanced. Started as a stringer for the *Times* in Beirut. Sold the magazine section a couple of pieces they actually ran. Sold stuff to *Harper's*, *Atlantic*, *New Republic*. But Sam pays better— and every week. My wife appreciates me more when I'm solvent." He sipped his coffee. "Just don't ever get me drunk."

"I'd been hoping to."

"Okay, you're on, kiddo." He got up and grabbed his jacket.

"The food editor is taking me out and getting me drunk," he called out to the room.

There were boos and catcalls.

They sat in a corner of the dark, rancid restaurant across the street from the office. It stood alone between two lots that were being readied for apartment buildings. As they ate they could hear the drilling and blasting. Jake ate a huge plate of spaghetti and ordered a second bottle of wine.

"To think you get to eat in places like this every day," he said.

They had restored their bantering relationship as soon as they left the office, but it was edged with tension as both waited for Jake to unleash the bitterness he had hinted at earlier. Jake loosened his tie, put his feet up on the chair next to him, and sat slouched over his plate, waving his fork at Tia when he spoke.

"So she gives the First Lady this massage and in walks the President and they start talking about some friend of theirs like our little hairdresser just wasn't there. They never acknowledged her presence. When he goes he says, 'It was great having a moment alone with you, honey,' or something." Jake laughed.

"What did you write about?"

"Huh?"

"Before the *Roundabout?*"

"Vietnam, mostly. I did some pieces on the Freedom Riders and that whole pot of stew."

"Were you in Vietnam?"

"Yeah. What a pit. After a while I got crazier and crazier and nobody would buy my stuff. The things that went on—men killing each other, stoned out of their gourds, blowing up women and kids and old men. And the other side just as crazed—boobytrapping little kids and sending them into bars. God, it was awful. Everyone was rotten and berserk and corrupt. I wish I'd never gone." He sighed and poured himself another glass of wine. "I tried a novel after that—to get it out of my system—but nothing worked. Sam offered me the *Roundabout*. Hell, Tia, I'm having fun. It's pretty easy for me. I like the kids there. I get home in time for dinner most nights. I can edit copy on the ten best ice-cream vendors in D.C. and get invited to a few interesting parties. So? At my age that feels just fine." He stared into his wineglass. "Most of the time I love my wife. My kid is okay. Every now and then I get smashed and screw some broad and feel like a heel and wonder what I've done with my life." He ran his finger around the rim of his glass. Sitting up straighter and looking around the room, he sighed. "So, kiddo, nothing works out quite like we expected. Right? But you make a few compromises. Don't you? Painting vegetables for a third-rate magazine?"

"Yes."

"Not what you thought you'd be doing at—what?—thirty?"

"No."

"But we have fun, right? My dad was a big-deal surgeon. Great man, everyone always said. I hardly ever saw him, and when I did he was so wiped out we had to tiptoe around the house or he'd flip out. He made plenty of dough and we lived in a big house in Brookline and always had a couple of maids and four new cars. When he died it was such a relief. We all took that hard-earned money and ran. That's how I could freelance so long. So, in the end, what does it all matter? We might as well be happy."

"Are you?"

"See my smile? See my big white teeth?"

Sloan was waiting at home for her.

"We wanted you to go swimming with us," said Daisy.

"Mommy, Mommy!" cried Peter.

"Priscilla had to leave early," said Sloan, "and Peter wet his pants and I can't find any more."

"They should be in his drawer. Or did I pack them all?"

"Oh, God, I don't know," Sloan burst out. He flung down his paper and went upstairs.

"What's the matter with Daddy?" said Daisy.

"He's had a hard day."

Peter started running around the dining-room table, pulling his truck. "Look at me," he cried, veering around the table.

Daisy stood with her hands on her hips, lips pursed. "Mommy," she said, "he's going to disturb Daddy."

"Vroom, vroom!" shouted Peter, careening out the door to the hall.

———

Tia sat by the edge of the small cracked pool. It was the local club, and the neighborhood prided itself on keeping it simple. Daisy held Peter while he fluttered his legs and beat his arms.

"Now just pull the water with your arms," instructed Daisy patiently.

"Look, I can swim!" cried Peter.

Daisy looked up at Tia and grimaced. "He splashes too much."

Tia lowered herself into the water. "Go on, darling, take a nice swim and let me help Peter for a while."

Peter soon tired of his lesson and joined a group in the wading pool. While they shrieked and splashed each other, Tia tried to read. She dreaded returning to the house. Sloan had not come out of his study before they left, though Daisy called to him through the door.

"I've talked to the Sykeses, and they both think I'm nuts to miss Klein's bash. He's such a prima donna and I'm really his number-one boy at the moment."

They were eating dinner in the garden. The children had fallen asleep together in the hammock. It was still hot but there was a breeze.

"Whatever you think," said Tia, peeling an orange.

"You won't change your mind?"

"Sloan, I can't. Please don't ask me to. It's the only time I ever see Robin and Gran." Her irritation had tuned her voice to a precise and condescending pitch.

He ate his peach and did not say any more about it. They carried the children to bed, and then Sloan watched television in the bedroom while Tia washed the dishes.

"Yes, Mrs. Pierce, I do love the house but Sloan hasn't seen it yet. I'm leaving this afternoon for Maine. Can it wait a week or so?"

"Mrs. Ensear, you might lose it."

"What do you suggest?"

"I'd suggest you make an offer and be prepared to put down a binder."

"I'll talk to Sloan and have him call you."

"Don't wait."

Sloan drove them to the airport. It was a quiet, unpleasant drive. He dropped them at the terminal and drove away. Tia stood for a moment, hoping he would look back and see her, surrounded by bags, a child at each hand. The moment passed quickly and she found a porter to take their luggage. Walking behind him, the children beside her, the trip secured, elation surged through her. It felt like the drug the doctor had given her when she was having Daisy, leaving her numb to pain and conscious of delight.

Still, it took a while to alleviate the children's gloom. Daisy sat, her forehead pressed to the plane window, refusing the bag of smoked almonds she generally coveted, and Peter tried to scale his seat and escape down the aisle. However, by the time they descended through the fog to land in Boston, both children were making plans for beach walks, purchase of toy boats, sailing with Aunt Robin.

Valery and Claudia were at the airport in Boston.

"You shouldn't have," said Tia, surprised.

"Owl's Head is fogged in, so we thought we'd come and get you," said Valery.

He looked very old. As they walked down the long, gray airport corridors, Tia tried to figure out how old he was. He had always teased Gran about her seniority but it was never really clear if it was in months or years. He must be well into his seventies, Tia thought, and for the first time his age was clearly marked on him. The vitality that had fueled his gestures, his alert eyes, the roaring laugh was dulled. His jacket seemed too big, and he leaned on Claudia as they walked.

"Gran is a little under the weather," said Claudia.

"Is she ill?" Tia looked at Valery. He stared straight ahead as they walked.

"Oh, you know how your grandmother is," said Claudia cheerfully.

Gran never discussed her body. She was rarely sick. Robin had persuaded her to have checkups but Gran came and went from them without revealing anything. No one asked. Gran's family and friends were anchored to her strength.

"What's the matter, Valery?" Tia said as they got into the car.

"We'll talk about it later, Tia," he said, inclining his head toward Daisy. Claudia tried to talk to the children but they soon fell asleep. Valery sat looking out the window.

"Robin came a day early," he said.

"Is it serious?"

"It's partly age," said Claudia.

They were going to tell her nothing. The trip was endless. She tried to close her eyes and not look out the window when they got to the place where her parents were killed, but she opened her eyes as they were passing it.

Myra greeted them when they got to the house.

"Helena is waiting for you, but don't spend too much time with her."

"What's the matter?"

"She's old, Tia."

"But what?"

"Her heart and a million other things. We'll talk later—she's waiting for you now."

Tia went slowly up the wide flight of stairs. She and Robin had always patted the window seat on the first landing and knocked each banister post once on the first day of an Easter Cove summer. Not resisting the old magic, she did it this time.

Gran was sitting in bed, propped against big pillows, her pale blue comforter covered with books and papers. Standing in the doorway for a moment, Tia watched her. The woman had always seemed old to her, with her white hair, long, high-collared dresses, strings of pearls, brooches, black shoes. Tia had never noticed changes before. The long hair braided and fastened to the back of her head, the faint violet scent, the well-arranged days balanced between work and household had seemed part of an immutable order.

Now, in the bright sea light of the July afternoon, Gran did look changed. Unaware of an audience, she had let her hands drop, palms up, on the comforter. Her head was back, eyes closed, her breathing labored. The hair she always kept so white and silky was faintly yellow, wisps escaping the coil.

"Ah, my dear," she said, when she heard Tia enter the room. She tried to sit up straight. She smiled. Her eyes looked faded, bleached.

"Gran, I didn't realize you weren't well."

"Just old age, my dear," she said, patting Tia's hand. "Are they keeping the children away too?"

"I'll bring them up later."

"Fine, fine."

Tia had not seen Gran since Christmas. Usually they spent Easter with her, but this year Peter had been ill and later Tia had been so busy that the long journey to Maine was postponed.

They had always operated loosely: Robin, Grayson, Gran, Tia. They did not see each other often, spoke and wrote sporadically. When she married Sloan, Tia had been surprised by Althea's constant demand on their time and attention. The bonds had seemed so forced and guilty, the visits so reluctant and fruitless.

"Oh, you're all so narcissistic," Sloan would say.

It had worked well for them. But no calls for help ever went out. Now, holding Gran's soft, cold hand, Tia wondered what happened when one of them was dying.

"It's her heart," said Myra, walking along the beach with Tia. "And it terrifies everyone. Valery with his young wife. Claudia. Masha."

Peter ran ahead of them, trying to keep up with Daisy, who was springing along the rocks in her new red sneakers.

"She's been treated for it for years. Dr. Buxton told me," said Myra.

Tia remembered the medicines Gran had always carried, the sudden retreats to her bedroom.

"I should have realized," said Tia. She should have been alerted by the changes in the rhythm of Gran's life. She had not gone to Paris for several years. She had sold the apartment in New York the year before, dividing up the furniture and paintings and the collection of birds and keeping very little. "It doesn't belong in Easter Cove," she said, when she parceled it out. The bulk of it went to Tia. It sat in a storage warehouse in New Jersey.

"The winters are too cold for her here," said Myra. "But it was too expensive to keep the New York place. Too big, and with just Masha—" Myra shrugged. "She's always been so generous.

Anyway, I spent most of the winter here with her. Masha gets hysterical if things go wrong. Poor old thing isn't much better off anyway. I got them fed, kept the oil burner going, got away from Pine Island."

"That's awfully sweet of you."

"Don't look so guilty, Ti, for God's sake."

"Poor Paul."

Myra didn't say anything. They sat on the rocks and watched the children try to sail their toy boats.

"Problems?"

"Yup."

They sat silently for a long time.

"Sorry to disappoint you, Tia, but my martyrdom on Pine Island began to wear thin."

"I thought you were happy—that you understood everything and—"

"For a while. I guess I was going on old nourishment. I had lots to give. Lots had been given to me. But I ran dry."

"How is he?"

"He'll be okay. He never really allowed himself to feel much again. I can't live like that anymore. Your grandmother understood. I'd wear her ear off talking about it."

"But back when I came out to the school—in those days— weren't you happy?"

"I loved it, or parts of it. It's not that I lived a lie. Just that time marches on. It's useless to keep trying so damn hard." She was in tears. "Sometimes you have to be rigorously honest with yourself—and make decisions no one but you can understand."

"Can you get back down Wednesday?" Sloan said on the phone that night. "Mrs. Pierce showed me a house on P Street that you'll love. It's bigger than we'd thought about, but Gran's things will look wonderful in it."

"Gran's very ill."

"Oh, no."

"I don't know how long I'll be here."

"Do you want me to come up?"

"Not yet."

"Do you want a referral? Is it her heart?"

"Buxton is up and he says there's nothing they can do."

"I'll call him tonight. Call me if you want me to come up."

Robin and Tia ate dinner alone in the dining room. Gran, insisted Masha, might come down and be upset if they were eating with her in the kitchen or on trays in the library.

"Why?" said Robin.

"She likes you to eat there like always," Masha had said firmly, "in nice dress." She waited until they had started upstairs. "See? Nothing changed."

Masha had fed Daisy and Peter in the kitchen. Tia had heard their laughter echo faintly up the heating duct while she bathed. Now, in the long, poorly lit room with its dark, oiled floor, narrow windows black in the evening darkness, Tia and Robin sat and tried to eat the thick gray meat that Masha served them.

"God, no wonder you were always so skinny," said Robin, putting down her knife and fork. "Is Sloan coming up?"

"Maybe."

"Can't he miss that picnic?"

"Probably not. You know, when we're together, at home, I can't wait to get away from him. Then—after a couple of days or so away—I start to miss him. Feel sort of amputated. What sort of feeling is that? Love or dependence?"

"Tia, you always have to make such puzzles out of everything."

Masha came into the dining room. She folded her arms and stood by the table. Jumping up and throwing her arms around her, Tia was surprised at how bony and small that round little body had become. Once the plump shoulders and big breasts were Tia's favorite retreat. She would lie against Masha at night and listen to her stories about Gran's father's house in St. Petersburg, about trips to Kaluga down wild roads, past rivers, willows, pines and fields, about wolves and wild beasts and people who rose from the dead.

In the morning Gran said she felt better. Tia and Robin helped her to the chaise by the window. The move tired her and she lay back in the chair, her eyes closed.

"What should we do for the Fourth, Gran?" asked Tia brightly.

"Oh, child," she said, her voice weak, "you plan."

"Since we won't go to town for fireworks, let's bring them here," said Tia.

"And have a picnic dinner on the porch."

"Yes. Have Masha get a nice roast," said Gran. "Ask the Petersens, Elizavetta, the Charetskys, the Hammonds, and that nice young couple that bought the Goddards' house. And Ferris. He still adores you, Robin." She opened her eyes and looked out to sea. "I think I'll get down. At least for dinner."

"I keep waiting for her to ask us to invite someone who's dead," said Robin as they went downstairs.

"Yes," said Tia, who often wondered about all the ghosts.

"Or for her to speak to us in Russian or French," said Robin.

"Or wonder what city or country she's in."

Gran was dying far away from the ocher house on the Neva where she was born, from the pine forests of Kaluga, from the apartment in Paris where her children were born, from the New York apartment with its tall windows overlooking the wide, dangerous river.

Sloan called the next day. He had talked to Buxton. Tia's heart sank. She recognized the soft professional purr.

"So there isn't much they can do but treat her with drugs. She's in no shape for a bypass."

"Does he know how much longer . . . ?"

"It could be soon or months or maybe longer."

He would call Jake for her. Priscilla was cooking him dinner. They would wait on the house, though if Gran seemed to stabilize, Tia could fly down for a day.

"Did you look at the one I liked so much?"

"Yes." He paused, and his voice was professional again. "It's nice—I see why you like it. It's just really too small. It isn't any better than this house."

"Sloan, I think it would be good for us."

"Well, let's not worry about that now."

She doodled on the phone book while they talked. Klein was having lobsters and clams shipped from Maine for his party. Sloan was going to fly down with the Jessups in their newly purchased Cessna. They were all going to drive to Rehoboth with the Sykeses for the rest of the weekend. He would miss Tia. The children would have enjoyed it. Klein had hired several teenagers to look after the children.

After she hung up she called Mrs. Pierce.

"I'm so sorry to hear about your grandmother," said Mrs. Pierce in her pleasant, southern voice.

"The house on Merriweather Street—can it wait for a couple of weeks?"

"Well, Mrs. Ensear," said Mrs. Pierce slowly, "I understood from Dr. Ensear that you would not consider the house."

"I am thinking about it seriously," said Tia, trying to keep her tone light.

Mrs. Pierce had already sensed the marital struggle. "I see," she said.

"I might fly back for a day or two."

"Dr. Ensear seems most anxious to make an offer on the P Street house," she said.

"Yes, I'll take a look at it."

"It won't be on the market long."

"What about the Merriweather Street house?"

"I've had the listing for several months. I think it will appeal to special tastes." Not, from the tone of it, to Mrs. Pierce's.

Walking upstairs to Gran's room with a lunch tray, Tia castigated herself for worrying about houses. She put the tray down by Gran's bed and watched the old woman sleep.

"Tia!" Gran woke with a start. "Don't stand there staring," she said irritably. Her voice was stronger.

Tia helped Gran sit up.

"Open the curtains, Tia. It's like a tomb in here."

Tia drew the curtains back from the bank of windows and then sat down on the window seat. Robin was sitting on the lawn with Daisy and Peter.

"Robin's wonderful with children," said Tia.

"Yes." Gran snorted. "But she's certainly unlikely to have any of her own."

"Why not?"

"Oh, child, it's too exhausting to have to explain everything to you." She drank her tea and pushed the food around her plate.

"Do you think about Russia, Gran?"

"When you get old, Tia, you think more about your childhood and your parents. I think about my father in the country. He loved that house. When I first saw Easter Cove I thought of it. It was near a river. My cousins and I used to play wonderful games in a big grove of willows. Like you and Robin on the rocks. We had a big meal around five, and everyone would go off and nap or play cards until supper, and my cousins and I would sneak down to the willow grove." She sank back into the pillows.

Tia watched her eyes grow distant. Three children, under the willows by the river, while the big, wooden house slept. The wonderful smell of the air that Masha recalled, and the sound of the woodsman chopping wood, and the horses grazing in the field.

"I had some wooden soldiers and horses that one of the men had carved for me. We had wonderful cavalry battles." She smiled. Her voice was weaker again. "My mother hated me playing with them. But she was usually ill and didn't know what we were up to. My father understood." She sighed. "It was so strange to live in Paris with Mama. She would never let us open the windows. She thought the air in Paris was poisoned. She was so used to having dozens of servants that she would order me and Masha and Masha's poor old mother around all day. But the loss of my father and brothers was so awful for her. . . . "

"And for you," said Tia.

"Oh, yes, for me." There were tears in her eyes for men who were lost more than half a century before.

"The mosquitoes were like a plague in the summer."

"In Paris?"

"No, no. In Russia. They were terrible." She sighed again. "My mother always played cards. She never went outside. She had lovely white skin but rather soft and slack from staying in bed so much. And wonderful dark eyes like yours, Tia." She sipped her tea. "I just could never like her." She reached for her glasses and went through the mail on the tray. Tia watched Gran bend over the letters, make a notation on some of them, throw others in the basket by her bed.

"Tia, dear, give these to Myra. She's been taking care of everything for me. Come up at teatime and bring the children for a little while."

Myra was in the kitchen talking to Masha. They were bent

over mugs of strong tea. They both looked up when Tia walked in.

"Did she eat anything?" Myra got up and inspected the tray. "Nope."

Masha shrugged. "Never. She never likes lunch. Madame eats very little," she said proudly.

"A sign of high birth," said Myra, winking at Tia.

"Yes, her mother was the same," said Masha placidly.

"Let's go for a walk," said Myra. She took Tia's arm.

"Not for me," said Masha, settling back down in her chair and drawing her cup of tea close to her.

Gran was sleeping when Tia and Robin brought her tea. Someone had pulled the curtains again and the room was dark and silent. They stood in the doorway, looking down at her. Her breath seemed to be drawn with great effort, her chest straining up, her hands twitching.

"I don't want to see her now," whispered Daisy, hugging Tia's waist.

"No, we'll let her sleep," said Tia, picking Daisy up and going back down the hallway.

Robin followed them. "Tia, she's just sleeping," she said.

"I know."

"Tia, you look like a ghost."

"For God's sake, Robin, butt out."

"Take it easy."

Tia hurried downstairs.

"Why are you and Aunt Robin fighting?" said Daisy, her face clenching with concern.

"We're both worried about Gran."

Tia woke up in the middle of the night and lay in bed for a long time. She could feel her heart beating, uncomfortably fast. There was a pain in her chest. Don't panic, she told herself, you're too young to be having a heart attack. She tried to remember what her yoga teacher had said about learning to regulate one's heartbeat. Breathing deeply, trying to concentrate on the sound of the sea washing against the rocks, watching the little square of light from the window that reflected on the ceiling, she found her panic was increasing. She got out of bed, went to the window and breathed deeply, feeling faint. The house was dark. She looked over at the music room and could see the light of the moon reflected in the panes of the French doors. The night air felt cold.

She put a sweater on over her nightgown and padded down the hall. She tiptoed over to Gran's door and pressed her ear to the door. It was quiet. Pushing the door ajar, she peered into the darkness.

"Masha, is that you?" Gran's voice croaked weakly.

"It's me—Tia, Gran. Are you all right?"

"Come in."

Tia crept across the room, found Gran's bed, and sat on it.

"Are you all right?"

"At this hour I used to be out dancing, off to breakfast at the docks. Now I wake up and stare into the darkness. I used to love this time of night, and now I dread it."

Tia reached for Gran's hand. "Do you want me to stay?"

"After your father and Tinka died, Masha used to come in and sleep on the chaise. Poor old dear, she snored like an engine."

"It must have been difficult for you—that time."

"For you too. And for Robin." Gran sighed. "When you are as old as I am, dear child, you find that very few survive. So many fall along the way."

"Not you."

"I've stumbled."

"I never saw you falter."

"Many times, dear child."

"You always seemed invincible. Pulling us all along."

"You never understood how strong you are, Tia. It's the tree that can bend in the storm, not the old oak that stands rigid in the wind that survives." She coughed. "You have so much of me in you, for better or for worse." She sat up. "Turn on the light, Tia. There are some things we must discuss. Get me some water. No, there on the table. Help me with my jacket." She put on her bed jacket and smoothed her hair. The room was pale and rosy in the dim light. It smelled of the sea and lavender.

"Are you happy with Sloan?"

"Yes."

"You sound unsure."

"I'm wondering why you ask."

"Answer the question, Tia."

"It's not mad, passionate love, but it's steady, dependable, pretty secure."

"Yes." Gran looked at her intently. "Not what you had with Ivan."

"No."

"I thought I was dying that year. The year Ivan went to England."

"What?"

"Yes. It certainly looked that way. I told Ivan. I told him he just couldn't take you away. He said he would wait a year. I said he couldn't tell you. We argued and argued and finally he agreed. After all, I was your family. Except for Robin, you had no one else. He couldn't support you."

"Oh, Gran."

"You were so young. Naive. Ivan was so difficult. He'd made Kathryn miserable. I could see what you loved about him but I was afraid for you. He'd used Kathryn's money for his work without thinking about it. I was afraid he'd do the same to you. Then rush off, leave you. He drank too much. Like your poor grandfather. I had to protect you from that. It had almost destroyed me."

Tia listened. Gran talked about her husband, the forgotten Gregory, and his frailties.

"He was so restless. He leaned on me, used my money, went out publicly with the most horrible women." Her voice was strong and clear. Her eyes blazed and her hands pounded the coverlet.

Tia sat on Gran's bed, the sea breeze blowing on her back, and thought about Ivan. It had been more than ten years since she had seen him off at the airport and time had faded and distorted her memories. It was only at Easter Cove that he still seemed real. There, looking down at the music room from her window, she could remember him bent over the piano, the disturbing fervor of his playing in the still summer night. In her room she could remember the feel of him next to her in bed, waking at first light so that he could leave her before the house awoke.

"Sloan is a decent man, Tia. I wanted to know someone was

going to take care of you. I was so used to taking care of everyone's needs."

"You don't really think I'm strong, do you?"

"Yes, yes. But I didn't want you to be like me. I wanted you to
have something more. Something better."

"Sloan?"

She took Tia's face in her hands. "I want you to forgive me.
Myra is right. She told me I played God with everyone."

"You helped people, Gran. You put people back together."

"I did too much, child. I went too far."

She sank back into her pillows. Her face was gray. Her eyes
closed. Tia stroked the pale blue-veined hands and watched her
sleep. When she married Sloan, Tia thought she had defied
Gran. "Callow," Gran had snorted. Why did Gran think it was
her idea?

In the dark dining room, Robin and Tia read the papers at breakfast. The children were eating in the kitchen with Masha. It was
a hot day. The cool breeze of the night before was stilled.

"How many coming tomorrow?"

"About fifteen."

"I called Bob, and he said he'd come up and do fireworks."
Robin stretched. She ate another piece of toast. "Ti, I've got to
go home day after tomorrow."

"I know."

They talked about the picnic and fireworks, about Robin's
friend Ferris, who was still a hopeful admirer, about Jenny and
her new husband, about Laura Landsdale's new play, about
Robin's trials at the children's clinic, about Tia's travails with
Capital Roundabout, about Masha's nocturnal nipping.

"I was very surprised by something Gran said to me last night
about Sloan. She seems to feel she created the marriage. I
thought she disliked him at first."

"Yes, she did. Said he had a bovine expression."

"Ah, bovine." They laughed. "Remember that boy she said
was too simian?"

"That was definitely worse than bovine." Robin laughed. "She
adjusted to Sloan. I think she likes him now. Of course she thinks
Althea is dreadful."

"You know how she says 'poor Althea' in that tone."

They walked out to the porch. It was hazy and still.

"Did she talk to you about Ivan?"

"Yes."

"She's been talking to Myra about him. I think you ought to know that he's visiting Elizavetta. He might come to lunch tomorrow."

"Oh."

"Yes, 'Oh.'" Robin laughed and put her arms around Tia. "So, look beautiful and let him eat his heart out. I'll bet he's gotten fat. And bald."

He was neither. Tia saw him from her room. She was brushing her hair and watching Daisy do cartwheels on the lawn when she saw him walk around the corner of the music room with Elizavetta on his arm. He stopped and watched Daisy, bending down and talking to her: two golden heads together. Sadness stirred in Tia. He picked Daisy up and she shrieked with laughter. Peter stood uncertainly, and Ivan bent down and scooped him up in the other arm and then whirled around with them. When he put them down they danced around him and begged for more. Tia could hear his laugh as he started toward the house, walking slowly with Elizavetta clinging to his arm, the children trailing him. He stopped under Tia's window and looked up.

"Tia," he called, just as she stepped back.

"Mommy, come down," called the children.

She walked back to the window and looked down. "In a minute." She ran to her mirror and looked at herself. The dress looked drab and baggy. She rushed to her closet and took out a white cotton dress she had bought years before and never worn.

"Ah, Tia," said Ivan, taking both her hands. "You're more beautiful than ever." He bent down and kissed her cheeks. He smelled of shaving lotion and baby powder. "We're early, but Mother wanted to see Helena before everyone else came." He smiled down at her.

"That's fine," she muttered. "I'll go find Robin."

"Pick us up, pick us up!" shrieked Peter, jumping up and down.

Tia hurried into the house. Robin was coming down the stairs.

She had let her hair down and it fell almost to her waist. She was adjusting the low bodice of her dress.

"I'm going to vamp Ferris," she said. "Maybe he'll give the clinic a grant."

"Ivan's here," said Tia.

"Good. You look great." She smiled, reaching over and smoothing Tia's hair. "Just keep remembering you're a wife and mother."

They sat out on the high lawn in white Adirondack chairs, facing the sea. Ivan stretched out on the grass in front of them, letting the children climb him, holding them up in the air, laughing with them. Gran sat in the center of the group, bundled in her thick shawl, Elizavetta beside her. Tia busied herself carrying trays back and forth, hurrying out of the kitchen, where Masha regarded her with portentous solemnity, back to the group on the grass.

"Everyone under seventy is being organized for a walk," said Robin when Tia returned with the cheese puffs. A group had formed around Ivan. There were almost a dozen children now, and they all held on to him. Parents and grandparents stepped forth and tried to calm them down, but Tia could hear Daisy's voice, loud and reproachful. "Mr. MacLeod is going to take us on a children's walk."

"That's right," said Ivan. "Who qualifies?"

"I do," roared the children, leaping around him.

"Come on, Valenkov cousins, and you too, Ferris. Myra?"

Myra declined. Robin took Ferris's arm. Tia walked along beside Ivan. The children raced out in front. Peter stumbled and bent over, weeping and holding his foot.

"It's okay," said Ivan, picking him up and examining the bruised ankle. "You can ride on my shoulders."

They walked down the narrow path through the pines, down between the rocks, to the spit of sandy beach. Ivan put Peter down.

"Now, be careful on those rocks."

"I've got new sneakers," said Peter proudly. He ran off to catch up to the other children, who were clambering over the jetty that separated Gran's beach from her neighbor's.

Robin had her arm in Ferris's, her head tilted up, walking slowly along the rocks.

"Come on," said Ivan. He took Tia's hand and led her over the jetty. She felt the jolt of his touch. She refused to look at him. She was not going to fall in love with his hair and eyes and profile again. "You never would have loved Ivan if he'd been short and fat," Jenny had said. "Or bald," added Robin. "Or dumb," said Tia. If Ivan had been dumb and bald and short and fat she would not have loved him.

Now, walking by the edge of the sea with Ivan, the children ahead, Robin's throaty laughter behind, not far from the big brown house on the hill, with Gran and her guests sitting on the lawn, Masha in the kitchen, the soft, damp wind blowing, she felt a roaring joy.

She tried to memorize it, imprint the quality of light and heat and summer, the feel of Ivan's hand in hers, the cries of the children as they tumbled ahead.

"You have to remember what feels right—profoundly and clearly right—and then hold on," Valery used to tell her.

"But nothing holds," she said aloud.

"What?" Ivan stopped and turned to her.

"Everything changes. One sickens, dies. You know."

He put his arm through hers and they walked on silently, on the sandy edge of the beach, until they reached the channel. The children were skipping stones in the smooth waters. Robin and Ferris had decided to walk on to town.

"Poor Paul," said Tia, looking across at Pine Island.

"He's painting well."

"Really?"

"I arranged a show in London for him last month."

"Are you married, Ivan?"

"No," he said, after a pause.

"But?"

"The work is pretty consuming. I'm no prize," he said, laughing. The conversation was awkward.

"Gran told me about her interference."

"I'm glad. I was a damn fool to allow it. That woman!" They stood looking out at the children playing on the sand. "It wasn't entirely her fault, Tia, or we wouldn't have let it happen. I've never been very good at making decisions that involve someone else."

"Were there other women?" It had been gnawing at her.

"What? With Kathryn? Once or twice. While you and I were together, and for a long time afterward, there was no one else. Don't you know that?"

"I'm never that sure of anything," said Tia.

Ivan brushed her hair back and ran his finger gently down her cheek. "We made a terrible mistake, didn't we?"

Later that night, after Gran had gone back upstairs, after the dinner and the fireworks, when everyone milled outside saying goodbye, Ivan stood close to Tia. She wanted to say something, to stop his departure, to pull him away from the throng, but she just stood, saying goodbye, hugging and kissing old acquaintances, acutely aware of him. Then he turned and, taking her hands, bent down and kissed her cheeks.

"I'm taking Elizavetta back to London with me tomorrow afternoon. Alexey's going to be with me for a month. I'm bringing them both back on August sixth. I'll come to Washington the next day."

He kissed her quickly on the mouth. He walked to the porte cochere and disappeared in its shadows as he helped his mother into the car. For a moment, when he opened the door, he was illuminated. He turned and looked out at the darkness and waved.

That night Masha woke Tia out of a restless sleep.

"Tia, Madame wants to see you."

Tia sat up in bed. "Now?" She rubbed her eyes and glanced at the clock. It was just past midnight.

Gran was sitting up in bed with her hair in two braids. She patted the bed. "Sit down, child. Were you already asleep?"

Tia sat down beside her. Gran's skin was gray, her breathing strained.

"Let me call Dr. Buxton."

"No," she said firmly and then coughed.

"Please, Madame," said Masha, tears flowing. "Please."

"Don't be an idiot," Gran said weakly. Before, she would have snapped it out, her eyes dark with irritation. "Tia, I want to talk to you."

"Gran, you can hardly breathe."

"Ivan," she whispered.

"He's coming to Washington in a month."

Gran closed her eyes. Tia watched her and thought perhaps she was sleeping. Then the eyelids fluttered and she smiled. "I've taken medicine," she said. "It's starting to work." Her eyes opened. "I should have left your grandfather and married Valery. We should have had children together." She paused. "I did the next best thing, didn't I? But that would have been the best."

"Are you giving me advice?"

"I want you to know that whatever you decide . . . "—she paused and took one of Tia's hands—"that I will approve, even if . . . " She sighed. "Your poor little mother. She had such a time with Peter. Such a little bird. She was happiest when he went off to war. Do you remember her at all then? She blossomed. She never had the strength to live with someone like Peter—his temper, his depressions, his schemes. Closed up in that little apartment. Both of them desperate."

"Were they that unhappy together?"

"Unhappy together? Not that they didn't love each other, or you. They made each other unhappy. It begins to tear away at people. They strike out, as he did. Or withdraw, as Anna did. You see them slowly tearing the life out of each other."

"And you think Sloan and I . . . ?"

"No, no, child. I don't know about that. Hindsight always helps." She closed her eyes again, for a long time. Just as Tia was about to leave, she opened them. "I feel I know what you should do, but this time I have promised myself I will not tell you."

"Why don't you and Sloan take some time together now? Get off for a week or two?" Robin buttered her toast efficiently. "Leave the kids with Althea."

"Leave them here with me," said Myra.

"Not with Gran so ill," said Tia.

"She might be like that for months," said Robin. "Or years," she added quickly.

Sloan responded vaguely to the suggestion that he come to

Easter Cove. "It'll be difficult to reschedule my patients," he said.

Tia did not press the matter. He did not mention houses.

She put down the phone and walked out to the porch. Robin and Myra had taken the children sailing. Tia could see Robin's boat as it rounded the point, the children in their bright orange life jackets. She looked down at the garden where now only the wild rambling roses grew and drifted back twenty-five years to the time when her parents were still alive and Gran barely fifty. Then the garden had been bright with lilies and daisies, the house always full of people; cars rolled in and out over the graveled drive. Anna sat in the sun in her white shorts and striped shirt, Tinka and Peter battled each other at tennis, Grayson and Valery sailed, Gran came down from her studio trailed by spaniels. It always seemed to be then, during one of those perfect slow summer days, that they would sense autumn. In the August heat they would smell the chrysanthemums, hear the cicadas, feel the sudden evening chill.

There would be those last days before the parents returned to the city when there seemed to be trouble between them all. Tia heard Anna weep in her room, saw Peter sit moodily staring out to sea. Tinka would take Gran aside, talk softly in her ear, clenching and unclenching her fist as she spoke. Grayson would keep reading briefs. When they all met for dinner, Tinka would do most of the talking in the throaty, musical voice that Robin had inherited. Gran presided coolly, politely, being sure to address Anna pleasantly, offering her more meat or dessert. Tia would put her hand in Anna's and wish that her mother would sit straight in her chair and speak up and laugh with Tinka. Once, after a dinner like that, she had screamed at her mother, some sudden outburst over brushing teeth or cleaning up her room, and Anna had stood, arms at her side, face limp with distress, saying nothing.

It was those sad eyes that had reproached Tia in dreams for years, banished only in daylight and finally by time.

"When do you think you might be coming home?" asked Sloan.

"Gran seems about the same."

"Yes, I talked to Buxton." His voice sounded cold, his words precise. "Of course, in her situation, she could go on for quite a while."

"Yes, so I gather."

"Why don't you come back Saturday, and if she takes a turn for the worse you can fly back."

"I think I will. We'll probably take a flight in the early afternoon."

"Fine. Give my love to the children."

She thought of asking him why he was angry, but at this distance she did not really want to know. Probably the Klein affair had not gone well.

Tia moved through the day of her flight in a dreamlike state. She menaced herself with fears about Gran. She walked around the house alert for every impression: the faded red runners on the steps, the light on the cherrywood table in the hall, curtains blowing in the sea breeze, the way the house muffled its sounds.

"Tia, you seem very abstracted," said Gran sharply. "You haven't answered me."

"I'm sorry."

"I've ordered some cold chicken and tomatoes for lunch," said Gran, looking at a list. "Valery and Claudia are coming."

"Gran, please call me if you . . . "

"Of course. Come here."

Tia sat on the edge of the bed.

"Tia, often you look so sad. Even as a child." Gran patted her hand. "Has it been very sad for you?"

"No, Gran, of course not."

"I never wanted us to dwell on sad things," said Gran. "I've seen that ruin so many people. One has to go on. Make the best of everything. See the glory in the weeds, as Valery used to say."

"You gave me a wonderful childhood, Gran. I have wonderful memories."

Gran sighed. Tia remembered when there were sighs of exasperation, sighs of disgust, contempt.

"It was my father who gave me everything. My poor mother . . . "

Gran rested against the pillows and closed her eyes.

"Did you love her?"

"Love?" She looked at Tia. "You know, Tia, I love very few people. Really love. You, your father and Tinka, Masha, my father." She paused and looked thoughtful. "My brother Serge."

"Valery?"

Gran looked surprised. Her mouth twitched.

"Yes, Valery."

Tia slid forward and put her arms around Gran's shoulders. She felt dry and weightless.

Sloan met the plane. He was standing, reading a newspaper, when Daisy sighted him. The children ran over and hugged him. He handed each one a wrapped box. They tore away the paper with delight and waved the new toys in the air.

"Look, Mommy, look what Daddy gave us," they cried.

"Mommy will have to wait until we get into the city to see her new present," said Sloan.

"That's not fair," said Daisy.

"Couldn't bring it with me," he said.

He put his arm around Tia as they walked through the terminal. "Glad you're home," he said.

Tia felt a stir of unease. There was a pale, flaccid look to his skin. He had put on some weight, and it showed around his middle and on his cheeks. Other women she knew got their husbands to jog, eat alfalfa sprouts, give up hard liquor. She had not even thought about it. Sloan seemed to worry so much about his health that she had always tried to ignore it.

"You need a vacation, Sloan," she said, feeling the unfair balance between her tan and his pallor. "You look tired."

"I'm going to take two weeks in August. I thought we'd leave the kids at the house with Priscilla and Althea and go sailing down the coast with the Sykeses."

She looked out the window, trying not to snap out an answer: The Sykeses? why on earth would we want to sail anywhere with them?

"I know you're not that fond of Joe," he said testily.

She waited for him to say something about her "arrogant, out-of-hand" rejection of Joe. He had said it several times before, and Tia would always find herself on the Sykeses' boat shortly thereafter.

"Anyway," Sloan said cheerfully. "Let's not think about that now."

Washington was bright and hot. The grass around the monuments was browning. They turned off the parkway, drove into Georgetown. Sloan was smiling as he drove up 31st Street and parked. He took her hand and put a key into it.

"I know this is very corny," he said, "but happy birthday."

Tia looked down at the key. The children peered over the seat. "What?" She knew.

"Happy birthday. Let's sing 'Happy Birthday' for Mommy," said Sloan.

"You bought a house?"

"It's yours. I'm putting it in your name. Tia, please don't spoil my surprise."

"You bought Mommy a house," said Daisy slowly. "Is it just for her?"

Sloan smiled. "I hope she'll let us live with her," he said.

"Where's Mommy's house?" Peter had his arms around Tia's neck.

"Come on, gang, let's go." Sloan jumped out of the car. It was a large, flat-front brick house with a gas carriage lamp in front of it. The jet flickered and sputtered. Sloan unlocked the door and led the way through an enormous front hall to a large high-ceilinged room.

"I fell in love with this room." He turned slowly, taking it all in again. "Isn't it beautiful?" The room was rectangular, with four arched windows facing a small garden. Except for a stack of newspapers, a telephone book, and a folding chair, the room was empty. There were two elaborate chandeliers hanging from the ceiling. Tia walked over to the windows and looked out at the garden. It was much smaller than the room, surrounded by a tall cedar fence. The ground was covered by a complicated network of bricks with a small, concrete fountain at the hub.

"Mrs. Pierce suggested getting in Otis Fessenden to do over the garden," said Sloan. "She said he'd done one like this on N Street for Senator Randall and really worked miracles. He uses planters and hanging baskets." He drew her along. "The kitchen's great, wait until you see it. I really want you to like it," he said, begging.

"I know," she said, trying to smile.

There were two kitchens and a narrow pantry. The first kitchen had an enormous gas range and two iceboxes and an ice-maker. The second had a smaller stove, one icebox, and a counter with six stools facing the dishwasher and dryer.

"Do you want to know something incredible? The people who redid this house? The Brisbanes!"

"My goodness," said Tia. The Brisbanes, royal family of haute cuisine.

"They wrote *French Sauces* here!"

"It's a wonderful kitchen," said Tia, trying to be amiable.

The house was very hot and close. It smelled of paint and shellac.

"I thought we could use window air conditioners for the first year and then maybe next year we can install central air conditioning."

"What have you done about our house?"

"Mrs. Pierce showed it Sunday, and she's taking someone through this evening. Priscilla's been scrubbing away," he said. He was sweating.

"How could you do this without me?"

"Tia, you know how you are. Nothing would have been right for you. We never would have moved. Someone had to take the initiative."

"I wanted the house on Merriweather Street. I would have compromised on something—but not this. This is ridiculous for us. How can we even afford it?"

"Let me figure that out."

"No!"

"God, I knew you'd be this way."

The children called from upstairs. Sloan and Tia walked up in silence.

Chapter Twenty-seven

"We might as well do it right," Sloan kept saying. He said it about the wedding, picking out the silver and china, planning a wedding trip.

They spent that summer writing and calling each other. Sloan had started his internship in Washington; Tia was working for Myra. They would wait, Sloan had decided, until October because of Toby's death. Sloan found a china he liked and sent a photograph for Tia. It had gold bands around navy blue bands.

"Rather formal," sniffed Gran.

Tia told him that Gran would give them silver. Sloan said he preferred Georgian silver, pointing out the few Ensear spoons that Althea had managed to keep intact. Most of the silver was with his cousins. Once he had seen a piece at the Museum of Fine Arts and had stared at it longingly. "On loan from Mr. and Mrs. Turner L. Ensear," said the card in front of it.

Sloan came up to Easter Cove for a few days in August and eagerly went over wedding plans. He was enjoying it. Even Gran was amused by his enthusiasm and let him persuade her to clear the music room for dancing. Wherever he could find a way to widen the scope of activities, he would. It did not seem very real to Tia, as she sat at dinner while Sloan and Gran fenced.

"The house is so big that we could really invite another fifty or so," Sloan said.

"Where would we put them?"

"We'd have to do it in New York," said Tia absently.

"That's a thought," said Sloan.

"Yes," said Gran, "that might be easier."

"No," said Tia. "This is getting out of control."

"Wouldn't it be easier to have people come if we were married in New York?" said Sloan.

"No," said Tia. She tried to calm her voice, restrain her irritation.

"Tia has spoken," said Valery. "You'll learn, Sloan."

Everyone laughed. Tia laughed too, but she was always surprised when Valery or Gran saw her that way. So often she felt she was without any will at all.

"Tia, you look like a little ghost," said Myra. "For God's sake, get married on Pine Island under a tree. We'll all drink too much and go for a long walk and see the sun set."

"That sounds wonderful." It was too late. Visions of engraved invitations, wedding dresses, flowers, caterers, silver, china danced in her head.

Althea had given them some money for a wedding trip.

"It's Toby's insurance money," she said, handing them a check.

Tia froze. Sloan looked out the window.

Later, Sloan said, "I wonder where she ever got together that much money. Awfully sweet of her," and Tia remained silent.

"We'll save it," he said. He only had four days off. Gran, who didn't know about the insurance money, took rooms for them at an inn in Ogunquit.

In September, Robin went down to Philadelphia to begin medical school.

"Of course I'll be back for your wedding," she assured Tia.

Tia sat in Robin's room and watched her pack.

"I won't see you for years. You'll be so busy."

"We'll have time up here every year. We'll promise. Every Fourth of July," said Robin.

"Swear?"

"Swear."

Robin packed in her usual careful, precise manner. Stacks of underwear, shirts, pants, were folded into neat piles. When they had gone to Europe together, Robin had washed out her clothes every night and hung them up to dry, tidied her handbag, and put her hair into rollers. Sometimes Tia envied that capacity for repetition and care.

By the end of September, Easter Cove was deserted. The houses along the cove and up on the hill above the bay were shuttered. In town the streets were empty, one of the two restaurants closed for the season, the library closed three days a week. People seemed to amble slowly down the streets, the air seemed purer, clearer, the sea more brilliant in the sun. It was cool during the day and cold at night, and the leaves were turning red and gold.

Gran went down to New York for a couple of weeks to help Valery arrange a show. Tia decided to stay at Easter Cove. Though Gran wanted to leave Masha with her, Tia finally persuaded them she would survive by herself. Seeing them off, she was swept by sadness. It was the old hollow sadness of loss that she had felt so long after her parents died.

The house seemed enormous and barren. Lawn chairs had been put in the storage shed for the winter, and the flower gardens had been cut down and covered. Clumps of chrysanthemums by the front steps had begun to fade. Wind rattled the windows and blew whirlwinds in the fireplace ashes at night. When the telephone rang it echoed.

Gran had left her spaniel behind and Tia took long walks with her. They climbed the hills and walked through empty properties, peering through windows into deserted kitchens, strolling along the piny paths to the beach. Nelly ran ahead, ears flapping, tail wagging. They walked along the cove, picking their way along the seaweed that covered the crescents of sand, climbed the rocks, and watched the breakers on the outer beach. Back at the house, Tia made pots of tea she forgot to drink, took her sketchbook out on the porch, built fires that she drew near to as dusk fell, sometimes drifted to sleep in her chair, book in hand, draped in a shawl like an old lady. The phone would usually wake her up. Sloan called when the rates were low and talked for three minutes. He sounded tired, and the time limit made it difficult to say anything. When she called he was always out.

After his call she would be wide awake and would wander

around the house restlessly, the earlier peace gone for a while. Eventually she would put a record on, find some crackers and cheese for dinner, rebuild the library fire, and read until she fell asleep. She'd awaken, the light from the big library windows bright on her face, the gramophone needle making its small circle with rhythmic insistence. Getting up slowly, she would turn off the record player, fold up her blanket, put away her teapot, eat a dry piece of cheese and a damp biscuit, and go upstairs to shower.

Once she tried on her wedding dress. She stood shoeless in front of the mirror, her hair in braids, skin still dark from summer, with the rich folds of silk and lace enveloping her. I look like I'm standing in whipped cream, she thought.

It was startling when Gran returned. She brought back a group of friends, three young Latin women who were to work through the wedding day, boxes of wedding presents that had been sent to New York. The house was filled with activity again, every room populated, meals served at precise times. The Latin women spoke only Spanish, argued, laughed, called out to each other, played the radio in the kitchen, and confused Masha, who retreated to Gran's bedroom in tears. Men came from town to polish floors and clean rugs. Tables were set up in the music room. Stacks of chairs waited in corners. More packages arrived: casserole dishes, vases, silver bowls, glasses, salt and pepper shakers, tea sets, trays. Tia spent her mornings writing thank-you notes and her afternoons walking, to escape the nuptial frenzy. The houseguests were caught up in the excitement and the air was filled with expectation.

"No, you don't look silly," said Robin as they tried on their dresses the day before the wedding, "we both do."

They looked at their reflection in the glass.

"Yeah," said Tia. "What happened?"

They both started to laugh and then collapsed in giggles. They sprawled on Gran's big bed.

"No, no," screamed Masha when she saw them, trying with her stocky little body to push them upright. "No, look what you do!" she cried.

Every time they sobered up, one of them would look at the

other and start to laugh again. Masha screamed at them.

"What on earth is going on?" said Gran coldly from the doorway.

"Look, look, madame," cried Masha.

The three Latin women stood in back of Gran, peering over her shoulder.

"You are both hysterical," said Gran. She strode into the room, the women in her wake. "Poor Masha will have to press those dresses again."

"Gran, we look hideous," said Robin, trying to recover.

"Nonsense, you've both just lost a bit of weight. Stand up, both of you," she commanded. The women stepped back and looked at each other.

"Odelia," said Gran, drawing one of the women forward, "is quite a good seamstress, and she'll fix the dresses."

Tia and Robin, chastened, spent the rest of the morning being pinned and seamed.

Sloan arrived the same day. Gran had arranged his flight and ordered a rental car for him. He was staying on Pine Island with Valery, Claudia, Paul, and Myra.

"Your grandmother is so well organized," he said, after he had gotten his orders for the day. Gran left nothing to chance.

They drove to Camden and walked down by the water. It was cold and gray.

"Ah!" Sloan exclaimed. "This is all exciting," he said, laughing. "We're going to have a good life." He put his arm around her shoulders as they walked. "It'll be rough for a while. But we can always get away to Easter Cove or New York for a couple of days."

"We should have gone off and gotten married by ourselves."

"And missed getting all those casseroles?" Sloan laughed. His mood was buoyant.

She wanted to prick his balloon. "It makes one so numb."

"Been hectic for you," he said. He stopped and looked down at a small sailboat. "It's all so difficult," he said sadly.

She looked at him. In the months since Toby's death she had learned to measure his moods by the tension on his face. Now, standing in the gray light, he looked drawn and tired.

"Are we doing the right thing?" she asked in a soft voice.

He turned abruptly and faced her. "What?"

"Are you sure?"

"Absolutely," he said firmly. He looked stubborn and defensive. "I love you very much. I can't imagine life without you." His tone was harsh. He stood in front of her, defying her to argue.

"I'm not as sure."

"You know I love you," he said angrily.

"What about me?" she said, matching his anger.

"Oh, for God's sake. You're never sure about anything."

Did he know her that well, she wondered, or was he just making a lucky guess?

"And you can make up my mind for me?"

"Tia, you need someone like me—to give you stability, goals—and I need you. . . . " He hesitated. He started to walk away, striding along the wharf with his head down, and then he wheeled about, strode back, and stopped in front of her. "You've had so damn much you take it for granted. You expect everything to be Christmas morning, and if it isn't, you start having doubts."

Once Valery had said that Gran made life difficult but exciting. "It's hard to imagine creating such a life away from her," he had added. Tia had argued with him that night but now she wondered if he was right. Ivan had had that quality too. But Gran provided a safe haven.

"I'm sorry," said Sloan. He put his arms around her and held her close. A cold wind blew off the ocean and chilled her back. "I've lost so many people. I just couldn't bear to lose you again."

"Please, don't be hurt."

"Don't leave me," he said fiercely, against her ear.

At dawn the next morning the clouds rolled out to sea and left the sky blue. Tia sat in the library and watched the sun clear the fog bank and rise in the sky. There was a strong wind and waves splashed over the top of the rocks.

With Gran's spaniel dashing ahead of her, Tia walked along the edge of the lawn, then turned down the path to the sea. She walked around the point to the channel and looked over at Pine

Island. The waves were high, frothed with white. She could see Paul's boat moored offshore, rising and then disappearing in the troughs. The dinghy that he lashed to his dock was dashing against the pilings.

"Child, where have you been?" said Gran, when Tia returned. "Valery called. They're going to have problems getting across. I've called someone in Camden to see if they can get a bigger boat over."

The winds increased, whipping branches off the pines and scattering gold leaves from the maples across the lawn. A bigger boat was sent but could not get close enough, and it seemed too dangerous to bring the dinghy out so far. Robin and Tia put on their heavy jackets and walked down to the channel. They could see Paul, Valery, and Sloan on the dock.

"It must be divine intervention," said Robin, at lunch.

"Nonsense," snapped Gran. "We've got two more hours, and the Coast Guard expects the wind to die down."

The guests looked anxious. The caterers busied themselves setting up tables. The Latin women were laughing in the kitchen. Masha had gone upstairs to press the wedding dress. The wind rattled the windows and roared down the chimney.

After lunch everyone decided to walk down to the channel.

"You stay here," commanded Gran. "I want you to let Masha do your hair."

Tia stood on the porch, her hair in braids, wearing Ivan's old blue sweater, and watched everyone walk down the lawn and then, by twos, start along the narrow path to the rocks.

"Tia," called Masha from upstairs.

"In a minute."

Tia walked across the lawn to the music-room wing and pushed at the door. It swung open, curtains blowing, wind whirling through the room. The furniture and rugs had been moved out, since there was to be dancing here this afternoon. Two big silver vases of roses were on the piano.

"Missy, missy, phone," Odelia called.

Tia went back up through the hall to the kitchen.

"Yes?"

"Tia? Can you hear me?"

"Ivan?"

"I called to wish you well." He was shouting into the phone. The caterers looked up from their sandwiches.

"I can hear you very well."

"Are you surrounded by a curious throng?"

"Yes."

"I've been agonizing over this call all day. I just felt something needed to be said. It's all been in letters."

"Thank you," she said awkwardly.

"Are you happy?"

"I think so."

"Some doubts?"

"Just a bit numb."

"He better treat you right, kitten, or I'll come and get him."

"Are you in London?"

"In Florence. It's lovely here. I spent the whole day at the Uffizi and thought of you."

Masha was calling her. The caterers clattered nearby.

"I missed you for a long time," she said, after a pause.

"I miss you all the time."

"Thanks for calling," she said quickly, afraid of what he might say next.

"I love you, Tia."

The Latin women were shrieking. The caterers ran to the windows. Tia looked out and saw Sloan, his clothes dripping, being escorted by the wedding guests. They were laughing and calling out for her.

"I've got to go," she said. "Thank you, Ivan." She hung up and stood by the phone for a moment.

"He swam!" shouted one of the guests. Sloan was being borne up the back steps by the admiring throng. He was smiling happily, letting himself be pushed along.

"The foolish boy swam to the launch," said Gran. "He might have drowned." She smiled at him.

"He'll never do anything like that again," said Robin quietly to Tia.

Chapter Twenty-eight

In the morning the haze had lifted and there was a breeze. Tia sat on the back porch, in a cotton robe, reading her mail. Priscilla was arguing with Daisy about breakfast.

"You don't eat, you'll be a midget," said Priscilla.

"A midget!" roared Peter.

"No, I won't, Priscilla," said Daisy, giggling.

"You want to be tall like your mommy? You finish this egg."

"Daddy says eggs give you heart attacks," said Daisy.

The conversation drifted on, the usual tug-of-war between Priscilla and Daisy, interrupted by Peter's repetition of key words.

Tia looked out at the garden. The roses had black spot and the phlox were covered with mildew.

"Tia," called Sloan.

"She's out on the porch, Mr. Snear," said Priscilla. She never varied her mispronunciation, and Sloan had stopped trying to correct her.

"Tia," Sloan said, as he hurried out to the porch, knotting his tie, "I'm off. I have a patient at six, and then I have to get to the institute. Klein's seminar is at eight, and I promised I'd be there early. I'll grab a bite somewhere."

"All right. I'll do the bills and then go down to the office for a couple of hours."

"Tia," said Sloan slowly, and then he paused. "Well, we'll talk later."

Tia got the checkbook and started paying bills. She noticed that the balance was low. Sloan had written a big check to Mrs. Pierce. Still, that would not nearly have covered a down payment on the 31st Street house. She went to his desk and looked for their bankbooks. They were not there.

"Mommy, you have a package," shouted the children.

She opened the box slowly. "It must be an early birthday present. Maybe I should save it."

"Open it," the children begged.

It was a box of books. There were novels, histories, biographies, garden books. "Look at this," she said, puzzled. Then, lifting the last, she knew they were from Ivan. He had included his book on Minoan villas.

"That's a lot of books," said Peter, admiring the collection.

There was no card or inscription.

Jake was away on vacation. He had left some notes on her desk, and she read them quickly. They were running her last piece in two installments, which meant she only had to do some restaurant reviews for the September issue. She talked to the copy editor about his brother-in-law's health-food restaurant in Bethesda. Someone had called about a feminist vegetarian café opening near Dupont Circle.

At noon, instead of heading for the Sister Sprout, she called Mr. Berger.

"Ah, Mrs. Ensear. Mrs. Pierce told me you have bought a house."

"My husband . . . you see, it's not—" She was garbled.

"Don't explain, please."

"No, it's not that. I'm really interested in your house still."

There was a pause. "I see."

"Please, may I come out?"

"Of course."

Mr. Berger greeted her with a glass of iced tea. He sat in his study, surrounded by piles of books and a haze of pipe smoke.

"Mrs. Pierce is upset about my pipes and piles," he said.

Tia walked to the doors overlooking the garden. "Your roses are doing well."

He stood next to her, looking out. "My wife brought them from her house on the Cape. Started them from cuttings. You have to keep pruning them back."

They went out on the terrace, sat in the shade of a dogwood tree. Mr. Berger sat back, sucked on his pipe.

"You are in trouble, aren't you?" He smiled at her.

She started to reply automatically, to say "What?" or "I'm not sure what you mean," but instead she nodded. "Yes."

"Your husband came in several days ago. He didn't like the place, I could tell."

"No."

"He wants something grander."

"Yes."

"Is that so terrible?"

Tia looked back at the house. "Yes, in a way."

"Would it be so hard to let him have what he wants?"

"It would be very hard."

"Mrs. Ensear, I'll make you a deal. I'll rent you this house for a year. I would just as soon travel for a year and then, at the end of that time, you either buy it or call Mrs. Pierce again."

"Really?"

"Would you let me leave my books here? I'll put everything else in storage."

"Of course."

He smiled. "And take care of the roses?"

"I promise."

"And now, we're really in trouble," he said.

"Yes," she said. They both laughed.

At first she was excited. It was, she thought, the exultation of just having committed a great crime. As she left the house she turned back and looked up at it. Mr. Berger stood in the doorway and smiled at her. Then, driving back, she decided to cut across the town and go to Lord and Taylor's. Prowling the bedding department, her adrenaline flowed. Quickly, before she could experience the fear that she knew was pushing up against her exhilaration, she ordered new sheets, comforters, towels. She stopped at the furniture department and walked around desks, chairs, tables, couches.

"Tia!" came a loud cry.

"Jenny," said Tia, shocked out of her trance.

"God, what are you doing here?" drawled Jenny.

"Getting some sheets," said Tia quickly. "What about you?"

"Just shopping. This is my big day in town. Wayne's working on Lowell Street, and I turn up like a good little wife with his lunch."

"Really?" Tia noticed that Jenny had put on weight. "You look well."

"Mother says too well," she said, patting her stomach. "Wayne's a dear. I've talked him out of breeding dogs. I'm just sort of puttering around. I even started baking bread." She sighed. "Disgusting, isn't it? If we had known how we would all turn out, we'd never have tolerated us."

Tia wanted to tell Jenny about the house on Merriweather Street but fought the impulse. Later, driving home, she knew Jenny would have insisted on a diagnostic conversation. Jenny abhorred ambiguity.

Tia walked Daisy up the street to her friend Lauren's house. Daisy, in a new dress, her hair neatly braided, clutching a birthday present, looked nervous.

"I wish I could go to a birthday party," said Tia.

"Sheila and Lauren are best friends now," said Daisy sadly.

"Oh, dear."

"Mommy, I have no friends now."

"What about Julie?"

"She likes Kim."

"And Leslie?"

"She's always pulling my hair."

"Is there going to be anybody at the party you are friends with?"

Daisy bit her lower lip and shook her head. A tear rolled down her cheek.

"Oh, sweetheart," said Tia, bending down. "Would you like to go and have an ice cream with me instead?"

Daisy looked at her, considering. The child had such cool green eyes. "I better go to the party," she said, almost apologetically.

Tia walked up the front walk, feeling leaden. She watched Daisy go inside, turn to wave, disappear into the darkened hall.

"We're going to have a magician," called Lauren's mother. "We'll be done at four. Come by and have a piece of cake."

Tia smiled and waved. She stood on the steps, imagining Daisy, in her flowered dress with its white collar and cuffs, her white shoes thick with polish, standing at the edge of the room. It was Tia twenty-five years before. But she had had Robin, always darting through the crowd to greet her and pull her into the center of the room, be her partner in games, see that she had her party favors.

"The party was wonderful. Why did you have to come so early?" said Daisy, clutching her prizes. "They had a magician and a puppet show!"

"And are you and Lauren friends again?"

"Yeah. She said she doesn't really like Sheila. But she wanted to go to Sheila's house because she has a pool."

"And Julie and Kim?"

"Yeah. We're going to have a club—me and Lauren. It's going to be the Detective Club." Daisy rattled on happily about how they were going to cover the neighborhood looking for spies.

"What kind of spies?"

"Just spies," said Daisy irritably. "We're going to have a newspaper," she added, brightening.

"I'm fine, I'm fine," insisted Gran on the phone. Her voice was weak and tired.

"I thought I'd come up for a few days at the end of the month."

"Darling, you were just here. Come in September for Labor Day."

She and Sloan had always come for Labor Day, sometimes with Althea.

"I might come in August."

There was a long pause. "I won't ask you any questions," said Gran.

"I'll call you tomorrow," said Tia quickly. "Much love."

Sloan was reading the Sunday paper. He glanced up as she hung up. "Going up in August?" he said coolly.

In the week that she had been home, they had not discussed the 31st Street house and Tia had not told Sloan about the Merriweather Street house. Mr. Berger had called and asked if she wanted to change her mind. She did not, but she had quickly shed her euphoria. She was unclear about her intentions, felt suspended, drifting, led by impulses she did not fathom.

"I can't pretend Gran is going to live forever, Sloan."

"No," he said. "I thought we might go in August. Before we go sailing. I can take off a long weekend. I think it's the weekend of the fifth."

Ivan would be in Washington the sixth.

"An old friend of mine will be in town then," she said.

"Oh?"

"Yes. I want to be here." She felt reckless.

"Okay then," said Sloan, taking up his paper. "Maybe the next weekend. Joe expects us to help him for a day before we sail."

"I'm not going," she said.

"To Gran's?" He put down his paper again.

"With the Sykeses."

"Tia," he said warningly. He stood up and walked slowly over to her and stood above her. "You're going." He was not going to beg, reason, or argue.

"I'm sorry, Sloan, but I'm not going." He stood close to her elbow. She did not look up at him.

"The hell you aren't," he said menacingly. He put his hand on her arm. "You're not going to fuck up everything again."

"Again?"

"The house. The Klein party. Last year you wouldn't go to the Sykeses for Labor Day. You're like Althea. You won't give a goddam inch." He was sputtering, clawing at her arm.

"They say men always marry their mothers," she said, reckless again.

He hit her across the face. "You asked for that!" he shouted, but he stepped back, holding his hand. His face was white.

Tia stood up. It had always been so reasonable between them. Sometimes bored, sometimes irritated, she had still always counted on their rationality. Now she wanted to hit him too, only she feared his greater strength.

"I'm sorry," said Sloan, recovering first. He went to his chair, sat down, and buried his face in his hands.

Sympathy stirred in her. She forced herself to sit and say nothing. Anna would have run to him and thrown her arms around him. It must have happened with Peter. Tia had seen Anna comfort him when her face was streaked with tears. But Gran would have thrown him out.

"So much is wrong," said Tia finally.

"No, it isn't," said Sloan looking up. "You're right. I married a woman who would give me as little as my own mother did. Who would think she was above groveling with the hoi polloi to help her husband's career. Who out of spite would—oh, what the hell." He got up and paced the room. "You never had to work for anything. It was all handed to you. You don't know what the real world is like. You made me come crawling to you. I know you had that other boyfriend. Robin warned me I was getting you on the rebound. And you made me pay, didn't you? Didn't you?" He shouted.

Tia watched. She let it go, waiting, not sure if this was what she had been waiting for.

"Didn't you?" he shouted again. He stood in front of her chair and then spun around and walked to the fireplace, where he put his hands on the mantel and talked with his back to her. She could see his reflection in the small round mirror Daisy had given them for Christmas. "You goddam spoiled people. I hear you all day long. You don't want to struggle. You don't want to work. You sit back and wait. You wait for engraved invitations. You wait to be begged and courted. Althea and her goddam stupid snobbery and her fucking pigsties. You with your fascist grandmother and her crazy lover and his stupid, illiterate wife and all those damn whining refugees and your know-it-all cousin. You sit there thinking you have it all, and you throw a bit to the poor outsiders." He turned and faced her. His face was purple, contorted, his eyes dark with rage.

Tia was frightened. She sat very still.

"Do you think it doesn't hurt when I remember all those months I begged you to see me?"

"It was so long ago," she said quietly. "Can't you forgive me now?"

"After all those goddam years of living with Althea in places I was ashamed to bring friends to, driving in her broken-down old cars, knowing the family thought she was crazy. . . ." He paced. "I've made a damn good life for myself. I'm a good psychiatrist. Klein thinks I'm one of the best people he's ever trained. I've bought us a beautiful house. I send the kids to the best school in Washington. I go out to your goddam restaurants with you and put up with Jake while he feels you up."

"Oh, come on, Sloan."

"I never asked you any questions about that professor. I took you for what you were the day you said you'd marry me. I try to understand why you don't like what I like, why you won't go along with me ever."

"You're being unfair, Sloan," she said. He was winding down.

"Unfair? Yeah? I'm just so sick and tired of your attitude, of your family's attitude. You and Robin never got over seeing me come up to Easter Cove that day in that old heap, feeling like an ass. You'll always see me that way. Our wedding day, when I swam across the channel, your grandmother and some of her friends saw me in a new light. But not you and Robin. You just stood there sneering at me."

"Oh, Sloan, this is getting absurd."

"I wish we'd met now. Now, when I've managed to . . . " He paused, searching for words. "It should be so easy," he said, his tone changing. "You are being asked to do what most women would give their eye teeth for. Move to a beautiful house, do whatever you want with it. Make yourself a studio. If you think you're such a great painter, why don't you paint? Your grandmother is going to die soon—God, you know that, Tia—and you'll have money to stay home and do whatever you want."

"Aren't you anticipating a bit?"

"Look, she's in her seventies and she's been ill for years. Buxton says it's a miracle she's alive." He turned away. "God, don't make me say these things. I sound awful."

"But it's reality," she said calmly.

"Exactly."

He looked ashamed. This was the right moment to tell him about the Merriweather Street house. She tried to start the sentence, but she didn't know what she was telling him. She felt she still had time.

———

The call came in the middle of the night. Tia had been expecting it, but when it came, tearing through the midnight silence, she was not prepared.

"Your grandmother died an hour ago," said Myra, her voice shaky. "She woke up and called out in such a loud, clear voice. You know, she called out to her mother. Isn't that strange? I ran in, and she turned and looked at me and she looked surprised, and then she closed her eyes." Myra stopped and sobbed.

"Did you call the doctor?" Tia had seen Gran close her eyes and seem to lie without breath and then wake again.

"Oh, Tia, of course. She was dead before he came. She was sort of smiling. I hadn't seen her look that way before."

Tia sat in bed a long time. Sloan put his arms around her and rocked her. She clung to him.

"I should have gone up," she said. When she spoke the tears started. "I can't believe it."

"It's all right, sweetheart," said Sloan, holding her.

Suddenly she started screaming. She pounded Sloan, threw herself away from him, flung herself on the floor.

She was vaguely aware of Sloan trying to get her up, of the children coming into the room, of Sloan taking them out, of the telephone ringing. Each time a cry went up from her throat she told herself she must stop, but she couldn't.

Sloan gave her Valium. She sat quietly on the porch, crying, feeling very sad and drugged. Priscilla was crying too. She sat down and put her arms around Tia and offered her comforting bosom. Someone had come and taken the children to the park. Sloan was on the phone, canceling patients, calling Buxton, making arrangements. Priscilla murmured soothingly.

"I want Mrs. Ensear to go lie down, Priscilla," said Sloan, in his professional purr. "Could you go to Mrs. Goldberg's house and see if you can help her with the children?"

"Yes, Dr. Snear," said Priscilla coldly. She squeezed Tia's hand. "You'll be all right," she said.

"Thank you, Priscilla," said Tia, trying to rouse herself.

Sloan led Tia upstairs. He offered her a glass and a pill.

"No, no more, Sloan," she said.

"I'm the doctor," he said gently.

"I feel so drugged."

"This will help you sleep. It's very mild."

She surrendered, swallowed, and lay down on the bed.

"I'm glad you're crying. Sometimes you detach so. This is much healthier."

He was trying to help. He smoothed the sheet over her, pulled down the shades.

"I just feel so awful about not staying with her. I think she wanted me there. When I was there she kept calling for me in the middle of the night. I think each time she thought she was dying. I should have stayed."

"You had other responsibilities. We always feel we haven't done enough. You were always very thoughtful," said Sloan. "Now, go to sleep."

"But she did so much for me. She'd lost so much. It must have been so scary for her. I was always trying to pull away."

"Now, Tia, don't be silly. She was an old lady. She lived a long and interesting life. You were always good to her."

"No, I wasn't."

"Try to get some sleep."

Tia could feel the pill take effect. Her body seemed to float. She tried to resist. "You gave me too much," she said.

"Trust me," he said. He patted her hand and then got up. She watched him through half-closed eyes as he tiptoed to the door. She wanted to ask him about the children but she couldn't speak.

"Mommy?"

Tia opened her eyes. Daisy and Peter were sitting on the bed, peering down anxiously.

"Mommy?"

"Yes, baby, what is it?" Tia tried to sit up, but she felt faint and let herself back down on the pillow.

"You wouldn't wake up," said Peter, in tears. Daisy was holding his hand and biting her lower lip.

"Oh, poor babies," said Tia, pulling them down. She glanced at the clock. It was ten in the morning. She must have slept for almost twenty hours.

Both of them burst into tears. Tia held them close.

"Children! I told you not to disturb Mommy," said Sloan, rushing into the room.

They wailed.

"It's okay, Sloan. I was awake."

"Okay, downstairs, downstairs," he said, pulling them off.

"No!" they cried, holding on to Tia.

"It's all right, Sloan," said Tia carefully. She felt strange.

"Oh, come on!" shouted Sloan. He could never stand hearing the children cry.

Slowly, Tia sat up. She gathered the children closer. "Gran died and I was very, very sad. I'm still sad but now I feel better. I'm remembering how much I love Gran and how much she loved us."

"I love Gran too," said Daisy, sobbing.

"Me too," said Peter, looking at Daisy. "I do too, don't I, Daisy?"

Tia talked to Robin. Tia would drive to Philadelphia and they would fly up together. Sloan would bring the children later.

"Dr. Snear won't like you driving," said Priscilla.

"I know." Tia looked at Priscilla and they both smiled. "I'll leave him a note."

"And those pills?"

"No more."

She packed hurriedly. Daisy and Lauren sat on her bed. Peter was stretched out playing with his trucks by the door.

"Lauren's grandmother died too," said Daisy.

"Just my Granny Mary," said Lauren.

"That's right," said Tia, searching the closet for a dark dress. Peter was looking up at her. "Don't cry, Mommy," he warned.

"She can if she wants to," said Daisy.

"Well, maybe later. We'll all cry at the funeral," said Tia.

She took her bags downstairs and kissed the children goodbye. Priscilla gave her a thermos of coffee and a bag of apples. They all stood on the porch waving. For a moment Tia sat in the car and watched the little group on the porch of that solid white house with the concrete steps and the pillared front porch. Then she started the car. They ran down the steps, waving to her until she turned the corner.

"I don't know how you could be so irresponsible as to drive to Philadelphia!" Sloan was shouting into the phone.

Robin sat on a pillow on the floor, sipping her drink.

"Robin sends you her love," said Tia.

"Did you hear what I said?"

"Yes."

"Tia, you were in no state to drive. I was very worried. Are you still taking the Valium?"

"No, I'm okay."

"Good. What about the service?"

"We're going to have it at the house on Wednesday."

"That's almost a week."

"We need time to let Gran's friends make arrangements to come."

"I'll be up Tuesday," he said coldly. "That is, unless you need me earlier?"

"Tuesday will be fine."

"Very well."

She hung up after she heard the click of the receiver.

"Trouble?"

"I don't know." Tia shrugged. "I keep thinking it's a stage, as Gran would say. That I'll get back into the fold again."

"Mmmm," muttered Robin, fingering her glass.

"We seem to be constantly at cross-purposes. Have you ever seriously thought about getting married?"

"No, I plan not to. I'm too self-centered to be married."

"Is that really it?"

"I think so. I've been tempted once or twice but counted to ten and came to my senses."

Robin's apartment was small. The largest room was furnished with pillows, brick-and-board bookcases, an old couch with a plaid blanket thrown over it, a table covered with books and papers, a wicker basket crammed with medical magazines. There were two tiny bedrooms, one filled with file cabinets, and a narrow kitchen where Robin kept a supply of frozen dinners in the freezer and diet soda in the icebox.

"It's so different from your house with Grayson," said Tia.

"Yeah. Gray says that when he dies he wants me to move to Brooklyn and take over the house. But I probably won't. I work so much. This suits me fine." She looked around the apartment with satisfaction.

"We'll take over the gardener's cottage at Easter Cove," said Tia. "Okay? Let's keep that. We can share it."

"Well," said Robin doubtfully, "let's think about it."

It was raining hard when they arrived at Easter Cove. Valery met them in the front hall. He looked exhausted and shrunken. His eyes had receded into dark hollows. When he embraced Tia she could feel his bones through his heavy tweed jacket.

She heard a buzz of voices from the library.

"Some people are already arriving," said Valery. "Myra's organizing everything." He leaned over to whisper. "And being a goddam pain in the ass."

"Tia," called Myra from the top of the steps. She was wearing a long black dress with one of Gran's amethyst chokers.

"Watch out for her," grumbled Valery.

"Darling," said Myra, hurrying down the stairs and throwing her arms around Tia. "So many people have been coming—Valery says it's almost like the old days—so I've put you and Robin together in your room. You don't mind? You remember the Ropers, Tia? You stayed with them after your parents died. They're here. Boris and Allie, the Charetskys." She rattled off familiar names as they climbed the stairs. "I've got Masha cooking up a storm. And Mrs. Pearson from town. Sydney is coming up from New York tomorrow to read at the service and Laura Landsdale said she'd like to do something too."

When they were alone together in Tia's room, Robin slumped into the chaise. "Oh, this is going to be awful," she moaned.

Tia went over and sat on the window seat. Through the rolling fog she could see figures moving about the music room, people strolling on the lawn, a dog running in circles around a small child.

"Tia," called a familiar voice through the door.

"Come in." It was Elizavetta. She threw her arms around Tia, sobbing.

"I thought you were in England," said Tia, jarred.

"We flew back last night. The minute I heard. Oh, I don't know how we'll manage without her," she cried.

Tia stood in Elizavetta's iron embrace. Robin rolled her eyes.

"Is Ivan here too?" Robin asked.

"He took Alexey back to Kathryn's. He put me on a flight to Owl's Head." She turned and looked at Tia. The face, seconds before soft with grief, was suddenly focused and watchful. "He'll be up tonight or tomorrow. We must all be together at a time like this," she said.

They sat around the dining-room table. Tia counted twenty-six. Myra sat at the head of the table, Tia and Robin on either side of her. Masha and Mrs. Pearson passed plates heaped with food. Chicken and noodles, bread, peas: Gran would have never allowed it. "All that starch," she would sniff when Tia described a dinner she had eaten at a friend's house.

Gran liked the dining room lit only by candles at night. Tonight Myra had brought in lamps. "Less funereal," she whispered to Tia. The room seemed far too bright. There was too much food. Valery sat silently, next to Claudia, whose head tilted to and fro in nervous conversation.

"I'm trying to keep Masha very busy," said Myra, spearing her noodles deftly. "We'll have to decide what to do with her."

Tia nodded. She felt as if she were sitting behind a partition. The conversation, in German, Russian, French, English, came to her ears muted and blurred. Nothing seemed to be connected to her; she could think of nothing to say.

She excused herself from the table, aware of the murmur of sympathy that followed her from the room. She wandered into the library and sat at the desk by the window. There were photographs she had spent hours examining as a child. Her father in short pants, his dark hair neatly parted, sitting under a large tree. Tinka, smiling over her shoulder, her hair in long ringlets, sitting on a pony. A young smiling Gran, without the long dresses and choker, a dapper, frowning husband at her side, her two children beside her, on a beach. There were lots of pictures of Tia, in pretty dresses, her hair neatly braided. A few with Robin, always much smaller, fair, plump and laughing. Tia looked at herself. Had she always been such a solemn, braided child? Vaguely she remembered the photographs on her mother's bureau were not so grave. She picked up a picture of Anna, standing beside Peter, holding the infant Tia. Peter was looking at the photographer with some impatience, his hand in his pocket, while Anna stood smiling beside him, so small she seemed overwhelmed by the bundled baby in her arms. Her face had that frightened, fragile quality that Tia remembered, the face of a very pretty child who had been held close and then abandoned.

"Are you all right, Tia?" said Valery. He stood in the doorway.

"Why aren't there any pictures of you here?" asked Tia.

"You know why," he said, coming to the desk and bending over the photographs.

"I'm never sure if life is far more complicated or far simpler than we seem to think," said Tia.

"I can't imagine it without her," he said, walking over to the fireplace. He looked up at the big painting he had done for her. When he turned back, tears were streaming down his face.

"You have Claudia," said Tia, trying to comfort.

"Helena was my past, my country, my language, my memories." He dabbed at his tears with a handkerchief. "Look at this. It was her father's." He sighed. "Now I have no bridge. I'm stranded."

Tia turned away from him and fought the impulse to rush out into the night and run into the darkness.

"Tia," said Valery, putting his hand on her shoulder, "you and Helena—you are both so cool. So steely." He sounded angry. "So little moves you. You miss so much." He slammed out of the room.

At lunch Myra stood up, rapping her water glass with a knife.

"Everyone, everyone," she called out in her rich voice, "can I have your attention?" She frowned. "Please!"

"Get on with it, Myra," growled Valery.

Myra leaned forward, her hands on the back of her chair.

"Ladies and gentlemen, friends of Helena Valenkova," she said, pausing as she surveyed the hushed table. "Tomorrow afternoon we are going to have a memorial service for Helena at St. Paul's Church in Easter Cove."

"What!" exclaimed Valery.

"We needed a larger space than we originally thought when we planned to have the service here," she said, ignoring Valery.

"She never set foot in St. Paul's," said Valery in a loud aside to Claudia.

"She was deeply religious," said Elizavetta crossly.

She and Valery exchanged some angry words in Russian.

"Please, please, we've come here to honor Helena—" started Myra.

"Not to bury her," finished Valery, rising from his chair. Claudia rose with him, her hand on his arm.

"Come now, Valery," said one of the guests, "let's hear Myra out."

"What right do you have, Myra?" shouted Valery.

"Sit down, sit down," said someone.

"Valery," said Myra good-naturedly, "it's all arranged. Four o'clock tomorrow."

"Who arranged it, I ask you?" Valery's face was crimson. Claudia tugged at his arm.

"This is terrible," cried Elizavetta, raising her hands imploringly toward the ceiling.

There was a murmur of conversation.

"Please, Valery," said Myra, her face stern, "there are a great many people here who—"

"Who what?" Valery was shouting, pointing his finger at Myra.

"Sit down, Malachenko," said someone.

"Everyone, everyone," said Myra, tapping her glass again.

Tia watched, her head turning back and forth as if she were at a tennis game. Robin was trying not to laugh. Several guests sat, stunned. Elizavetta and Masha were standing behind Myra, in a profound embrace, weeping. Claudia had run out of the room in tears.

Tia stood up. "I'm going to talk to Myra and to Valery, and then Robin and I will decide where and when the service will be held."

Robin stood up.

"No, Tia." Valery was shouting again, with someone trying to take his arm. "She doesn't care!" he bellowed.

"You're going to have a stroke, Valery," said Robin coldly as she followed Tia out of the room.

Sitting in the library again with Robin, Tia poured them both a drink and then started laughing. Robin was laughing so hard by now she had slumped to the floor and was doubled over.

"This is awful," they both kept saying.

They sat on the Adirondack chairs, in the hazy morning sunlight, drinking coffee, making final plans for the service. Tia, Robin, Myra, Elizavetta, and the Reverend Oldslinger, all politely skirting Gran's lack of religious affiliation, all disagreeing on the service. Valery and Claudia had been dispatched to Owl's Head to pick up noon arrivals. Sloan had decided to fly to Portland and drive up the coast and was not due for another two hours.

Myra, it turned out, had spent two days on the phone. Hundreds of people were arriving at St. Paul's for the service at four o'clock. It was too late to change anything except Myra's suggestion that Daisy and Peter come and put a spray of roses on the altar as the service started. Everyone vetoed that.

Mr. Oldslinger was pleasant, wary, obviously somewhat confused by the phone calls he had been getting from Valery.

"Is he all right?" he asked, bending confidentially toward Tia.

"Oh, thank God, there he is," cried Elizavetta.

Tia turned around and saw Ivan walking slowly down the lawn. He had some books under his arm.

"God, he's brought some poems too," said Robin.

He walked over to Tia and bent down and kissed her cheek. "Rough? Mother says everyone's been crazy."

"It's getting straightened out," said Robin testily.

"Of course." He laughed, bending over to give her a kiss. "Little Robin Roughneck."

Robin smiled. "It's good to have you here," she said, springing up and giving him a hug.

Ivan sat on the arm of Tia's chair. He put his hand on her shoulder. Elizavetta smiled benevolently. Myra pulled her chair closer. The rector, seeing peace at hand, looked pleased.

Sloan arrived late. The service had started when Tia heard the doors bang shut and saw Sloan and the children slide into a rear pew. Tia indicated the seats she had saved for them in her pew, but Sloan shook his head. When Tia turned back she saw Ivan was watching her. The service seemed interminable. Several times Robin nudged Tia and said, "Gran would hate this."

Afterward people kept hugging and kissing Tia, their faces

inches away, misty with sympathy. Sloan and the children had disappeared. Masha was crying on Elizavetta's shoulder. Ivan stood with them, watching Tia.

"Let's get back to the house," said Robin, reaching Tia through the crowd, her face smudged with lipstick.

"Come on, let's go in my car," said Ivan, suddenly at their side. "We'll go around through the sacristy."

He led them up over the altar and out a side door. They hurried into the car, slammed the doors, and started off.

"What happened to Sloan and the children?" Tia asked Robin.

"Your little boy was getting wiggly," said Ivan. "They must be back at the house."

Sitting between Ivan and Robin in the little car as it made its way through the pines, above the sea, Tia wanted the ride to go on forever.

"Keep driving," she said, as they reached Gran's driveway.

They drove on up the hill, to the high curve on the road. Ivan pulled the car off and parked.

"I wish we could stay here all afternoon," said Tia, resting her head against Ivan's shoulder.

"There will be all the other afternoons," said Ivan.

They sat for a long time, until the car started feeling hot.

"Okay, gang," said Robin. "Let's go before we melt."

Sloan was deep in conversation with someone on the lawn. The children were racing around the chairs. Myra was directing the group of waiters she had hired. Masha stood in the kitchen, slowly buttering slices of bread. She threw her arms around Tia.

"It's important for her to keep busy. We can all cry after everyone has left," said Myra briskly, pushing Masha back to her bread and butter. "Come on, everyone has been looking for you," she said, taking Tia's hand. "You too, Robin."

There were more eyes to look into, more hugs, handshakes, murmured sympathy. Tia watched the white-coated waiters moving among the guests on the wide lawn above the sea, the sun, already caught in the high branches of the trees, casting shadows in their midst. She closed her eyes for a moment. Then she knew what it reminded her of: her wedding ten years earlier. There was no music this time and Ivan was standing beside her and she had two children playing on the grass, but it felt like the same day.

"I met Rainer Haffner," said Sloan. "Isn't that amazing?" He was delighted. "I didn't know your grandmother knew him."

"He was married to a cousin of hers."

"Tia, why didn't you ever mention it!"

She went into the bathroom and turned on the shower. The water felt good and cool running down her head, over her face and breasts.

"What are we going to do about Masha?" called Sloan.

"I don't know."

"What's happening to the house?"

"Don't know."

"Who's staying for dinner tonight?"

Not Rainer Haffner, she wanted to say. "I'm not sure."

She turned off the shower and dried herself slowly. Gran's towels were always big and white and thick. Gran believed in white sheets and towels, no monograms.

"Was that . . . ?" He paused.

"Yes?" She knew the question. She smiled pleasantly. "What?"

"The tall man who was standing with you this afternoon." Sloan stood in the doorway, his face flushed.

"Hmmm?" She looked at him innocently.

"Was he—you know?"

"Ivan MacLeod," she said, the words clearly enunciated.

Sloan winced. "Oh."

"Don't be silly, Sloan," she said blandly. "He's known us all his life. He used to come to Easter Cove before I was born."

"God damn it, Tia, you can stop playing games with me. I want him out of here."

"That's impossible," she snapped.

"You heard me."

He was going to make a stand. Why had she not been more careful?

"Sloan," she said, trying to put her arms around him. "Please don't."

He stood rigidly. "How long is he staying?"

"You saw how Myra is running the show. I don't know." She kissed his cheek and went to her closet to find something to wear.

"You wearing that?"

"Why?"

He looked at her coldly. "A bit young for you, don't you think?"

"Maybe," she said. She took out another. "This pass?"

"I don't care," he said and left the room.

Rainer Haffner did stay for dinner. Valery and Claudia, Laura Landsdale and Jenny, Elizavetta and Ivan, Robin and an old summer beau, Grayson and a young woman, Sloan, Tia, and Myra sat on the porch, watching the waiters pick up glasses and napkins on the lawn below. It was almost dark and the air was damp with dew and fog.

"What do you think of Grayson's newest? This one must be Daisy's age," whispered Robin.

Grayson was holding the young girl's hand while he talked to Sloan. Ivan sat on the porch rail with Valery, who seemed subdued at last. Elizavetta and Myra were discussing the service. Tia sat and watched them. A year ago on an August night, Gran would have been at their center.

Sloan had brought her a vial of Valium, and she rolled a small yellow pill in her fingers, wondering if she should take it. She wanted to be calm, to sleep. Instead, as the evening passed, she started feeling raw. It had been too familiar, eating in the dining room, hearing Elizavetta's accented voice, Ivan's laughter, Jenny's prickly observations, Valery's sarcasm. They were all here too long, marking Gran's death with too much confusion.

"Tia, what are you going to do with the house?" asked Claudia. There was an embarrassed silence.

"I don't know. Robin and I will have to think about it," said Tia quickly.

"It must cost a fortune to run," said Sloan. Heads turned. "In this day and age," he said. He looked up, his face flushed, his eyes unfocused. "It's too bad. My grandmother's house in Ipswich was like this, and none of us could afford to keep it up." He was slurring his words.

"I've never seen Sloan drunk before," whispered Jenny.

"You're right," said Ivan. "These houses are wonderful but anachronistic."

"Anachronistic?" Sloan grinned, his head dipping and swaying. He said the word slowly, tripping over the consonants.

"Yes," said Valery, his voice smooth with geniality. "Helena said it was hopelessly inefficient."

"Oh, but it's so wonderful," said Laura Landsdale.

"Helena made it wonderful," said Valery.

"I hadn't seen it for years, and nothing has changed," said Rainer Haffner.

"This family is very complete," said Sloan. Then he laughed.

"Sloan, darling," said Laura Landsdale, "take me upstairs and let me peep at those lovely children at yours."

Sloan frowned, but Laura put her arms around his neck and kissed his cheek. "I adore that little boy of yours—the image of Tia as a girl. And Daisy, what a beauty!" She led him out of the dining room.

"Good old mother," said Jenny. "She'll get him to sleep it off. She was always brilliant with my father."

Tia walked into the shadows of the porch, looking for Ivan. She heard his voice and walked toward it. He was sitting on a wicker couch, talking to Grayson.

"Tia? Come join us," he said.

She sat beside him, feeling the warmth of his body and listening to the low rumble of his voice. He put his arm lightly around her shoulder and pulled her closer. After a while she put her head back against his shoulder and closed her eyes. She drifted in and out of sleep, hearing his voice, trying to find her way back from a dream, sometimes sitting up suddenly and then feeling his arm tighten around her until she slumped back against him.

"Tia, Tia." Myra's voice penetrated her sleep.

Myra was bending over her.

"Myra thinks we better wake you, kitten," said Ivan. He was still sitting beside her, with his arm around her. "I think she's afraid to leave us in this compromising position."

"Laura got Sloan to lie down, but it would be awkward if—"

"Yes, Myra, you're a good girl." Ivan laughed.

Tia sat up slowly. "What time is it?"

"Two o'clock."

"I'm sorry, you must be paralyzed," she said, touching Ivan's arm.

He bent over and kissed her cheek.

Myra stood back, waiting for them. Tia got up stiffly and stretched. Ivan pulled himself up and stood beside her. She didn't want to move away from him. He put his arm around both women and walked them down the porch.

"Good night, fair ladies," he said, when they reached the hall.

"I'm going to stay down here and talk to Ivan for a while," said Tia firmly.

Myra looked doubtful. She hesitated on the steps.

"Go on, we'll behave," said Ivan.

"It's not that," said Myra. "It's that this is a difficult time for Tia. She's vulnerable. . . ."

"I can take care of myself, Myra."

"I know." She kissed Tia on both cheeks.

The moon was almost full and the night was clear. They walked down to the beach and sat on the rocks, listening to the surf.

"I'm always surprised to see the stars at night here. In Washington you can't see them at all."

"Can you see more clearly here? Tonight?"

"Yes."

"And?"

She hugged herself tightly and shook her head.

"Tia, don't always look away," said Ivan, his voice suddenly angry. "Why didn't you come to London? Why?"

"I was waiting for you to come rescue me," she said.

"I'm not very good at lifesaving, am I?" He put his arms around her.

"I miss Gran so much. First you and then Gran. I feel like Valery—stranded, without a bridge."

"But I'm here, Tia, right in front of you."

"And?"

"Do you want me to ask you now?"

"No."

———

"You slept with him, didn't you?" Sloan was shaking her, his face inches from hers. She sat up in bed and pushed him away. "Don't you push me away, young lady!"

"The children," she said warningly.

"They're downstairs. They've been up for hours." He paced the room.

Tia walked over to the window. The children were playing on the lawn with Robin. Jenny and Ivan were sprawled nearby.

"Every time you came up here," Sloan was saying, his voice rising with each word. "You goddamned hypocrite!"

"Oh, for God's sake, Sloan," she snapped, "don't be such an ass."

"Don't call me an ass." He leaped for her, grabbing her wrists.

"Leave me alone!" she roared. He stepped back.

"Quiet," he said. "Everyone will hear you."

"Just leave me alone!" she said, as loud.

He hovered near her, his own frustration and rage barely controlled.

"You're upset," said Sloan suddenly. "Of course, Gran's death—though we knew it was coming—is a great loss for you. But it might also be a release, a liberation."

"I can't stand the sound of your voice."

"Oh, but you love his voice, don't you? That phony accent, that well-trained basso profundo."

"Get out of here."

"Don't tempt me."

"Get out," she said.

"I've had it with you." He swung at her. She stepped back.

"Getting to be a habit with you," she said.

"You bitch," he said, advancing again.

In the sunlight below, the children chased each other around the Adirondack chairs. Robin knelt in back of Ivan with her arms around his neck. Jenny was talking and they were laughing as she gestured.

"This is so ugly," said Tia.

Sloan stopped. He looked out at the lawn.

"That's your little club out there, cheering you on," he said.

"Is it?" she asked, surprised.

"Oh, you'll never walk alone," he said. "I used to think it was just Gran. There you were—alone in the world. What a fool I was—or, as you so kindly put it, an ass."

Sloan decided to leave that afternoon. To be safe, he told her in front of everyone.

"I told Laura I'd drive her down to Boston," he said. "I'll turn in the car there and take the shuttle to Washington."

"The children can stay here with me," said Tia.

"Yes, that's what I thought."

"I've got to get on too," said Ivan.

Tia sat tensely while they made their plans. Valery and Claudia would go to Pine Island with Paul for the rest of the month. Masha and Myra would stay at Easter Cove with Tia. Robin and Jenny would stay a couple of days too.

"Don't worry, darling," said Laura as she left. "Sloan is just a spoiled little boy who doesn't like to be out of the limelight."

"Mother should know," murmured Jenny.

"Goodbye," said Sloan formally. "I'll call you tonight."

Ivan was putting bags in his car. Elizavetta was hugging Valery. Masha stood in the doorway, her face submerged in a big white hankerchief.

"Drive carefully," said Tia. She picked up Peter. "Say goodbye to Daddy," she called out to the children.

Sloan turned away from her and got in the car.

"Let's go, darling," said Laura, putting her hand on his knee.

He looked up quickly. Tia saw the look on his face.

"Don't fight it, it'll solve all your problems," said Jenny, as Sloan drove away.

"Really?" Tia watched the car go around the curve of the drive. She started to laugh.

Ivan walked over to Tia. He took her hand. "I'll be back in about three weeks."

She watched him go down the path between the hedges and waited until she heard his car start.

That night Tia lay in bed and thought about Sloan making love to Laura in a Boston hotel room. She treasured the stabs of jealousy. She tried to imagine them together, envision their bodies entwined, Sloan's face as he bent over Laura. But even the most painfully blissful scenario she conjured was interrupted by thoughts of Ivan. It was Ivan she wanted next to her now.

She got up and turned on the light. Three o'clock in the morning. The hour that Gran could not sleep through. The hour of her death.

She went quietly down the corridor to Gran's room. The windows were closed and the room was stuffy but it smelled of Gran: her perfume, the bowls of spicy potpourri, the beeswax and rug shampoo. The bed was made up neatly. The dressing table had been cleared and all her brushes and bottles were in a small cardboard box. On the bed table were some books, a letter from Robin that had not been opened, a list made out in a shaky hand. Tia bent down and tried to read it. It was a grocery order and a reminder to send Daisy a birthday check.

She opened the closet. There were the rows of long dresses and, on the shelf above them, hatboxes. Tia pulled some down. The hats brought back memories of Gran, much younger, standing in the sun with the shadow of a brim across her face. The last box was full of letters. Most of them were from Tia. Early letters written on lined paper, followed by horseheads and dog profiles, blue notepaper from college, the large *Roundabout* letterhead. There were boxes of shell pictures, potholders, unglazed clay animals, glazed clay figures, files of school reports, notebooks cataloging vaccinations and illness, charts of shoe sizes, records of height and weight. She groped among the dusty, brittle papers and the files at the back of the closet. There were old leases, records of paintings and jewelry sales, and a box of photographs.

Tia opened them and sorted slowly through them. They were the faces of strangers, sitting in strange places: women in long dresses, men in high collars. In one Tia recognized a small child with large dark eyes as Gran. She stood between two young men in uniform and stared solemnly at the lens.

As Tia put back the photos she saw a pack of letters, held together with a narrow, faded ribbon. She recognized Valery's hand. They were addressed to Gran, Paris postmarked. Tia looked at the top envelope a long time and then pushed them back under the photographs.

"Can't sleep?" Robin walked into the room. "Hard to believe, isn't it?"

"I didn't expect to feel so devastated."

Robin walked over to the window seat. "Once she made me sit here all afternoon because I had come into her room without knocking," she said.

"She was hard on you."

"And you too, in a different way."

"Sloan said I'd feel released."

"From him?"

"Sometimes I wish."

"Well, then?"

"I just can't."

"I know you, Tia. You'll arrange it so he thinks he's doing the leaving. There you'll be, shining with goodness and innocence. 'Poor little Tia.' And not even Sloan will realize you left him years ago—if you were ever there at all, which I doubt."

"Is that the way I operate?"

"Sure. Guess why it was always me that got blamed for all the schemes you cooked up? Remember the time you got us out on the roof and Jenny almost broke her leg rappeling down the side of the house?"

"I told Gran it was my idea."

"Tia, it was the way you said it. I always figured Ivan was good for you because he didn't let you do all that stuff with him." Robin opened Gran's candy box. "Look, it's still full." She popped a chocolate in her mouth. "Remember how Gran would watch everything we ate? She'd read me the riot act every summer when I'd arrive looking like a little porker." Robin's mouth was full of candy. "One damn chocolate a week." She took another. "Have one. They're delicious."

They sat on the window seat eating chocolates until dawn.

At the end of the week, Tia left the children with Myra and went back to Washington. Jake had called several times and, after one sympathetic statement, had started complaining about her last reviews. She'd better get back for a couple of days at least. Two big new restaurants had opened and of course he could send that new copy editor out but— Weary of the sad chores at Easter Cove, Tia seized the excuse to leave for a few days.

"I'm glad you're back," said Sloan at the airport. "I'm glad the kids are in Maine. We've got lots to straighten out."

"Yes," she said, looking over at him, assessing how much guilt he might feel and how much he was assigning to her.

He glanced at her and then back at the road. He looked tense. His face was red and shiny with heat.

"You look tanned," she said.

"Joe and Liz and I went down to Rehoboth to see the Hunters last weekend."

"Good."

"Diana got smashed and Liz ended up cooking dinner for twenty people."

"Wasn't Liz smashed last weekend?"

"Cut it out, Tia. You know she's got her drinking under control."

"I hadn't noticed."

He clamped his mouth tight and drove faster.

They drove down the parkway, across Memorial Bridge, around Abraham Lincoln, high up in his memorial, and into Georgetown. He pulled up outside the 31st Street house.

"Come in and take another look," he said.

She followed him in. The front hall was not quite as big as she remembered it but the chandelier was brighter and hung lower. He led the way into the big living room. They stood, looking around the long bare room. Pacing up and down, Sloan told her that their house had been sold. The buyers wanted to do some work on it and wondered if, since the Ensears already had bought another house, they could move out in six weeks.

"I rented that little house on Merriweather Street," said Tia suddenly, interrupting him.

"What?" He wheeled around. "When?"

"Recently."

"My God!" He clutched his head. "Did Laura . . . ?"

She stood very still. Robin was right.

"My God, are you that damn perfect? That phony professor and that sleazy Jake . . . "

"You're way off, Sloan. I'm really pure as the driven snow."

"You know, whatever you say about Liz Sykes, she's there for her husband."

Sloan walked up and down the room, his voice echoing between the bare walls, saying what he had said so often before. He is really disappointed, thought Tia. Victoria Valenkova of Summerlea turned out to be a spoilsport. What would he say, if Valery was right, when he found that Gran had not left her much money? The disenchantment would be terminal. It would be his Althea luck, the curse of the poor Ensear.

He stopped in front of her. He was getting weary. His eyes were bloodshot, the lids puffy. Tia could see his anguish but feel nothing. She watched him, his tortured gestures, his disillusion, his anger at his prizes, so close, so nearly grasped, spun away from him again on the whim of someone he had put his faith in.

"You don't give a damn, do you?" he said, spent.

It hadn't been said. During the silent ride home, the door-slamming evening, the night in separate bedrooms, not a word had been spoken. When Tia woke in the morning, her head aching, her body stiff, Sloan was gone. She stood in the doorway of his study, wondering what secrets it concealed. In all the years she had been married to Sloan, she had never really wondered about him.

She went downstairs and made herself some coffee and took it out to the porch. The day was hot, with a milky sky and no wind. She sat back in the big wicker armchair that Gran had given her when they bought the house. It was from the porch at Easter Cove. The dark, shellacked wicker and faded floral pillow were incongruous on the narrow, white screened porch overlooking the small, patchy garden.

Perhaps she should go up to Sloan's study and open all the drawers, study the appointment book, search his coat pockets, go over their credit-card bills. She could call the institute and see if he was really leading a seminar on Tuesday nights. Following the clues, she could decipher his covert life.

As she sat drinking the hot coffee in the heat of the August morning, she felt uneasy. Having grown up with half-told tales, she still felt confounded by obscurity. "Why do you have to have all the answers?" Robin would say irritably when Tia pursued the verity in a carelessly told anecdote. "Use your imagination."

That, probably, was the trouble. They did not understand

how far her imagination traveled. Better to take another's framework, better to stay in their enclosures.   ·

"Well, Mrs. Ensear, how is your trouble?" Mr. Berger sounded merry.

"You were right."

"Come and have coffee with me."

She took a cab out to the house, watching eagerly for it as they drove down the wide suburban street. Mr. Berger was trimming back the roses that had grown wildly over his fence.

"For someone in trouble, you look well," he said, as they went inside.

"It's so nice and cool," said Tia.

"My wife insisted on the air conditioning," he said apologetically. "It was Mrs. Pierce's favorite selling point."

They sat in Mr. Berger's library. He pushed aside a stack of books and cleared a chair for Tia.

"You haven't changed your mind?"

"No," she said, starting to laugh. He joined her.

"So, now, will you come and help me pack?"

"I'd love to."

They ate lunch in the kitchen at the white enamel table with a black chip on one corner. There was a big bowl of pink roses in the middle. "Every morning, Louisa would pick some roses for this bowl," he said. "They only last a day, these rambling roses."

While Mr. Berger talked, Tia surveyed the lines of Mexican tiles: red flowers, alternating with plain yellow tiles. She would like sitting here in the afternoon with the winter sun slanting through the two long windows overlooking the garden. She would finish the table she had started making out of some cherry planks Jake had given her. It was lying, half finished, in her basement.

Sloan was not at home when she returned. There were several messages for him with the answering service, as well as a call from Mrs. Pierce.

"You need to sign the sale agreement, Mrs. Ensear," she said, "and the Potters want to know when they can settle on the house."

"I'll let you know tomorrow."

She called Masha, who had gone to live with Laura Landsdale in New York. It was a trial arrangement, approached with enthusiasm by Laura and trepidation by Masha. Though Masha complained about having too little to do, she did not ask to come to Washington. Laura had, apparently, convinced her that she was too old for a household with children.

"It's okay," said Masha, using the one colloquialism she had learned in more than thirty-five years of living in New York.

Relieved, Tia made arrangements with Jenny to try a new restaurant on Jake's list.

While Tia changed she called Easter Cove. Valery had been right, Myra told Tia: Gran's estate would not be large, though there were jewelry, paintings, and furniture that had not been assessed yet. There had been several inquiries about the house. Gran's will, said Myra, left Tia the house and Robin the gardener's cottage. It would take a while, probably a year, before the will was probated. Meanwhile Myra had gathered as much jewelry as she could and put it in Gran's safe in the library. Tia pulled on her stockings as Myra cataloged the possessions that would have to be divided. She didn't want to listen.

"And Ivan?" Myra's question was sudden, coming right after a description of the Porthault linen she had found in an attic closet.

"What?"

"Gran left him Pine Island."

"What?"

"She asked me if I wanted it, about three months before she died. She changed her will about a month later. She knew Paul was going to teach in London, and Valery can't take the winters."

"But Ivan?"

"I was surprised."

Sloan was sitting in the kitchen, reading his mail. He looked up when Tia came in and then back down at his letters.

"You were lucky to miss Chez Henri," she said, sitting across from him.

"Mmmm," he mumbled, not looking up.

"I talked to the children tonight. Claudia and Valery took them sailing."

"Fine," he said absently.

She sat, waiting. What are we doing to do, Sloan? What are we going to do about the houses we have acquired? She wanted to ask but she did not really want to start their final argument.

"You mean, you and your husband haven't discussed this?" said Mr. Berger, waving his hand around the half-filled boxes.

"No," said Tia.

Mr. Berger packed for a while in silence.

"It's crazy to live like that."

Are you waiting for Ivan to come and spirit you away? Jenny had asked. What are you waiting for? said Mr. Berger. They were both irritated. Tia could feel their irritation mixing with her own.

"I seem paralyzed. Maybe because my grandmother . . . "
Because I'm an orphan, as she had once said to Jenny.

"For goodness' sake," said Mr. Berger. "You're a big girl. You can afford to make an alliance with someone. Someone besides old men who lecture you and school friends and children."

"Is it necessary?"

He stood up and looked over at her. "No, not necessary. But, I think for you, enriching."

She bent over and sealed the box she had packed, near tears. "Perhaps," she said finally.

"I have a feeling, Mrs. Ensear, that you surround yourself with people like me, don't you?"

She was tired of questions and answers, hearing herself described, analyzed, criticized. She walked over and looked out at the garden. At that moment nothing seemed magical anymore. The house was dusty and crowded with packing boxes, the garden small and dry in the August heat. The canvases she planned to paint in the study were not going to be very good. The articles she wrote for Jake were silly and often untruthful. She had married a man she did not love, without a great deal of thought. While she felt that her children were the core of her life, she was eager to leave them with Priscilla. Once she moved to Washington she had not thought of Gran often, not written or called her much, often resented her calls. Robin's life in Philadelphia was a mystery to her. Jenny worried her but also exasperated her. She found Sabrina boring.

"So, you're not a saint," said Mr. Berger, when, with her back to him, she confessed her sins. "But there's no harm in trying." He laughed.

"Tia," said Sloan, "this isn't going to work out." He had called her in as she passed his study. She sat on the chair his patients used. He leaned back in his own chair.

"But the children," she heard herself saying.

"I know, I know." He looked down at his hands.

"Are you talking about getting a divorce?"

He looked up at her. "I'm not sure. Perhaps."

"Oh," she said.

"It has nothing to do with Laura," he said reassuringly. He felt in control. Tia wasn't going to make it difficult. She was sitting in the right place. "Strangely, I love you still. It's just that—"

"You want someone to go to Klein's picnics with."

"Don't take that tone, Tia."

"Have you got it all planned?"

"I understand from—well, I gather that Gran hasn't left a great deal of money. But you'll have the house to sell, and her stuff should bring in quite a bit."

"That must have disappointed you," she said.

"Tia, don't. Let's not get ugly. Let's have a good divorce."

"Let's have a wonderful divorce," she said, getting out of the chair. She picked up his leather engagement book and threw it at him.

"Of course you can't move out of the house until Mr. Ensear has agreed to support payments," said Granger, the divorce lawyer. Jenny had recommended him.

"He's closed out our bank accounts," said Tia.

"His attorney told him to." Granger smirked. "Peter Rosenberg, a great guy." He smiled with large capped teeth, waiting for her to be surprised. "He won a dandy settlement from my client last month—I told him this time it's my turn." He chuckled.

"Sounds like fun," said Tia.

"No, no," said Granger. He sighed deeply and settled back into his big leather swivel chair. "No, I wish it was." He settled his solemn gray eyes on her for a moment. Over his shoulder a row of sons, daughters, and wife with planeless faces and deep red lips smiled from silver-framed photographs: Granger's fortune, never shared with the victims of accident and divorce who straggled woefully into his office.

"It's ridiculous for me to live in that house—we have two others, and the buyers are suing us."

"Dear, you'll thank me for this. The kids still in Maine?"

"Yes."

"If he abuses you physically or verbally, call me right away."

"You'll be the first to know."

"I know, sweetheart," he said, getting up and going around the desk to put his hand on her shoulder, "it's rough. But try to keep your perspective. You know, Jumbo Sydney says you're a pretty sweet little gal." Granger smiled down. "Oh, boy, I'm due in court," he said, looking at his watch and sweeping her to the door in one practiced motion.

Jumbo Sydney had taken over the management of Gran's estate from old Mr. Parker of Parker, Pennyman and Cooke. Mr. Parker had written Tia a scrambled note of sympathy after Gran died, assuring her that young Sydney was "top notch." Mr. Parker must have known or retained some faint, discomforting memory of how muddled he had allowed Gran's affairs to become. Of course, it was hardly his fault that Gran's own records were twenty or thirty years out of date, that money once counted on for bequests was no longer in the estate, that Valery was threatening to sue Myra over her share.

In his glass office in New York, Jumbo, as he preferred to be called, seemed quite adept at straightening out some of Mr. Parker's oversights. There were taxes that had not been paid on the sale of the New York apartment, taxes that had not been paid on stock sales, a packet of missing stock certificates, a question of whether the last will had been properly signed.

"How much money will there be for me?" Tia asked. "I need to know," she added hastily, "because I'm getting divorced."

"Yeah, I've talked to Granger. Don't worry, Vicki, your husband won't be able to lay a hand on your money."

"I'm sure he has no intention of doing that."

"Don't bet on it, honey. We'll probably delay probate. Don't worry, Granger and I will work together on it."

"It's really a question of me knowing what my prospects are— about what I can plan for. . . ."

"Look, didn't Granger tell me your husband has a girlfriend? And you have very young kids. So keep your nose clean and you'll have no problems."

Many of the items in Gran's will could not be found. She had left several pieces of jewelry to Myra that no one could remember, a choker to Claudia that Myra felt had already been given to her, paintings to Valery that were "currently in storage," but there was no record of where. Tia and Robin flew up to Easter Cove with a list that Gran had attached to her will. They searched for tables, looking glasses, silver, china. The IRS, warned lawyer Sydney, would not understand their absence.

"I remember that table," said Robin. "Do you think she sold some of these things?"

"I don't know," said Tia, tired and depressed.

They sat on the porch rail and watched the children doing cartwheels.

"I'm having awful thoughts," said Robin.

"That they were taken?"

"You know how crazy Valery had gotten. None of us really knows Claudia. And, God knows, Myra has had free run of the place."

"It's not worth it, then," said Tia.

"Shit, Ti, that stuff is worth lots. We don't want to pay taxes on it."

"Gran was always so well organized."

"Exactly," said Robin. "God, after living with Grayson and his obsession to make his house perfect, and Gran with all her treasures, I thought I'd like to be free of all that. But I'm just as greedy and jealous of possessions as they were."

"You'll overcome it," said Tia.

"Jesus, you're getting to be a goddam nun," said Robin. "Let's hope Ivan arrives on the scene and rescues you from your order."

Back in Washington, with the children still with Myra in Easter Cove, Tia packed. Priscilla helped morosely, slowly filling cartons. "Sure is a pity," she'd say, holding up a doll or a truck before letting it fall into a box. But she brought Tia dinner on a tray before she left and hovered nearby, waiting for her to eat it. "I hate to leave you alone," she'd say, putting on her hat and standing by the front door. "House seems so quiet," she'd say, looking past Tia at the empty rooms.

The moment the door closed behind Priscilla, Tia would feel a lurch of fear, tension would grip her bowels, and then she'd go upstairs to the third floor where her small studio was still intact and go to work. Hours later she would come downstairs and pour a glass of wine and go out onto the screened porch and smoke a cigarette and listen to the cicadas and the muted sounds of traffic and neighbors. The house behind her would be dark, quiet, locked up for the night. The smoke from her cigarette would twirl slowly above her head in the light of her neighbor's gas lamp. The sky above the locusts and the cherry trees was always lit by the city below it, sometimes dense and rosy, sometimes opaque and navy.

She'd pack for a couple of hours, and then there would be a long bath and an hour of reading in bed before she fell asleep. It was all so perfectly quiet and comfortable. She sometimes wanted to hear music but hated to break the silence. It was a wonderful intermission, oddly peaceful and productive, those August nights. On weekends she would get up early and take a long walk down to the park and back up the hill. Then, with a thermos of coffee, she'd climb up to her studio and lose any sense of the passage of time. When it grew dark she'd clean her brushes, tidy the studio, stand for a time and look at what she'd done.

Downstairs she would fix dinner, still moving slowly, among the packing boxes. Often the roar of the phone would jolt her, and she would find her tongue and voice thick from disuse. "No, I wasn't asleep," she would explain.

Ivan called from England. He had been offered a job at a small Virginia college where he would have only one course to teach and could finish his book and think about the next. They'd written him about a stone house on a hill near the college with a fine view of the Blue Ridge and the Shenandoah.

"And Pine Island! Isn't that extraordinary? If I go on teaching we'll have three months a year there."

"Yes," said Tia.

"Would that be hard, kitten? Pine Island and Easter Cove? Would you like to cut all those ties?"

"Oh, no."

She listened intently to his voice.

"Is the divorce going to take long?"

"It could take a year." A year on Merriweather Street, with Mr. Berger's books and Louisa Berger's roses.

After she hung up she sat down and waited for a sense of excitement, elation.

"What's the matter?" asked Priscilla, walking by with an armful of towels. "You okay?"

"Yeah, just tired." She got up and helped Priscilla with the towels.

In September the children came back, and it was clear that the quiet time of August and early September had been just an intermission.

"People turn into monsters when they're dividing up their property," said Jenny, who had had to give quite a bit of hers to Wayne. She often came to dinner and sat out on the porch with Tia, when the children were finally in bed, trying to decide what to do with her life. "Laura thinks I should be her dresser. Can you imagine—waiting on my mother in all those rancid dressing rooms?" The tour was to start in October, and Jenny was increasingly unhappy about her promise to join it. "As Sabrina says, Mother thinks she's helping me. Being motherly comes so hard for her, I hate to set her back." She sighed. "You're so lucky, Ti."

Daisy cried out often in the night and Peter clung to her when she left him at school. Sloan was usually late picking them up on weekends and they would sit on the back of the couch, watching the street for his car. They both seemed to get sick every week, and Tia found herself writing articles at midnight, alert for a feverish voice calling her, feeling increasingly weary and incompetent.

She forced herself to go up to her studio every morning after the children left for school. Often she would stand in front of her canvas, absorbed in a reverie so profound and so dissociated from anything around her that when the spell broke she could not remember what had so abstracted her. Once, when she saw herself unexpectedly in the mirror above the sink, it was like catching a glimpse of someone's private, hidden face. It made her turn away quickly.

There were days when she froze with terror, listening to her heart pounding, faster and louder at every beat, and she seemed to be succumbing to disease and death. She'd wake up in the quiet darkness of the house, gasping for breath. Her dreams were often grotesque, twisted and vivid. The panic would strike suddenly, in the middle of a conversation with Jake, shopping at the supermarket, at the dentist's, waiting for Daisy's teacher for a conference, driving home. She'd wonder that no one seemed to see it on her face, the inward alteration was so enormous, but Jake would go on talking, the dentist would go on drilling, Daisy's teacher would not pause, no one averted his eyes from the stricken beast. Even the house offered no refuge.

At night she took out Gran's spaniel, Nelly, and they would trot up the block, around the corner, in the late-night emptiness of her Washington street. Sometimes a police patrol would slow down and drive alongside. "Be careful," called an officer once, into the still, hot night. Nelly was old and they couldn't go far.

When Sloan came to the house to pick up the children he would stand in the hall, arms folded in front of him, face set grimly, while the children got their bags. Every day the lawyers were calling each other and making impossible demands.

"When are you moving?" Sloan asked one evening while Daisy ran back upstairs for a toy. His voice was studiously toneless.

"I'm not sure," said Tia.

"Don't let your lawyer destroy every vestige of our relationship," said Sloan, his voice suddenly pleasant. "We can decide some of these things between us."

"I think it would be easier to let the lawyers do it," said Tia.

"I hope you don't delay the divorce," he said. His voice was harder again, cold. He wanted to get on with it. She could feel his impatience. All the Ensear—and now Valenkova—roadblocks. The perishable Liz waited in her Ferrari. He had prospects again.

Ivan moved into the stone house overlooking the Blue Ridge. Tia ignored Granger's orders and drove down to see him for a weekend in October. It was a hazy, warm Saturday morning with leaves blowing across the parkway. She turned on the radio and listened to Haydn as she headed west into the blue hills of Virginia. Rolling down the window, letting in the autumn air with its mellow dampness and smoke, she felt herself relax.

"Well!" Ivan laughed as she flung her arms around him. Their telephone conversations had been strained, and he was surprised. The house was small and sturdy, with a terrace in back that faced yellow, hilly fields and, far away, the long even line of the Blue Ridge. Lying in the sun, drinking the warm champagne she had brought, they talked about the time that had separated them. Here, Ivan was the star of the faculty, the distinguished archaeologist and former Harvard professor, and he was clearly enjoying his role.

"I like it here," he said. "I have plenty of time to finish my book, and they seem eager for me to take any term off I want so I can go work with Wilson or go to Crete. Amazing."

Tia lay back, shielding her eyes from the sun, high overhead, and watched him bound from his chair to refill her glass, watched his face with its deep lines around the eyes, the wide mouth, the hair growing silvery, listened to the deep rumble of his voice. He was talking about his students and she felt herself drifting to sleep, tranquil with champagne and sun.

When she woke she was covered with a blanket and the sun had gone to the other side of the house, casting deep shadows across the terrace and lawn. For a long time she did not move, listening to the birds and the wind in the trees and the faint sound of a Brandenburg Concerto, breathing the cooling air.

That night, lying against Ivan in his narrow bed, she told him about the lawyers, the houses, and the lawsuits and finally about the terrors.

"Death, divorce, and old love renewed," he said softly. "It has been quite a summer."

It was peaceful in the circle of his shoulder, in the quiet of the soft southern night.

In the morning Ivan brought coffee upstairs. He sat on the edge of the bed and watched her as she drank it.

"When are we going to get married?"

"Married?"

"Victoria MacLeod," said Ivan, laughing.

She remembered that long ago she had had a fantasy that they would run away to Connecticut and get married and she would be Tia MacLeod. It was a name she had practiced in the margins of her schoolbooks.

"We can get married down here," he said.

"Here?" She was sleepy still and strained to think clearly.

"I'd like to have another child," he said, smoothing back her hair. "Wouldn't it be wonderful to have our own baby! I've missed so many years with Alexey."

"Yes," she said vaguely. Once she had wistfully wanted his child, even wished that Daisy had been Ivan's daughter. When she had seen them together that first time, so strangely alike, she had realized how often she had wished it.

"It would be wonderful," he said, springing up and pacing the room, his face lit with enthusiasm. "Wouldn't it be wonderful to have our child?" he exclaimed.

Now she no longer wanted it.

"Do we have to move?" cried Daisy, throwing herself on the floor. Peter hugged his teddy bear and sucked his thumb. Priscilla waited in the front hall, carrying her large handbag.

"Come on, Daisy, we're going to be late," she said.

The movers were due. Priscilla was taking the children to Georgetown for the day.

"No, I won't go. I hate you!" shrieked Daisy. "I hate you!"

"I'll go, Mommy," said Peter, rushing over to Tia. "I'll go with you."

"We're all going together." She hugged Peter and then bent over Daisy, who was thrashing around on the floor. "Look, I know it's tough. But that's too damned bad for all of us. Now get up and get going."

Daisy looked up, surprised, her face streaked and red. "I hate you," she said fiercely.

"Okay, let's go," said Priscilla.

"She's being a baby, right, Mommy?" Peter had an arm around Tia's legs.

"I am not, poo head," said Daisy, jumping up and lunging for him.

"That's enough," said Tia, grabbing Daisy. She forced a hug on the child's rigid little body and kissed her wet cheek. "I love you."

Daisy looked grim but she stalked over to Priscilla. The three of them walked down the steps and started down the street. Peter and Priscilla turned back and waved but Daisy marched forward, arms rigid at her side.

The excitement of the new house and their new rooms carried the first few days. Priscilla brought Daisy a kitten, and one of her sons came and helped Tia put up a swing in the back garden. There were lots of children in the neighborhood, and they gathered around the house to check out the new occupants. Peter soon had a friend who brought his trucks over and played for hours in the garden. Lauren came to stay with Daisy the first weekend.

"Sheila lives two blocks away!" Daisy announced. "Now Lauren is afraid me and her are going to be friends."

"What about the Detective Club?"

"I think we should have Sheila too." She thought. "Maybe we could have some extra people in it."

"I told you you'd like your new house," said Priscilla.

"I don't. I want to move back to our old house," said Daisy, hands on hips. "Daddy's house is much bigger."

"I like this one," said Tia.

"It's okay," said Daisy.

"Did you know that Liz and I separated too?" asked Joe Sykes. He had come to the door with a bouquet of flowers and a bottle of wine. "God, is this where you're living?" he said, looking at the front of the Merriweather Street house. "It's charming, of course," he said as they walked in.

Daisy was putting away silver in the kitchen while Peter sat on the floor, making ramps for his trucks from the packing boxes.

"Joe, if I'd known you were coming. . . ." She shrugged. There were lots of evening visits these days from men like Joe Sykes.

"Mommy," said Daisy, displeased to see another visitor on an evening they had planned to go out for ice cream, "will we be staying in now?"

"No," said Tia. "Joe, why don't you join us for ice cream?"

Joe seemed delighted. He drove them up the street, down Connecticut Avenue, past the row of small shops to the drugstore that Tia pointed out.

"Oh, no, I'm going to take everyone to the Café Glacé."

Daisy nudged Tia. "Thanks, Joe, but this is the children's favorite place."

He was disappointed, following them into the crowded soda fountain sullenly. He sat, sipping coffee and eating stale pie while Daisy and Peter slowly finished their sundaes.

When they returned to the house, Tia gave the children baths and put them to bed, knowing that no matter how she procrastinated, she would find Joe downstairs. She did. He was sitting in a big wing chair from Easter Cove, drinking a glass of Scotch.

"How long have those two been screwing is what I want to know?" he said, his tongue already thick.

"Who cares?" said Tia.

"You should. You know when your mother—or was it your grandmother?—was dying, that bastard would spend every waking minute with us. I thought he was helping Liz shape up."

"She seems better, Joe."

"Oh, yeah, Liz is always wonderful in the service of love. Give her a few months with Sloan and she'll be bored enough to start boozing and screwing around again."

Tia took up some knitting she had started months before. She would hear him out, as she was hearing all the other people who came to her door with their tales of woe. They would look around at her small house, standing at her studio door and comment on the nice view of the garden, mourn briefly over the children, and, feeling they had seen pathos, reveal their own.

———

Her friends had warned her not to expect too much from Merriweather Street, but even as she was moving in, putting away her books, hanging her paintings, finding space for dishes and pans, she knew this would be what Valery called "exactly right."

She'd spent several days with Robin in New York, going through the storage bins, finding chairs and tables and lamps she wanted. Though Robin had argued that Tia should sell the rest, that she could ill afford the storage bills, they both decided to keep everything.

"One of these days, maybe," said Robin, not entirely ready to change her mind.

Now, on Merriweather Street, the few pieces Tia had brought from New York took on new life. She hung Gran's small Russian scenes, Valery's late large oils, her own paintings of the Easter Cove gardens. Tables, chairs, lamps, chests, liberated from the dark, crowded vaults of Gran's New York apartment, looked suddenly smaller and simpler. The furniture from Tia's bedroom went into Daisy's room, and Myra sent Peter Valenkov's old toy soldiers and big painted chest to Peter from Easter Cove.

Tia immersed herself in the house, often wandering around it, rearranging and assessing the day's work, until midnight. Its siren song diverted her every morning, luring her off the straight path from kitchen to studio, calling her back for another look, another alteration. She would stop work, brush in hand, and think that perhaps Gran's Kaluga paintings would look better in the dining room where there was less furniture. Or that she could build shelves in the children's rooms and perhaps window seats too. The demands of her canvases seemed a harsh intrusion— and the work was progressing at such a slow and uninspired pace. Often she would rub out an entire week's work with a few drops of turpentine, painting and repainting the same small patch of tortured canvas.

There seemed to be so little time. All the tasks she had once accomplished quickly, as she hurried to the office or returned home, seemed awesome and taxing, commanding her entire attention for their commission. Now she felt she must spend as much time with the children as possible, and yet her attention did not focus easily or for very long and the children were learning to pull at her and call out for it. By late evening, after Daisy's protracted bedtime and Peter's last glass of water and trip to the bathroom, Tia would fall into a chair and read for a few minutes before dozing off. Usually she would wake up at midnight and go to her bedroom and lie sleepless until dawn.

"I should" were her watchwords that autumn. "I should be better to the children," "I should call Jenny," "I should shop for Daisy's new shoes," "I should finish one painting before I even think about another," "I should get a checkup," "I should be getting more exercise," "I should be earning money," "I should talk more to Ivan," and so it went, with few of the "shoulds" imperative enough to force action. There were more of them on the list each day.

"Yes, ma'am," said Priscilla one day, eyeing her coldly.

"I'm sorry," said Tia quickly. "I know I've been awfully irritable," she added, wanting to make a more elaborate defense.

"Mmmm," muttered Priscilla, bending over the sink.

Swept by a sense of the familiar, Tia remembered her mother facing Polly's broad back in the small Washington Square kitchen, apologizing.

"Priscilla, please forgive me," said Tia.

"You're in that study, shut up all day, too much, if you ask me," said Priscilla crossly.

"Perhaps."

"You ought to get out more," said Priscilla, warming. "Have some fun."

"Fun?"

"Goodness, girl," she said in exasperation, "it's no sin."

Tia called Ivan. His voice was tense. Tia remembered listening to him through the thin walls in Brittany when he talked to Kathryn: edgy, impatient.

"When am I going to see you? I thought you said the separation papers were going to be signed yesterday?"

"I'm sorry," she said.

"Tia, what is it?"

"Can we meet at White's Ferry?" It was halfway between them.

"Sure. In two hours?" He sounded puzzled.

Don't be mad, she started to say, but stopped herself.

The day seemed overabundantly clear and soft, discordantly fair for someone who felt so meager and gray. Tia arrived early and sat at a picnic table by the ferry landing. She felt like an old lady on a park bench, the sun warm on her stiff body, eyes closed, her bag on her lap. One day, she thought, I will be here in an old tweed coat, a hat with a feather in it, elastic stockings, sitting by the river in the sun.

"Sleeping Beauty," said Ivan, bending to kiss her cheek. "I'm sorry I'm late," he said, helping her up.

They walked in the woods along the river, shuffling through copper leaves, away from the picnickers. Ivan took Tia's arm and she leaned against him, feeling faint. He led her to the bank and helped her sit down on the rocks. Looking down at her feet, she wondered if her shoes would fall into the river.

"Tia, what is it?"

He had his arm around her shoulder and his face was so close to hers that she turned away.

"Ivan, I feel so drained," she said slowly. There was a long silence. She looked at him. He had pulled away. His face was stiff.

"I know," he said.

"I can't feel anything."

"For me?"

"Feel anything at all."

"Or sometimes too much?"

"Yes."

Ivan took a pack of cigarettes from his shirt pocket. "I know I've been pushing you," he said, looking at her over the hands he had folded over his match. He puffed at the cigarette until the end glowed red. "I didn't want us to drift apart again." He blew out smoke quickly. "You see, Wilson has been after me to come to London and give some lectures with him at the university."

"You're going to London again?"

"The thing is, Tia, I love Virginia, but it's not enough and they're willing to give me—"

"Are you going to London?"

He sighed and looked across the river. "Yes, Tia. I think so."

"Damn you," she said, "you never give me any time."

"It's not that."

"You just go off! You just leave."

"But I don't leave you." He took both her hands in his, but she pushed him away. "I want you to come with me. Marry me. Be part of the planning."

"Your planning, your damn planning. Not my planning." She stood up and looked down at him. "We can never settle down together. You always go off, or change, or leave. What am I going to do every time? Leave school, leave children, leave work, leave every damn thing, and live like a gypsy?"

"Tia, I'm never going to live in one place forever."

"Then what do you want from me?"

"I want you to be with me, but I'm not going to throw you over my saddle every time I have to go off."

"I can't go to London—uproot the children, go off with you when nothing is really settled." They were walking now, close to the river. "I don't want to have death, divorce, remarriage all running together."

She did not want to tell him how very much she wanted to be in her house, alone, how reluctant she was to allow anyone inside it, to interrupt her, to need her, even to love her. And how little her feelings for him surfaced now, even as she looked over at him and saw dark shadows under solemn eyes, shoulders slumped wearily. Other images crowded her vision: Ivan drunk in New York, pulling at her, retreating from her into a dark entryway; Ivan driving too fast, cursing Kathryn; Ivan disappearing into the plane the day he left for London, almost forgetting to wave to her as she stood with her nose pressed to the glass.

Now, in this autumn sun, he looked wan and unsure.

"You know, Tia, perhaps last time you were ready and I wasn't. Then it was me that was feeling rotten and resentful. Later, when I thought about that time we had in Cambridge and on the Cape, it would have been—if there had been no Kathryn—the most natural progression for us to marry then. For you to come to England with me. If I'd waited until the end of your term, you would have, don't you think?" He paused and looked across the river and sighed. "Of course there was Gran's heart drama. And I felt so turbulent that winter. I had to escape. I wanted you with me—but I wasn't going to force you. I assumed you'd come eventually. It never occurred to me—never—that you would marry someone else."

"You didn't try to stop me."

"Of course not," he said impatiently. "Did you expect me to?"

"I think so."

"That's silly, you know."

"I know."

"That's not what you want now, is it?"

"No."

He came over and put his arms around her. "You know how much I love you. Isn't that enough to tide you over?"

She thought of Anna. Anna, sitting in a corner reading, tears falling on her book.

He stepped back and looked at her. "So it's your turn to be turbulent?"

She nodded.

"It's a damn strange thing to be in the middle of someone's ambivalence," he said.

"I know."

"I'm not going to sit around weaving like Penelope."

"I know."

She wanted to be back in her car, driving swiftly through the woods and fields of the Potomac shore, back to Merriweather Street.

"Damn it!" he cried out and strode ahead of her down the path, never looking back until they got to the ferry landing.

Later she thought often about those last minutes, when he bent down and kissed her cheek, his eyes teary and jaw stiff, and then got into his car. Tia had climbed the grassy bank above the ferry and looked down at his car and seen his head resting on the steering wheel. But she had watched him as if he were a stranger. After a while, she had walked slowly to the ferry house and stood inside, gazing vacantly at racks of potato chips. When she heard the ferry engine start she had gone out to her car and started driving slowly back to Washington.

"I'm hibernating," she explained to family and friends who wanted to see her.

"What about Christmas?" said Myra, disappointed. "I thought

we were all going to Easter Cove. I even made up with Valery."

"Next year, Myra. I've asked Sloan to take the kids. I'm going to work through Christmas. I don't dare stop."

They all tried to rescue her. Especially at Christmas. There must have been something about the way she refused them that finally kept them at bay.

"Don't worry, I'm fine," she kept telling them. "I'm working hard."

It was, aside from crawling out of bed in the morning and getting the children off to school, almost all she did. Priscilla said nothing, kept cooking casseroles and leaving them in the freezer with carefully printed instructions. Jake, after seeing her, agreed to another month's leave. Sloan offered to find her a therapist.

"I'll be okay, really," she said, seeing the guilt on his face. "Honestly, Sloan, it's nothing to do with you."

She went upstairs so he would not see the tears. They came readily now, as readily and unbidden as sleep. At times they offered her luxurious self-pity but more often they stung her with a sense of loss and remorse. Sleep would follow tears, finding her curled up in her old quilt, in the quiet of the dark house, sniffling. It was only when she was working in her studio that she escaped the sudden onslaught of either state, where, in fact, her world mercifully shrank to the size of her canvas. Focused there, she was not attacked by rogue thoughts.

Sometimes, when she was painting, she would catch sight of what looked like alien flesh: a hard, bony arm streaked with charcoal dust and paint, and then she would look down at her worn skirt and pale legs and wonder if she would be forever dry and chaste. There was not, in this brown winter, a carnal impulse in any part of her.

Sloan took the children several days before Christmas, almost apologetic as he took their bags from the hall, pausing for a moment on the threshold.

"You'll be okay?" he said.

She laughed, which startled him. "Yes, I will," she said quickly.

She closed the door after them and pressed her head to the cool glass. Then she went up to her room and crawled into bed. She slept for twelve hours and then got up and worked in her studio for a few hours and then, with no need to stay awake for the children's lunch, she went back upstairs to sleep again. But for the first time in weeks, sleep did not sweep over her. She lay in bed a long time. In the dark, listening to the street noises, she let her mind wander, only half conscious of its meanderings. She was aware of fleeting images of Gran, Anna, Peter, Ivan, Elizavetta, Kathryn. She did not try to sort them out.

Later, she got up and went to the kitchen and made herself tea and toast and wandered into the study to look at the painting on her easel.

"Good lord," she said, suddenly recognizing her subject.

During the past few weeks, when her mind had been so empty she had trouble finding anything to put on canvas, Daisy had suggested she paint "a secret garden." Tia had sketched out Gran's Kaluga garden from old photographs, but Daisy was disappointed. It didn't look secret, she said gently. So together they had spent an afternoon making sketches of what Daisy called "secret places." They drew weeping willows, brooks, walls, gates, rose banks. Tia had begun, on this canvas, a rustic cottage. Several times she had tried to change it, level the pitch of the roof, widen its windows, but it seemed to resist alteration. It was, with its resolutely steep roof and small windows, the MacLeod house in Connecticut, the way she had seen it the first time, with leaves turning, high yellow grass in the field, hazy autumn sky. The first day she had seen Ivan standing in the window as they drove up to the house. Glorious golden Ivan, who had read to her, talked to her, taken her on walks, let her ride home on his back when her legs grew weak with exhaustion. Those were days that Ivan could barely remember but that Tia had never forgotten.

Then, once recognized, it was difficult to get right. It took her weeks: Ivan's shining head in the front window, Elizavetta's small figure in the doorway, the rusty, smoky dampness of that fall day. Used to painting fast, with what Paul had called her facile touch, it frustrated her to have to keep wiping out the figures, trying again and again, not satisfied. She would rise from her stool, her body aching, tense and angry.

"Damn it," she'd mutter, sometimes cry out, into the silence of the house. She'd wander out to the kitchen, leaving the study door open so she could look at the painting, and stand for a long time, trying to remember.

"Do you want some photos of the place? I might have some," said Myra when she called.

"No," said Tia quickly. "It's almost finished."

"How's your nervous breakdown?"

"What?"

"You feeling better?"

Tia laughed. "Yes. But I've got to get back to the *Roundabout*."

"Oh, no."

"I'm trying to buy this house."

"Buy the house! Christ, that's all you need."

"No, I want to," said Tia.

Mr. Berger had written from San Francisco about a place he had seen, near his daughter's house, with a wonderful view. It was not really a request but she saw her obligation. For a while it unsettled her. The Merriweather Street house had become her refuge, for weeks she had hardly left it, and its not being hers gave it a greater safety. The benevolent spirit of Otto Berger lingered.

Mrs. Pierce tried to be helpful. "I know we can work something out for you, dear." She talked about loans and mortgages and points. Tia sat, baffled and tense.

"I don't understand," she said.

"It really is very simple."

Tia went home and sat in her study and looked out into the late winter garden, bare and spiny rose stalks rattling against the bricks, and thought about amortization tables.

"Your money is still in probate, dear, but you can probably get a loan against it," offered attorney Jumbo.

"Get an appraisal," said her neighbor. "Get at least two."

"You sure you want to buy it?" said Sloan. "If you do, when the lawsuit is settled you'll have enough to put down from the sale of our house."

She had forgotten.

"How could I forget that?" she said.

Mrs. Pierce looked down at her papers. Finally she sighed and said, "Well, then, I'll cable Mr. Berger."

The roof would need new tiles and some work done on the chimney, said the bank. The engineer who looked at the house said the furnace was iffy, the house was dangerously under-wired, and she ought to reputty the upstairs windows. Then the bank called again and asked what her income was, since she had left that space blank. Oh, they said doubtfully.

"You can try another bank," said Mrs. Pierce.

So, instead of quitting the *Roundabout*, Tia asked for a raise.

"A raise," muttered Jake thoughtfully.

"I'll never get a mortgage approved with what you're paying me now," she said.

"But you told me you're cutting down your hours so you can work on your painting."

"I am grossly underpaid."

"True."

The day she spent hauling Mr. Berger's boxes from the cellar, loading them into the car, and driving them through torrential rain to a UPS outpost in a cloverleafed, concrete part of Maryland, she thought up angry letters she would send him. You never told me the roof leaked, the window frames were crumbling, the chimney needed pointing, the study neaded a space heater in the winter, the cellar steps were rotting. "You never told me!" she screamed, aloud.

The raise must have helped, because the second bank agreed on a mortgage and Mr. Berger agreed to wait for the down payment until the litigated house money was freed. That happened the day the real estate tax bill on the Easter Cove house arrived.

There were days when Tia dreaded night because that was when everything seemed impossible, when ruin threatened with every bill, death with every heartbeat. Sleep no longer slipped in easily behind a veil of tears. By now she was well acquainted with the cracks on her ceiling, the shadows cast by the street-light, the buses on Connecticut Avenue heralding dawn. These lustless nights, she thought, when she felt Nelly's old body heave in her sleep.

Still, in the morning it was always easier. Sloan called to say the money from the house was out of escrow, Jumbo said that Gran's estate would pay the Easter Cove taxes, the roofer's bill was no greater than the estimate, she was getting her magazine work done in record time, and she was painting every day. Peter stopped wetting his bed and Daisy organized her Detective Club in the basement room that Tia had fixed up for her.

Robin came to visit and talk about selling the property at Easter Cove. She was curiously indecisive about it. We should sell the whole place and be done with it, she'd say, and then later she would say she could not bear the thought of never spending another summer in Easter Cove.

"I don't know if I want to be rid of Gran or hold on to her," said Robin finally.

Tia looked at her curiously.

"Well, she was a big part of my life too," said Robin defensively.

Tia wondered how it would be to lose everything from the past and live on here, a hundred miles from the sea, in this flat swamp of a city, stay on here, in the pale green heat of its summer, the celibate Sabbatarian.

"I think we should keep the gardener's cottage. We could share that, remodel it, sell the big house," said Tia.

"Perhaps."

"We'll have it all done legally," said Tia. "I'm a legal veteran."

Robin roamed around Tia's study, examining the paintings. She stopped in front of the MacLeod house and said "That's nice" and then stopped and turned back.

"Ivan, still."

"Do you remember how we adored him as kids?" said Tia.

"Yeah, I guess."

"Come on, Robin, you did too. Remember how furious we were when he married Kathryn?"

"I had the most beautiful dress for that wedding. Do you remember?" She sighed. "I suppose I was always jealous because he liked you so much."

"Everyone was always lusting after you."

"Never Ivan. Besides, he always scared me. That's probably why I liked Sloan. Never could tell with Ivan."

"Scared you?"

"What do you need Ivan for? Your life seems fine."

It was fine: this snug house, the children, the painting, her friends. Except for the times when the car failed, the children were sick in the night, pipes burst, bills piled up, it was more than fine. The torpor was receding. There were changes. She was aware of them in fits and starts. It didn't happen as she expected it to, all at once, shimmering lights announcing glorious direction. It's time, it's time, she told herself, but it was such a delicate balance she'd achieved. I'm waiting for a sign, said a woman in the movie she was watching. I'm waiting too, thought Tia.

"You're waiting for an abundance of clarity," said Robin one day.

Actually, Tia was no longer waiting. The finer it seemed, the more she missed Ivan. It had started stirring slowly, the knowledge that the emptiness now lay in his absence. It was becoming painful to think of him in London, not waiting. It was not that she had the answers but that the concerns, if anything, had grown less cosmic in this season of window putty and roof tiling.

She had called the Virginia college and was told they did not have the London address, only his Pine Island box number in Easter Cove. She had called Elizavetta, gotten no answer, and then a card came from France: She was there with Claudia and Valery. Myra had not heard from Ivan since before the New Year, and neither had Masha. Once Tia woke with a start from a dream where she had seen Ivan in bed with a woman. Lying in the dark, she wondered if she was, at last, prescient.

All this made her reluctant to admit to Robin how hard she was trying to find Ivan, her search growing more urgent as the trail grew colder. Maybe it's past time, she thought the day the letter she had written him, care of London University, came back. Trying to make sketches of him, she found she could no longer clearly recall his face.

She had finished the MacLeod cottage painting, working on other paintings while it dried, examining it each morning and resisting the temptation to put it back on her easel. Ivan's half-hidden face, in the shadows of the house, was too ethereal, she thought. But when Sabrina called to ask Tia for a painting for an art show to benefit Save a Pet, she decided to send that one.

"I'm trying to get these damn painters—no offense, Ti—to exhibit something with an animal in it. Do you have one like that?"

Thanks to one of Sabrina's stepfathers, she had the use of the lobby of a corporate headquarters in New York.

"I've got a landscape with two dogs in it, but you can hardly see them," said Tia.

"Well, that's okay," said Sabrina.

Tia wanted to be in the show badly, so she returned to the MacLeod canvas and painted in two tiny dogs in the field beyond the cottage.

In April, Tia went to Easter Cove. She had to pack up Gran's house and find a contractor to work on the gardener's cottage. She had looked forward to leaving the children with Sloan, to being alone in the house in what, with Washington's advance on spring, she thought would be balmy weather. She would walk down to the rocks while the sun rose over the islands in the sea. She would gather spring flowers. She would light the library fire at night, curl up with design books, and plan the cottage alterations. Instead, she had arisen from her mildewed bed the first morning to find rain pouring out of a dark sky on a brown land, the house cold and damp, and had quickly set to work, far too tired by nightfall to make a fire or plan anything. Much of the furniture was already in storage, leaving many of the rooms empty. Still, spread around the house, in closets, on shelves, in forgotten cabinets, there were things to be thrown out or packed. Scattered as they were, they did not look formidable until she started after them with packing boxes and green garbage bags.

When finally, on the third day, the clouds rolled inland, she ventured out into the spring sun. She walked across the wet grass to the pines, down the worn, slippery path to the rocks. She stood for a long time listening to the surf before she started toward the point. She walked carefully, remembering the places where the rocks had worn smooth, where there was a jagged rise to climb, where they dropped sharply into the sea and rose again on the other side of a crevice with the churning sea between them. When she got to the point she started up the hill to the pines that skirted the village. She heard a launch across the channel and, shielding her eyes from the sun, watched the boat rounding the far buoys, making the turn so fast that water plumed over its stern. It skimmed past the offshore rocks, roaring back toward Pine Island and then making a wide figure-eight, rocking and rolling across its wake, passing close below her.

"Ivan!" She saw him clearly as he passed. "Ivan!" she screamed into the ocean wind. She ran along the rocks, waving at him, calling, but he roared past, standing at the tiller, looking straight ahead.

"Look up, look up, you dope," she cried. She stumbled on a tree root and fell to her knees and, crouched on the rock, watched his boat disappear around the northern tip of the island.

She waited for it to reappear, strained to hear it. Clouds covered the sun. The wind was cold. She ran back to the house and dialed the Pine Island number but there was no answer. As she rushed outside to her car she wondered if she had been hallucinating. Why would Ivan be on Pine Island in April? He would never spend a winter there. He had said, that day at White's Ferry, that he would go to London after Christmas.

It took her a while to persuade the man at the marina to rent her a boat. He followed her down the dock, issuing warnings about the tide in the channel as she backed out of the slip. To reassure him she turned slowly out of the harbor, heading north toward the island. There was a steady wind from the sea, and the water was choppy. The little boat slapped across the waves, shipping a little water. The wind whipped her hair, tugged at her coat. As she got in the lee of the island, the water was calmer. She opened the throttle and the boat roared along, below the high, shadowed coast of Pine Island. Approaching the point, she slowed the boat down. The launch she had seen earlier was tied to the dock. She had to turn and make a second pass because she had come in too fast. Catching the stern of the other launch, she pulled her boat alongside.

"Ivan," she called as she headed up the path to the house. She knocked on the door and called again, but there was no answer.

"Anyone here?" she called as she reached for the doorknob. Then she hesitated. Since the moment she had seen Ivan turn his boat toward Pine Island, she had pushed away a disquiet that had grown untended until now it paralyzed her on his doorstep. Why would he choose to come here? She remembered this house as dank, with pink, peeling wallpaper, boarded-up fireplaces, oily window shades, cheap rugs, full of Paul's venom and loss. Why would Ivan come through winter seas to this grim house? She wondered if this was to be, after all, a sign.

She pushed the door open and stepped across the threshold into a house bright with sea light, white walls, furniture, and paintings from the MacLeods' Connecticut house, floors bare and varnished, empty of the ghosts of Hanna and Lisl, of Paul and Myra's dying marriage. She wandered through the rooms. Ivan had hung some of her paintings, sketches of his own, a big oil of Valery's, a group of Gran's small Russian scenes. He had cut a large window that looked east, toward the sea. The fireplace had been opened and logs and kindling piled beside it. Bending over his desk, she inspected his papers. There were some letters from Wilson in London, a pile of galleys, stacks of typewriter paper, books of notes. She pulled open the top drawer. There was a large photograph he had taken of her the first weekend she visited him in Virginia, laughing at him as he fiddled with his new camera. Under it was a picture of Alexey on the beach in Brittany in Elizavetta's arms with Robin and Tia on either side of them. They were all very brown, smiling, and in the distance was the small house they had shared for a week. In other drawers were boxes of slides of his digs, diagrams of sites, files of archaeological papers. As she pulled out the bottom drawer, she paused. There were stacks of letters she had written him, cartoons and drawings she had done for him, photographs of her, a pair of cheap cuff links she had bought him with her own money as a wedding present. In a frame, under dusty glass, was a photograph she could not remember seeing before, of the two of them at Easter Cove, their backs to the camera, walking across the lawn. His face, in profile, was smiling and she was looking up at him, most of her face hidden by blowing hair, saying something.

"Ivan," she called again as she started upstairs. She paused on the bottom step. What if she had blundered in, too late, foolishly expectant? He might rise from another women's side, come peer sleepily over the banister.

"Ivan," she called again, walking slowly upstairs. The first two rooms were furnished but clearly not occupied. At the end of the hall was a large room with an unmade bed, clothes draped over chairs, books piled on the bed table. She heard a door slam downstairs and stood frozen.

She came down softly, on carpeted stairs, and paused. Ivan was bending over, laying a fire. She stood for a moment watching him.

"Hello."

"What?" He wheeled around. "Tia!"

His face was ruddy, leaner, and his hair, longer, almost covered his eyes until he brushed it back with a quick, self-conscious gesture.

"I tried to call you."

"My God!" He stood staring at her.

"You didn't go to London."

"No. No, I came here."

"I've been looking for you."

"Really?"

She nodded.

"I thought I'd left a trail full of clues." He laughed. "I told the college that I'd be here."

"I was so sure you were in London."

"Came here to weave," he said.

"Did you?"

He nodded. He stood stiffly, still holding a piece of kindling in his hand.

"Am I too late?" said Tia.

"Too late?"

"Is there a big redheaded Peggy upstairs?"

"Peggy!" He laughed and came over to her. He put a hand on her arm in a tentative gesture. "No, certainly not. You remember Peggy! I think I lost her to a banker at one of Gran's Christmas parties."

She put her arms around his neck and he grasped her in a crushing hug, lifting her off the floor.

———

Later, waking up next to him at dawn, she looked out the window, across the channel at Gran's house. Half hidden by pines, shrunk by distance, it was hard to distinguish from its neighbors, similarly shingled and shuttered, arrayed on sloping lawns above the sea.